BLOOD COVENANT

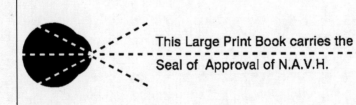

This Large Print Book carries the
Seal of Approval of N.A.V.H.

BLOOD COVENANT

LISA HARRIS

THORNDIKE PRESS

A part of Gale, Cengage Learning

GALE
CENGAGE Learning·

Detroit • New York • San Francisco • New Haven, Conn • Waterville, Maine • London

GALE
CENGAGE Learning

LIBRARY OF CONGRESS CATALOGING-IN-PUBLICATION DATA

Harris, Lisa, 1969–
    Blood covenant / by Lisa Harris.
        p. cm. — (Mission hope series ; 2) (Thorndike Press large print Christian fiction)
    ISBN-13: 978-1-4104-3988-8 (hardcover)
    ISBN-10: 1-4104-3988-7 (hardcover)
    1. Civil war—Africa—Fiction. 2. Refugee camps—Africa—Fiction. 3. Measles—Fiction. 4. Large type books. I. Title.
    PS3608.A78315B56 2011b
    813'.6—dc22   2011020837

Published in 2011 by arrangement with The Zondervan Corporation LLC.

Printed in Mexico
1 2 3 4 5 6 7 15 14 13 12 11

To every man, woman, and child who
longs for freedom.
May you find it in Him.

ACKNOWLEDGMENTS

To my husband and sweet children — without your love and support I would never be able to write these stories. I love you guys!

To Joyce Hart, my agent — thank you for always being such a great source of encouragement to me.

To Sue Brower and all of the incredible staff at Zondervan — thank you for not only believing in this series, but for the energy and creativity you pour into each book.

To Rachelle and Ellen, editors extraordinaire — thanks for forcing me to dig deeper into my characters and story.

To my fabulous experts — I would never have been able to complete this book without all of you! Faith Walker, who's always willing to answer my medical questions. Paul Simpson, who helped with the military scenes and provided incredible photos of an actual medivac mission so I could see the desert. Randy Burrows, who ensured Nick flew like a real pilot. And last, but not least, Dave Lindsay, who not only helped me flesh out and give Taz his name, but who also became my number-one nitpicking fan and extra pair of eyes!

BLOOD COVENANT

Republic of
DHAMBIZAO

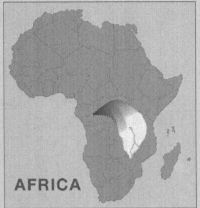

AFRICA

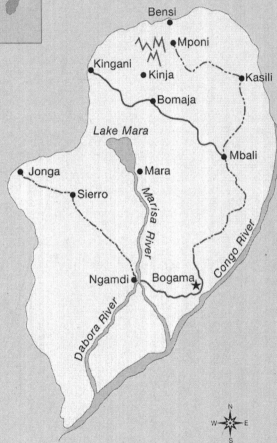

Bensi

Mponi

Kingani

Kinja

Kasili

Bomaja

Lake Mara

Jonga

Mara

Mbali

Sierro

Marisa River

Ngamdi

Bogama

Congo River

Dabora River

N
W E
S

★ National Capital
• City, Town
ᴧᴧ Mountain Range
— Main Road
--- Secondary Road

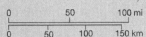

0   50   100 mi
0   50   100   150 km

PROLOGUE

Thursday, January 29, 3:48 p.m.
Republic of Dhambizao (RD), Anamadi Township

Jonas Moya moved from the narrow alleyway onto the dusty street, then disappeared into the late afternoon crowd. The country's elite, with their fancy government buildings, commercial strips, and plush houses, had all but forgotten the tangled web of muddy alleyways that laced the sprawling slums of the capital. Which made the high-density township the perfect place to hide.

He breathed in a lungful of acidic smoke from the piles of trash burning in the distance, then glanced again behind him. A group of women balanced buckets of water on their heads. Children played along the edge of the road. A drunk loitered in front of a shop. But there were no signs of anyone following him.

11

He shook off the uneasy sensation. Rarely did President Tau's soldiers set foot inside the rambling settlement, known for its high crime and corruption — even with the recent order to round up every member of the Ghost Soldiers in the countrywide manhunt stretching from the capital to the base of Mt. Maja. It was an order that had left him on the run.

Anger replaced his unease. None of the president's government officials had complained about the generous financial kickbacks they'd received from the dozens of slave-labor camps the Ghost Soldiers set up throughout the country's fertile mines. But their fat payments didn't change the fact that he and the others would take the fall for their crimes, while the current government remained innocent before the UN and the rest of the world.

The crowd thinned and an eerie silence settled across the humid afternoon air. It took a full five seconds for Jonas to grasp what was happening. By then he stood fully exposed to a dozen uniformed soldiers converging on the leaders' rendezvous point less than ten meters in front of him. Automatically he dropped for cover behind a battered pickup, but not before catching a glimpse of his brother, Seba, and four others lying facedown in the dusty street. If he'd arrived five minutes earlier, he'd be lying there as well.

Clinging to the truck's rusty bumper, he searched for an escape route, weighing his options one by one. His best bet was to take the alley across the street and get lost in the endless maze of cinder block houses. But running would do nothing for his brother and the others.

Squinting in the bright afternoon sunlight, he peered around the dented bumper. One of the soldiers kicked Seba in the ribs. "Where are the rest of your men?"

Seba rolled over, sprang to his feet, and slammed into the soldier. Instinctively, Jonas pulled out the weapon hidden beneath his thin jacket, but not before a shot ripped through the humid air. Seba dropped onto the street. Blood seeped through his pant leg and spilled across the brown dirt beneath him.

Jonas fought rising panic. There was still no sign of Ngozi. Together the two of them might stand a chance, but alone, any heroic rescue would prove foolish against President Tau's elite.

The soldiers began to spread out, searching for the missing rebel leaders — and making his hiding place vulnerable. Another group of soldiers approached from behind. Jonas dropped to all fours and cursed. He'd waited too long, and now his only escape was blocked. Another gunshot echoed in the air. The few remaining curious onlookers scattered toward the surrounding compounds. A soldier yelled. Jonas' jaw tensed as two of them headed toward his position.

For a split second he considered the odds, then made a run for the alley. Halfway across the street, he felt a bullet rip through his shoulder. He stumbled, pain searing his senses. Blood dripped down his arm, but he couldn't afford to slow his pace. He flew toward the narrow alley lined with someone's laundry, trying to ignore the thundering footsteps behind him. Yanking a shirt from the line, he pressed it against the wound. Behind him, the two soldiers closed in.

Anger and adrenalin drowned out the pain. For years, he and the other men had been nothing more than puppets in the hands of their own government. Hundreds of them had been recruited and trained as the president's secret guard. Today they were called insurgents and rebels. Used for the government's purposes, like the running of their slave-labor camps, they were then easily disposed of when the rest of the world caught on.

Jonas slipped into the afternoon shadows of the deserted alley, took a sharp left, then a right, managing to put distance between him and the soldiers. A plan began to form in the recesses of his mind. That same government believed they could get away with watching them rot in some dark prison in exchange for more foreign aid and UN support.

Not if he had his way.

ONE

Dr. Paige Ryan hesitated in the open doorway of the Cessna Caravan before stepping
down onto the grassy runway. An early
morning mist lingered along the edges of
the clearing, but even the cloudy veil wasn't
enough to mask the handful of thatched
huts smoldering on the far side of the landing strip.

The familiar feeling of helplessness
pressed against her chest. The last time
she'd gone out with the mobile medical
unit, the pilot had been forced to do a low-
level pass before landing to scatter the herds
of goats and the children playing soccer with
their homemade balls on the airstrip. Today,
all that greeted them was an eerie silence
coupled with the bitter smell of burning
huts.

Simon Love, head of emergency relief,

stepped up beside her and tugged on the bottom of his Volunteers of Hope T-shirt. "Apparently the government's statements that the rebel's threats are nothing to worry about were exaggerated. It looks as if most of the villagers have fled this area."

Except those slaughtered by the rebels. A lump swelled in Paige's throat. She hadn't wanted to believe the rumors. Seventeen dead in Mkondi. Six in Latasha. Fifteen near the border town of Marani . . . But if Simon was right, those deaths could easily be the tip of the iceberg.

Their pilot, Nick Gilbert, grabbed Paige's medical bag from the storage compartment and handed it to her, temporarily distracting her from the haunting scene. Given another place and time, she'd have given his boyish good looks a second glance, but today all she could see was the smoky destruction in the distance.

"I'll wait here with the plane, but we need to be in the air by eleven if we're going to have time to visit the other villages and still make it back to Kingani before dark."

The pilot's strong southern drawl sounded out of place in the middle of the African bush, but to Paige it helped soothe the recent renewed pangs of homesickness. Tennessee had never seemed so far away.

She slung the bag over her shoulder and shot him a smile. "Then I reckon we'd better get moving."

Nick's reply was cut off by the loud rumbling approach of a beat-up 4×4, replacing any feelings of familiarity with the reality of the situation. Fighting between government forces and renegade Ghost Soldiers had escalated in the past seventy-two hours, with the villagers scattered across the base of Mt. Maja caught in the crossfire of the conflict. And while the government insisted that President Tau's army was maintaining control over the situation, the senseless killings being reported only reinforced her helplessness.

As soon as the boxes of hygiene kits and medical supplies were loaded into the back of the waiting vehicle, Simon wasted no time in making introductions to their ground contact. "Abraham, this is Dr. Paige Ryan and Michael French, my logistician." Simon turned to address her. "Abraham used to work with Volunteers of Hope but now is the full-time director of the four clinics here in the Mponi region."

"It's nice to meet you." Paige shook the man's weathered hand.

Nodding good-bye to the pilot, she stepped over a trail of ants crossing the dark red earth, then jumped into the back of the vehicle with her colleagues. Abraham slipped the vehicle into gear. It sputtered and sped off down the runway.

"What can you tell us about the situation?" Simon shouted above the roar of the engine. "We've had a hard time contacting you until this morning."

"Most of the cell-phone towers in the vicinity are down, and despite the government's propaganda about what's happening, in this village alone we buried forty-seven after the attacks. It is impossible to know how many are missing, because of the hundreds fleeing the area." The jeep crashed through the thick brush edging the bumpy dirt road that was barely wide enough for one vehicle. "Those who remain fear the rebels will return, so most of them are staying inside the hospital compound. I'll take you there first."

Paige's fingers tightened around the door handle as the hot breeze from the open window dried out her eyes. Any hopes that the number of deaths reported had been exaggerated faded like the morning mist. The International Criminal Court had sent out dozens of warrants for the rebels involved in the forced enslavement of hundreds of Dzambizans in the nearby mountains. The rebels' response to the arrests of five of their commanders had been a vow to fight until the indictments were dropped and their demands for amnesty were met. A stance that meant until a resolution was negotiated, innocent people of the RD would continue to be slaughtered.

A minute later, the narrow bush path merged into the main road of town. A dozen cinder block buildings lined the street with colorfully painted walls advertising soft drinks, toothpaste, and cell-phone providers. But no one walked the dusty road through town today. Even the market, normally bustling with vendors and buyers, lay bare. Bensi had become nothing more than a ghost town.

Abraham parked inside the large compound of the hospital, where at least a hundred people waited beneath a thatched shelter sitting adjacent to the medical structure. At the sight of the aid workers their faces lit up with expectation. Paige undid her seatbelt and slid out of the vehicle. Three months in the country had taught her that a couple of hours were barely enough time to scratch the surface of everything that had to be accomplished. Today's crowd had multiplied those odds against them.

A uniformed nurse met them at the door of the main ward, determination registering in her dark eyes. "I am Patience. We were afraid you were not coming."

"We came as soon as we could. I'm Dr. Paige Ryan."

By the time Paige entered the long, rectangular ward behind the nurse, several men had transferred the medical supplies to the floor by one of the pale-green cinder block walls. The nurse jutted her chin toward the other side of the room where two rows of metal beds lined the walls, each one holding a patient. "Most of our staff has left and our supplies are almost gone, including our generator that was stolen by the rebels. But I stay . . . hoping this will all be over soon."

Paige caught the heavy note of desperation in the woman's voice and stopped at the end of one of the rows. "They stole your generator?"

Obviously the hospital's six-foot-high perimeter wall strung with razor wire had done little to deter the rebels' rampage.

"And left three of my patients to die."

Paige's jaw tightened. Constant power outages made generators essential for surgeries and other critical life-saving operations. Without one, the death rate would automatically climb.

"I'm sorry. We had no idea things had gotten this bad." Paige stopped at the end of one of the beds where an old woman lay sleeping beneath a tattered sheet. "The local media has reported outbreaks of fighting in the region, but always with assurances that the president's army is in control of the situation."

Patience shook her head. "I have yet to see one of President Tau's soldiers come to our aid. The government only says what they want the world to hear. And they do not care if our women are raped and our children murdered in their beds as long as their pockets and bellies are full."

Paige expelled a sharp breath. The past few months had taught her to think fast on her feet and find solutions to what often seemed to be impossible situations, but those scenarios hadn't included rebels in the equation. Any solid answers to resolve the problems facing this woman and her people escaped her.

"We should get started." Paige pushed aside the dismal reality that seemed all too prevalent in this country — and the lingering guilt. In four days she wouldn't have to deal with any of this anymore. "Even though our time is limited on this initial visit, I want to do everything I can to help, especially by evaluating your specific needs for this clinic. But for now, if there are any patients you'd like me to see . . ."

"Where do I begin?" Patience pointed to one of the women. "Sari's seven-and-a-half months pregnant. We managed to stop her contractions, but without the generator, if her child is born anytime soon, the chances of the infant surviving are small." She nodded at the child in the next bed. "We diagnosed Tayla, who's six, with pneumonia and have done what we can, but she is not responding. She's so weak . . ." Patience's words faded as she turned toward the mother.

Paige picked up her medical bag and crossed the cracked cement floor of the clinic, stopping at the metal-framed bed. A woman sat on the edge of the thin mattress next to her daughter, a vacant expression covering her ebony face.

Paige rubbed the little girl's fuzzy, black hair and studied her lips and the tips of her fingers. Both were a dusky, unhealthy shade of gray.

"I cannot lose my daughter." Tears filled the young mother's eyes. "They killed my sons and husband in front of me. Tayla is all I have left."

She'd heard stories of other countries

24

where villagers were forced to hide in the forest at night in fear of the rebels who stole their children, raped their women, and murdered their families in front of them. But she'd never imagined being thrust into the center of a similar nightmare. She eyed the stack of hygiene kits they'd brought and felt the nausea return. Free hygiene kits, with their limited contents of toothbrushes, chlorine tablets, and mosquito nets, seemed useless compared to the needs of these people.

The clear tremor of fear lacing the mother's words filled Paige with a renewed sense of determination. Back in Tennessee her niece had just celebrated her seventh birthday. Tayla deserved the same chance.

"I'll do everything I can to help your daughter." Paige touched the woman's hand, wishing she had a better answer.

She turned Tayla onto her side to listen to her lungs with her stethoscope. The crackling sound confirmed the nurse's diagnosis. Upper respiratory infections in young children and infants, especially those who didn't have the chance for adequate nutrition, could quickly turn lethal. If she were back in Tennessee, she'd have sent the child to the ICU. Here, listening to the grunts of the small child as she fought to breathe, she didn't have that luxury.

The handheld radio she'd brought with her buzzed inside her bag. "Hello, Echo Lima, this is November Gold, over."

Nick?

She picked up the radio and pressed the Transmit button. "Roger . . . November Gold . . . Send, over." One day of practice on the field radio wasn't nearly enough.

"I've just received a radio communication with orders to fly you out immediately. Over."

Paige dropped her stethoscope around her neck and moved toward the screened window overlooking the dozens of people who'd come seeking safety inside the hospital compound. If she and Michael and Simon left now, it could be days until another team was sent, which meant more lives lost. There was no way she was leaving.

Two

Monday, February 21, 9:27 a.m.
Bensi

Paige gripped the radio. "November Gold, I have patients I need to treat, and Simon and Michael are going to need more time to evaluate the situation. I need a couple more hours minimum."

"You don't have that kind of time, Echo Lima."

"Wait out, November Gold." Paige released the Transmit button, excused herself, and hurried from the building. Simon and Michael stood outside talking to Abraham and several other men from the town.

Simon turned to her. "Is everything okay?"

"Nick's just received a radio transmission with orders to pull us out immediately, but he didn't give an explanation."

"Nick wouldn't transmit security-related information, which means the rebels must have returned."

She shook her head, unwilling to accept the order. "The rebels have no reason to return here, and these people need me. I can't leave."

Paige caught the look of conflict in Simon's eyes. "As much as I hate to pull out, I don't think we have a choice. I'll have Abraham drive us back to the plane immediately —"

"Wait a minute." Paige moved in front of him, blocking his way. "I know our safety is on the line, but the situation here is serious. The rebels stole the hospital's generator, and I've got a woman in there who's gone into labor six weeks early. Without a generator, a baby born premature doesn't have a chance —"

"I understand how you feel, but Nick wouldn't call us back to the plane without a serious reason, which means that, like it or not, we're leaving."

"Without any regard to the needs and safety of these people?"

Simon's jaw twitched. "You have to know by now I'm committed to ensuring that these people receive the help they need, but I will not put the lives of my own people in danger. We're leaving. Now."

Paige marched back into the clinic, yanked her stethoscope from her neck, and dropped it into her medical bag beside Tayla's bed. Throwing a tantrum wouldn't change anything, but she still hated the helplessness of the situation.

She ran her finger down the rounded face of the young child that glistened with fever. "I'm sorry, Patience. They've ordered us to leave the region and fly to Kingani immediately."

"The rebels . . . They are back?"

Paige shook her head. "I don't know."

Patience's voice pleaded with her. "Please . . . please, don't forget us."

"I'll do everything I can to make sure someone returns with what you need. I promise."

Guilt squeezed again at her chest as she said good-bye, then ran to catch up with Simon. "There's got to be another way. Something we can do to help these people."

"I'm sorry, Paige. You have to know this isn't a call I take lightly. I'm as determined as you are to make sure every single person in this country gets the medical care they need, but sometimes it simply isn't possible."

She tightened her grip on the handle of her medical bag. "I know, but all of this seems so preventable. There's got to be a way to stop these insurgents."

Simon stopped in front of the jeep and caught her gaze. "I've been here for a year and a half, and I don't think I'll ever fully get used to the horrors I've seen. But we do what we can and that has to be enough. Life here . . . It's like dangling precariously on the end of some flimsy thread, and sometimes there's just nothing we can do to stop it from breaking."

"It's not right."

"No, it's not." He helped her into the back of the vehicle and climbed in beside her. "But it's the reality."

Abraham floored the gas pedal, and Paige watched the cinder block hospital disappear around the corner as they headed back toward the plane. Wind whipped through her hair and fanned the injustice smoldering inside her. She caught sight of a couple of villagers sifting through the charred remains of broken clay urns. How was it that life had become this unfair paradox? Those needing her the most were the very people she couldn't help.

The crackling of gunfire ripped through the morning air. Fear closed in on her, constricting her lungs, and she ducked beneath the door frame. Rural Tennessee had its problems, but they had never included being chased by rebels with machine guns. This wasn't Tennessee.

Another round of shots split the air. Simon slumped beside her.

Abraham shouted from the front seat. "Everyone get down."

Paige ducked, then reached for the patch of red soaking through the fabric of Simon's shirt. Warm blood covered her fingers. "He's been shot."

"How bad?" Michael shouted from the front seat.

"I don't know. Simon? Can you hear me?"

"Yeah." He rolled his head backward. "I always wanted to go out with a bang. Please . . . please tell April I'm sorry."

"Stop. You're going to be fine. You're not going anywhere except on the plane and out of here."

Paige's fingers tightened against his chest as she fought to keep pressure against the bullet's entrance to stop the bleeding. The vehicle bounced across the uneven ground, jarring loose her hold.

Michael was already on the radio with the pilot. "November Gold, this is Mike Foxtrot. Request that you are ready for immediate takeoff. Over."

"Roger that, Mike Foxtrot. Over."

Paige strained to look behind her, searching for any sign of the armed rebels. Trees waved in the morning breeze, along with the tall grasses lining the runway, but there were no signs of the insurgents.

Panic engulfed her. "I don't see them."

"I don't either. They're probably on foot and meant it as a warning."

"A warning?" Paige shouted. "That was no warning shot. They hit Simon!"

Abraham slammed on the brakes beside the plane and within a matter of seconds the men had hoisted Simon inside behind Paige.

Michael turned back to Abraham. "Come with us."

He shook his head. "These are my people. I'll be waiting for your return."

Nick pulled up the ladder and closed the door. "Fasten your seatbelts, everybody. We're taking off."

THREE

Nick crossed the well-kept lawns toward his plane, grateful for the long, narrow field that allowed for emergency landings at the back of the hospital. Especially on days like today. They'd been lucky to escape, but that did little to take away the lingering trauma of the past two hours. Anyone of them could have been hit by the rebels' bullets. Simon had been.

He grabbed a stick of gum from his backpack, mentally thanking his sister for her occasional care packages. Her last box had taken four months to arrive and had been filled with snack foods and DVD reruns of the television series *M*A*S*H*. But it was the photos of his four-year-old nephew Malachi that had turned his thoughts toward home. The sweet, blue-eyed boy was growing up far too fast and made him wish he could

33

bridge the distance between Africa and Louisiana more often.

A rare wave of homesickness struck, making him long for his small hometown, fishing in the bayou with his grandfather, and Sunday dinner with his sister's fried chicken and shrimp fritters. His stomach grumbled at the thought, and he hesitated beneath the thick, tangled branches of an African tulip tree, wondering if he should find something to eat at the hospital or go ahead and leave for his base in Kasili. With today's attacks, his flight itinerary had been indefinitely postponed, which meant he'd probably end up running maintenance checks on planes until the government found a way to squelch the rebel uprising.

Still debating, he caught sight of Dr. Paige Ryan sitting on one of the concrete benches behind the clinic, wearing blue surgical scrubs and staring out across the lawn, now brown from the summer heat. He'd only met her twice during the short time she'd been in the RD, but the shared connection of a home country and mother tongue tended to bond expatriates quickly. Her independence, obvious sense of adventure, and the fact that she was beautiful were all added bonuses.

He breathed in the musky fragrance of the

orange-red blooms above him. Memories of his own first days in the RD swept over him like it was yesterday. When he'd arrived, Ghost Soldiers were nothing more than rumors brushed aside by government officials. Today, with the rebels demanding amnesty for their involvement in the slave trade, the situation had exploded into something far worse than anything he'd had to deal with outside the Middle East.

Making the decision to delay his lunch plans, he crossed the lawn and slid onto the bench beside her. He dropped his backpack on the ground. "Mind if I join you?"

"Simon didn't make it."

Nick felt the punch to his gut at her brusque announcement. He'd seen life snuffed out a dozen times before in the throes of war, but every time death crossed his path it reverberated within him like the first time. "I was just going to ask you how he was, but I thought . . . I assumed he'd make it."

"The bullet was lodged in his chest. He might have had a chance somewhere else, but not here." She stared across the lawn toward the colorful bougainvillea climbing up across the high walls of the hospital compound, her hands trembling in her lap. "He has a sister who lives in St. Louis and a fiancée in Cincinnati. Her name's April, and they were planning to get married this summer."

"I'm sorry." Nick digested the news . . . and the dozens of memories it dug up from his own past. "I know firsthand how tough it is to lose a colleague."

"We had breakfast together this morning." She rubbed the back of her neck with her hand. "I've treated gunshot wounds, saved some and lost others, but this is different. We're aid workers trying to save lives. Simon wasn't supposed to die."

He watched her shoulders slump and hoped it would take more than a rebel's bullet to send her running. As tough as the situation was, this country needed more people like her. "You did everything you could, both in the plane and here on the ground. That's all you could do."

"But it wasn't enough to save Simon's life." Paige shivered, even though the temperature was well into the nineties. "I thought I could come here and make a difference, but it's always the same. Today I left a hospital full of people needing medical help and watched a colleague die. I'll never get used to this."

Poignant memories surfaced in the form of random snapshots. Nomads dressed in their desert garb. The flash of light from the grenade. He'd been in her position before. What happened in places like this was rarely expected — or fair.

"I don't think any of us get used to the death and poverty we see every day. Between stalled plans, hard-nosed officials, injustices, and the feeling of powerlessness, most of us end up realizing that we'll never change everything."

Her jaw tensed. "Then why come if we're not making a difference?"

"I never said we couldn't make a difference, but we'll never be able to save them all."

Despite his affirming answer, Nick cringed at the question he'd heard asked again and again. He, of all people, knew that no matter how much good they did, or how many lives they saved, it was never enough to erase the sting of losing someone. He'd dealt with the same discouragement in his own life, but knew that he could never let those intense feeling of failure and loss wipe out the good they did. That was what she needed to hold onto in moments like this.

"I always saw myself as an optimist." Her hands fiddled with the hem of her scrubs as she broke the silence between them.

He nodded at her to continue. Talking was

a positive step.

"But I've watched that part of me slip away over the past few months until I catch myself feeling cynical about everything around me. Simon was a good man, one who wanted nothing more than to help the people here."

"Someone once told me that there are two kinds of people who end up here: runners and seekers. The runners are fleeing their past and the seekers are hungry for adventure."

"Which one are you?"

He'd run the first time at twenty-one. Adventure had become the perfect escape. Thirteen years later, there were still days when he felt as if he was trying to find a way to buy his redemption.

"Honestly? I suppose a bit of both. What about you?"

She looked up and caught his gaze. "I don't know that it really matters anymore. I'm leaving for the capital tomorrow to finish up some paperwork and debriefing, then catching a flight on to Nashville on Friday. I'm going home."

FOUR

Paige felt the tension that had been building in her shoulders begin to release at the thought of going home, but even that wasn't enough to dissipate the lingering anger. Something had snapped the moment Simon took his last breath. Life had turned into a game of Russian roulette and she wanted out.

Three months ago, she'd left for the RD as a naive doctor who'd intended her assignment with Volunteers of Hope International to be the first of many. It hadn't taken long for that idealistic dream to shatter. In a matter of weeks, the stark reality magnifying the gap between the haves and have-nots had left her reeling. She'd watched mothers lose their babies and children lose their parents, all because of the lack of clean water, inadequate medical care, and harsh

39

living conditions. And no matter how many lists she wrote or how many improvements she tried to implement, the pain and suffering she saw around her only seemed to multiply.

"Are you ready to go back home?" Nick's question broke through her troubled thoughts.

"Honestly, I never thought I'd be so ready to leave." She wiped a stray tear from her cheek, self-conscious of her display of emotion in front of a man she barely knew.

"Give yourself some credit. Jonga is said to be one of the hardest assignments in the country."

Paige couldn't help but smile. "It isn't exactly a thriving metropolis."

Before being transferred to Kingani for the last month of her assignment, she'd worked alongside twenty Dzambizian nationals and a handful of foreign volunteers in Jonga. The remote Volunteers of Hope compound had consisted of a row of white-washed buildings and thatch-roofed huts. Electricity had been sporadic, telephone lines nonexistent, and relief from the heat impossible to come by.

She shoved her hands inside the front pockets of her scrubs and felt the worn photo of Marila. The ten-year-old orphan's

40

plight had been the significant factor that had not only brought her here, but had kept her going when the reality of living in a third-world country hit with a vengeance. And was why her relief to return home was tinged with traces of sadness.

"Despite all the frustrations, there are parts I love about the work. The children's smiles, the mothers' love for their babies, and their dedication to family. I've been able to run mobile clinics, set up cholera treatment and therapeutic feeding centers, and oversee vaccination campaigns. There are days I've felt as if I were making a difference."

"You are." Nick's solemn expression intensified the worry lines on his forehead. "But then sometimes, like today, there's nothing else you can do but walk away. Humanitarian efforts often become high-value targets and a way for rebels to leverage their demands, which in turn can strip us of our role as provider."

Which was what haunted her the most. She was used to finding solutions to problems and making things work. Her medical knowledge and experience helped keep her in control, and being told she couldn't do something made her want to fight back.

But even those intermittent feelings

weren't enough to make her want to stay.

Nick's cell phone rang. He spoke briefly, flipped his phone shut, and caught her gaze. "That was Digane. He wants to see us."

The hospital administrator sat in his office at the end of the green, cinder block hallway deep in the middle of a phone conversation. He signaled for them to sit down in the two open seats in front of his desk before finishing his conversation and hanging up. "I appreciate your coming to see me. I just heard about Simon."

Paige's jaw tensed at the visual image the reminder invoked. While declaring a patient dead had always been a heart-wrenching duty for her, having it be someone she knew and worked with had made the task even more difficult. "They shot and killed him in cold blood."

"I know that the conditions you are forced to work with are difficult enough without having to witness the murder of a colleague." Digane slid his thick glasses up the bridge of his ebony nose. "I truly am sorry you had to go through something like this, and I want you to know we are doing everything we can to ensure this doesn't happen again."

Her fingers pressed against the edge of

the desk. "I was told when I arrived that all foreigners have been warned to leave the Mponi region."

"That's why we pulled you out. The warning from the government has now turned into an order for all foreigners to leave."

Suspicion closed in around Paige. "I'm glad to see the government doing something about the situation, but if Abraham is right — and we saw evidence that he is — the official government death toll doesn't even begin to scratch the surface."

"You may very well be right." Digane nodded. "I just finished an emergency conference call. As you might have already heard, due to these escalating attacks a refugee camp has sprung up north of here near the border. Already there are over ten thousand people who've arrived needing shelter, water, sanitation, and food, with hundreds more arriving every day. We sent in a skeleton team and a convoy of supplies a week ago to deal with the basic needs of food, water, and shelter, but it's not enough."

She'd heard the scenario before. It was rarely enough. "I'm not sure what this situation has to do with me."

Digane didn't hesitate with his response. "I'd like you to lead the emergency medical team we're sending in."

The request took her off guard. "I'm returning to the States in a couple days —"

"I realize that, but we've got a serious situation on our hands. What started out as a small cholera outbreak has quickly reached epidemic proportions."

Paige shivered. She'd seen it happen before. While relatively simple to treat if discovered early on, controlling the spread of cholera was an entirely different matter. And unlike other diseases, it could kill within hours as the result of dehydration.

"The minister of health is helping to coordinate with our efforts," Digane continued, "and is prepared to send additional medical personal, but their resources are scarcer than ours."

She wasn't going to do this. "Digane, I'm going home —"

"All I'm asking for is three days. The illness is spreading faster than a veld fire, and they're already stumbling over the dead bodies. The local government has asked for our help, and I need yours, Paige. If this situation isn't contained immediately . . ."

She tried to smother the guilt, but even with her readiness to go home, she couldn't dismiss the gravity of the situation. "I know how serious it is."

"Yesterday, the lead doctor who was in

charge of coordinating the setup of the medical facilities was called home because of a family emergency. I've got another doctor who has experience working in refugee camps lined up to take his place but he can't get here until Thursday. Until he arrives, I need a field coordinator to help get that cholera treatment center set up and running in the next twenty-four hours."

Paige felt her blood pressure rise. The idea of returning to another emergency situation made her stomach turn. All she wanted to do was to go home.

"You know if I had someone else with experience who was able to step in on such short notice, I wouldn't ask you." Digane pulled off his glasses and began cleaning them on his shirt, giving her time to consider his request. "There is a national staff as well as a logistician, nurses, and local workers already in place. All you have to do is say you want an addition built, and they'll have it up for you within the hour."

Digane made it sound like setting up the treatment center in a refugee camp during an epidemic would be a piece of cake compared to the past three months. She wasn't so sure. "Somehow I don't believe it's going to be quite as easy as you're making it out to be."

45

"Can I take that as a yes?"

She wouldn't go empty-handed. "I'm going to need supplies."

"A convoy left from the capital this morning with twenty-five hundred liters of Ringer's lactate for rehydration, along with food and other necessary items. We can fly in additional supplies for the treatment center immediately."

"Oral rehydration salts, IV sets, antibiotics —"

"I'll make sure you have everything you need."

"There are also all the logistical items. Chlorine, soap, and buckets —"

"Done."

"And I'm back in Bogama by Thursday night for my flight out of the country the next morning?"

Digane smiled for the first time, revealing his gold front tooth. "I'll get you out of there in time, but I need you, Paige. You're the only qualified doctor I've got at the moment who's free."

She forced down any remaining doubts. "You know I'll go wherever I'm needed."

Digane turned to Nick. "I'm glad you're here as well, because I need a pilot to fly in the emergency team and run supplies. Think you can get permission to lend a hand for a few days?"

Nick didn't hesitate. "I'll need to speak to my boss, but considering the situation, I'm sure he'll agree."

"Good." Digane's smile said he was pleased he'd gotten his way. "How long until you both can leave?"

Paige glanced at Nick. "Is an hour too long?"

FIVE

Monday, February 21, 12:54 p.m.
Mt. Maja, Senganie Route, 7,800 Feet
Brandon Collins leaned over, hands against his thighs to catch his breath, and stared out across the glistening landscape of Mt. Maja. After six hours of trekking up the slippery slopes of the rainforest, the thick canopy had finally given way to the open terrain of grassy moorlands, where yellow rays of light spun patterns of gold across the dozens of colorful wildflowers. With the first day almost behind them, the seventeen-thousand-foot dormant volcano still hung above them in the distance. In another three days, they'd reach their goal: the summit of the mountain's icy peak.

Unzipping his waterproof jacket, he drew in a lungful of frosty air, then glanced at his wife, Jodi, who was making her way up the narrow slope behind him. He shouldn't worry, but he couldn't help but be concerned that even the year of training she had under her belt for this trek wasn't going to be enough.

Jodi's expression shifted from one of deep concentration to panic as she lost her balance on the loose gravel. She grabbed for a tree limb, missed, then slid back down the incline.

"Jodi!" Brandon skidded down the worn path to where she'd fallen.

She wiped her bloodied palm against her pants. "I'm okay."

Brandon knelt in front of her, unconvinced. Blonde hair peeked from beneath her fleece hat, framing her flushed cheeks. "You just slid a good fifteen feet down the mountain. Don't tell me you're okay."

"I lost my balance and cut my hand. It's nothing."

"I want to check your ankle."

She grinned up at him. "Is that my husband or my physical therapist speaking?"

"Both." Brandon removed her boot and carefully rotated the scarred ankle with its metal pin. "Does that hurt?"

"It just feels a little stiff."

There was no swelling, no heat —

"I told you I'm fine, Brandon." She slid her boot back on and tied the laces.

He frowned, still unwilling for her to take

any chances. "Stand up carefully."

She shot him a disapproving look, but complied by testing out her foot on the ground before she put any pressure on the ankle.

Brandon pulled a tissue from his back pocket and pressed it against her palm. "You feel hot."

"I'm hot because someone convinced me to wear too many layers of clothes." She reached up and kissed him on the cheek, then grabbed a bottle of water from her pack and took a long sip. "Stop worrying."

Looking into Jodi's dark-brown eyes reminded him again why he'd asked her to marry him. Several friends had questioned their decision to spend three months trekking across Africa for their honeymoon, but eighteen months ago Jodi had faced off with death and won. Neither of them intended to let life pass them by without really living.

But that didn't erase his concern. She might be convinced of her ability to reach the top, but he knew her limitations as much as she did. Even with the relatively slow pace of today's climb, she'd need to conserve energy in order to make it to the summit.

He laced his fingers with hers. "We're almost to the camp and you can rest."

Jodi screwed the lid back on her bottle. This time she didn't argue. "Lead the way."

At the top of the hill, their camp, already set up by their guides, spread out before them. One of the other climbers, Ashley James, dressed as if she'd just stepped out of a pricey outdoor sports catalog, jerked back the flap of the small orange dome tent, and set her hands on her hips.

Brandon slid off his jacket. "Is there a problem?"

The twenty-something's frown deepened. "Where's the wash tent?"

"Wash tent?" Brandon pointed to the bowl of water at the edge of the tent.

Ashley picked up the bowl and dumped the warm water into the bush. Her success on last season's surprise-hit sitcom might have made her a household name — and given her temporary job security in Hollywood — but apparently the tabloid rumors of the actress being difficult to get along with had been right on target.

"My father and I climbed Mount Kilimanjaro in Tanzania two years ago and we had a private bath area." Her frown deepened. "He told me I could expect a similar experience, but this . . ."

"Similar, yes." Robert James walked up behind Ashley and grabbed the empty bowl

51

from his daughter. "But I also told you that climbing in the RD would be a more rustic setting. I was hoping you'd enjoy the experience."

"Enjoy the fact that even though I can call home from my satellite phone and receive text messages from the office I can't take a decent shower or have any privacy?" She tugged on the edge of her knit beanie. "You'll need to talk to the guide. This is not acceptable."

Brandon watched Ashley saunter off toward the other side of the camp and forced himself to hold his tongue. With less than twenty-four hours on the trail together, he already found the woman's constant complaining intolerable.

Robert dropped the bowl back in front of the tent. "I know what you're thinking. I love my daughter, but that doesn't mean I'm not aware of her faults." He glanced toward the edge of the trail, where Ashley now stood beside a fallen log, talking on her satellite phone. The girl's roaming charges were going to cost a fortune. "She thinks I drag her on these expeditions so I don't have to travel by myself. But the truth is I keep hoping I can ingrain a better appreciation of life in her."

Brandon chuckled. "I suppose I can see

the benefits of heavy discipline and a sense of accomplishment this trip provides."

"I hope so, but I'm starting to wonder if it hasn't all been a waste of time."

Brandon caught the tinge of disappointment in the older man's voice. Their group had met at the base camp last night for dinner and Robert had kept them laughing with anecdotes from a recent business trip to Brazil. Ashley, on the other hand, had complained that the food was too salty and the service too slow, then escaped to her room before most of them had eaten half their dinner. Whatever her father had tried to ingrain in her thus far had obviously failed.

Robert jutted his chin in his daughter's direction. "For now, she's gone and gotten herself engaged, so I figure in four months she'll be her new husband's problem."

Brandon sat on one of the provided chairs and helped Jodi take off her boots, wondering what kind of man would want to saddle himself with someone as high maintenance as Ashley. Or how someone as nice as Robert James had failed to pass on any of his charm to his daughter.

Robert pulled an energy bar from his pocket and ripped it open. "I don't want my daughter to know this, because it will only give her one more thing to worry about, but have you heard what the porters are talking about?"

Brandon looked to Jodi, then shook his head. Gossip about the actress had no doubt become fodder for conversation during the uphill trek.

Robert took a bite of the bar. "There was an attack at the base camp a couple hours after we left."

"An attack?" The older man's words took Brandon off guard. Whining and complaining could be tolerated, but unrest on the mountain potentially put all of them in danger. "What happened?"

"A group of men carrying automatic weapons broke in and stole a bunch of supplies."

"Was anyone hurt?" Brandon asked.

"I don't think so."

"I know there's been unrest in parts of the country, but we were told that this route was far enough away from the conflict that we'd be safe."

"The last thing the government wants is to scare away potential tourists." Robert stroked the bottom of his salt-and-pepper beard. "But even so, I can't imagine them hiking up this far for a handful of electronics."

Brandon glanced at Ashley, who still held the phone to her ear. Between her electronic collection and the porters who carried communication devices as a precaution during the climb, their group could easily be viewed as a prime target for a bunch of desperate rebels. "What were they looking for? Electronic equipment?"

"Satellite phones, radios, and food. And while I don't think we have anything to worry about, I do think we should all be on the lookout for anything unusual." Robert crumpled the foil wrapper in his hand. "Maybe I shouldn't have said anything . . ."

"No, we're glad you did." Brandon dropped Jodi's boot onto the ground beside him and started rubbing her foot, wondering if he might have more to worry about than the hardware embedded in his wife's ankle. He tried to shake off the slivers of alarm while at the same time hoping the man's prediction was correct.

Six

Monday, February 21, 2:21 p.m.
American Embassy, Bogama, RD
Paul Hayes downed the extra packet of cold
medicine his secretary had left on his desk
with a swig of lukewarm coffee, trying at
the same time to forget the ultimatum his
wife had just left him on his voice messages.
Three months ago, he'd have sworn their
marriage would last forever, but that was
before Maggie had left to spend the holidays
with his family in Denver, amidst promises
that he'd be there by Christmas. Now
Valentine's Day had come and gone and
he'd yet to join her. Which translated into
the dismal reality that their marriage was
on the line.

How had it ever come to this?

He cleaned his glasses with his shirttail,
rubbed his eyes, then slid the glasses back
on. When they first married, Maggie hadn't
seemed to mind his long hours at work.

56

She'd been caught up with advancing her own career as an associate in a small firm in Denver. Even their six months apart while he was on assignment in Afghanistan hadn't left any permanent damage to their marriage.

Nine months after his return, their twin daughters were born and everything changed. Maggie, who'd once reveled in making a name for herself in the corporate world, found everything she wanted in motherhood.

When the girls were seven, he'd been assigned the position of deputy chief of mission at the U.S. Embassy in the RD. The hardship pay and adventure of a new place had seemed worth it at first. But the novelty of living in a peaceful country had recently been replaced by not only the current turmoil facing the government, but also the fact that the ambassador was currently out of the country, making him the acting chief of mission. And he had no idea when he was going to be able to leave.

He sneezed, willing the congestion in his lungs to vanish. Or if nothing else, for the cold medicine to numb his heart. Picking up the phone, he hesitated, then jammed the receiver back in the cradle. While he couldn't blame her, Maggie's ultimatum couldn't have come at a worse time. Daily reports from the government continued to downplay the situation brought on by the attempted assassination of the president two months ago — an act that had plunged the country into political chaos. And just when he thought everything was settling down again, the legendary Ghost Soldiers had come forward with demands of amnesty for the leaders who'd been arrested three weeks ago.

He took another sip of his coffee before shoving the bitter drink aside. Everyone hoped the situation would be resolved as soon as possible, but he knew how quickly circumstances like this could spiral out of control. Rebel soldiers had put the entire country — and himself — in a precarious position and a quick resolution wasn't likely.

Sighing, he glanced at the photo of the twins propped up on his desk and ran his finger across the silver frame. He had tickets to return to the States on Friday, but he'd yet to tell Maggie that more than likely he'd have to postpone the trip. Not that she wanted to see him. She'd made it quite clear that unless he resigned from his post immediately, she was filing for divorce.

Despite everything that had happened between them, he still missed her like crazy and wished they were here. The girls turned nine next week and in January had started third grade at the local elementary school down the road from his parents. A thread of helplessness wound its way through him. With hundreds of lives potentially at stake it didn't seem fair to have to decide between his country and his wife and children, but the life he'd picked had been full of unfair choices.

Isaac knocked on the open door, then plopped a stack of folders onto the edge of his desk. "Mercy asked me to drop these off and tell you she is being bombarded with calls from expats wanting to know if rumors of rebels raiding villages and slaughtering villagers in the north are true."

"How did my Foreign Service National investigator get drafted into the role of gopher?"

Isaac's smile broadened. "That's a good question, sir."

Paul flipped through the stack of folders Isaac had given him. As a Foreign Service National investigator, Isaac was the head liaison between the embassy and the RD's security and law enforcement. He'd become Paul's right-hand man from day one of his assignment, especially with the ambassador out of the country. "I've got an e-mail box full of the same thing, despite your government's assurances to the contrary."

"You sound as if you do not believe them."

"To be honest, I'm not sure what to believe. They might be labeling the death of the American aid worker this morning as a misfortunate accident, but it's hard to know who's telling the truth, especially when no one will give me a straight answer." Paul pushed the folders to the edge of his desk. Any nonessential operational issues would have to be dealt with later. "The rebels, no doubt, want to repress what's happening so it doesn't become an international affair. That would call for the UN to come in and clamp down on them, and I'm quite sure that the government doesn't want to lose their international aid or turn away tourists."

"Or maybe the reports are right, and it was just a case of being in the wrong place at the wrong time."

Maybe.

Paul rotated his neck in a slow circle to try to loosen some of the tension that started at his jawline and made its way down to the small of his back. If he could find a free moment in the next twenty-four hours, he'd take an hour off and go running. But until then, his bottles of Tums and Tylenol would have to ease the ongoing symptoms of stress. "All I know is that it's getting hard to distinguish fact from fiction. For now, we've got to make sure we keep all local wardens and volunteers in the loop in case we have to recommend an evacuation for the rest of the country."

"Do you think it will come to that?"

"At this point, I don't think so." Paul caught the concern in Isaac's expression and felt for the man and his family. As an American citizen, he could leave before the situation spiraled out of control, but for Isaac and most Dzambizians, there was nowhere for them to go. He cleared his throat and pushed away the guilt freedom often brought with it.

"I hope you are right." Isaac's smile had faded. "But we all know how situations like this can turn into an international incident overnight. Three months ago the RD was hailed as a poster child for not only a peaceful election, but as an example to other African nations."

"And now that has all changed." Paul picked up his pen and tapped it against his desk. "I want you to get a hold of Digane Olam at the hospital in Kingani. It was his aid workers who were involved in this morning's incident. I want to hear his version of what happened."

"Yes, sir."

"And while you're on the phone with him, tell him to call me once the convoy makes the refugee camp."

"A convoy?"

"It left early this morning from here full of medical supplies, food, and equipment, and a dozen aid workers. Tell him I want confirmation the minute it arrives at that camp."

"I'll let him know." Isaac started to the door, then stopped. "Before I forget, how are Maggie and the twins? I promised my wife I would ask."

"They're good." Paul again felt the sting of guilt and wished he could avoid the subject. "She told me how much she hated missing your daughter's birth. How is she?"

Isaac smiled. "She turned four weeks old yesterday. She is beautiful."

"I'm sure she is." Paul steepled his hands in front of him and rested his elbows on his desk. "How long have you been working here?"

"Four and a half years."

"What does your wife think about the long hours?"

"She has always been supportive. I think right now she is more worried about the

62

rebel attacks in the north where her family lives."

Paul shook his head. "Don't lose her, Isaac. I know we come from different cultures and different backgrounds, but this job has a tendency to come between you and everyone you love and pull you apart. You don't have to let it."

No one had given him that advice twenty-five years ago. His father had been a workaholic, and he'd followed blindly in the old man's footsteps. At this point there was no turning back for him. He knew what his choice would be. Maggie knew what his choice would be.

Isaac nodded. "Of course not, boss. I have no intentions to."

"Good." Paul cleared his throat. Dumping his personal problems on his employees wasn't in his job description.

But neither was sacrificing his wife and children. He'd seen how unrest could escalate overnight, and with armed rebels on the move, he was left to try and ensure the safety of the Americans living in the country. Those in the Mponi region had already been ordered to leave. Next, they'd contacted all the local wardens and volunteers throughout the rest of the country who'd been organized to ensure everyone was in the loop and received the latest warnings. If things did end up spiraling out of control, the next step would be to recommend all Americans — who were mainly humanitarian workers, missionaries, and a handful of tourists — leave the country. A task that could end up involving the U.S. military and miles of red tape on his end.

"Anything else you need me to do, sir?"

"Get your people to tell you what's going on while I run through a few contacts of my own. And I'll want hourly updates on what's happening out there."

"What happens if this conflict spreads beyond the northern region?"

Paul shook his head. "Let's pray it doesn't get to that."

SEVEN

Monday, February 21, 2:58 p.m.
Rebel Base Camp

. . . In other news from the African continent, talks continue in the capital of the Republic of Dhambizao between the government and spokesmen for the rebel leaders, but many fear that the resolution to the three-week-long standoff is nowhere in sight. Rumors continue to spread that villagers are being butchered in their beds by rebel soldiers, giving way to fears by some of a possible genocide. President Tau insists that his army is in control of the region and denies that the rebels are gaining any ground, despite their threats. He also denied rumors that the RD is heading toward a civil war.

On the other side of the controversy, rebels maintain that they now control over seventy-five percent of the Mponi region, where their camp is believed to be located. It is also estimated that in the past week another five thousand have fled to escape the heart of the conflict, leaving aid organizations over-whelmed with high numbers of refugees and few resources.

To assure his people, Tau addressed the country yesterday from his home in the capital and told those listening that the army is still in control, and that despite the rebels' demands no group would be able to coerce the govern-ment.

Later, a spokesman for President Tau even went so far as to say that the RD is willing to offer amnesty to the leaders of the Ghost Soldiers in exchange for an end to their reign of terror. But the International Criminal Court says that their organization will not withdraw the international arrest warrants they issued last month.

Because of this, many fear President Tau's assurance that everything is under control is simply not true. An American aid worker was shot and killed earlier this morning, fueling fears for foreigners living inside the country and forcing the president to implement a forced evacuation of all foreigners in the Mponi region.

Washington has repeatedly said that it will not intervene in the conflict, though a spokes-man from the State Department did say that marine expeditionary units have been alerted to prepare for a potential rescue mission to pick up evacuees if necessary . . .

Jonas tossed the cigarette butt onto the ground and watched the orange tip smolder for a few seconds before it turned into a pile of pale ashes. His own heart had been extinguished years ago, making revenge far more palatable. But even the numbness couldn't completely hide the raging anger inside. Or the guilt.

A mosquito buzzed in his ear. He swatted at the nuisance, wishing the late afternoon held more of a breeze. The shaded compound held little relief from the sun's fury, for him or the dozens of other soldiers and their women who made up the newly formed camp. The success of the past few days hadn't been enough to sway the outcome of the situation. They were going to need to do more to convince Tau and his army they had no intention of backing down until their commanders — including his brother — were released. He'd worry about the next step after that.

Ngozi slid into the wooden seat beside him, a bottle of beer nestled between his fingers. "I am worried."

Jonas tried to shove aside his own tremulous thoughts, but knew the nightmares and the constant worry would never leave him. Ngozi's stature resembled his own lean frame. Too much drinking and too many women killed a man on this continent. But he never took time to worry about tomorrow. Getting through each day was enough.

"Why are you worried? Nelson radioed an hour ago and told me that their attack was a success. They'll be back in a couple hours."

Ngozi shook his head. "Successful? They were supposed to return with satellite phones and equipment. Instead they left a man dead. How well do you think that will go over with the International Criminal Court?"

Jonas laughed. They'd killed dozens in the past three weeks, and Ngozi was worried about one man? "There are always casualties in war, and I have never known you to worry about a few dead bodies."

"Getting the Americans involved does not equal success."

Jonas had wanted to ignore that detail. Few cared when the rebels spent their time burning down villages and raping women, but kill a white man and the world reacted.

Ngozi leaned forward. "They will send more troops, the UN will get involved, and then where will that leave us?"

Jonas shrugged. "It doesn't matter. By the time President Tau assembles his troops and comes after us, it will be too late. We will have squeezed Tau until he has no choice but to give us what we want."

"And then what? You think they will actually honor any promises of amnesty to your brother, Seba, and the others?"

Jonas turned and studied his friend. The hard lines on his face displayed the scars of the rough life they'd both lived. "It will not matter. We will disappear somewhere and live like kings."

"And how do we do that when we've lost a dozen of our own men and do not have the resources of the army."

"All we have to do is strike back faster and smarter."

"And that means burning down more villages to prove a point?"

"When did your conscience start bothering you? We wanted to get their attention, which is what we have done. And until our demands are met, I have no intention of stopping. Have you forgotten why we're doing this?"

"No, but —"

"We cannot forget that our government once promised us far more than the status of *renegade.* If we do not win, we will end up nothing more than cowards like the rest of them."

"Maybe, but how much longer can this continue? Or is this nothing more than revenge because the army murdered your wife and children and now your brother sits rotting in prison?"

Jonas bit back the acidic reply that hovered on the tip of his tongue. Right now he needed Ngozi on his side. "My brother and the others are why we will continue to fight. And the fact that they murdered my wife and children puts me in the perfect position. They have taken everything I have and I have nothing more to lose."

"What about Eshe?"

Jonas' gaze flashed to the thatched hut where a young girl lay on a reed mat, their child growing within her large belly. Yara toddled beside her, then fell down, her brown legs covered with sand. His gaze dropped. Children didn't belong in a camp run by a bunch of renegade soldiers, just like he hadn't belonged in one at seven. But he'd had no alternative. Eshe had chosen to stay. Or so he liked to believe. He'd heard little complaints from the woman he'd chosen as his second wife.

"Do you plan to risk the lives of your children for . . . revenge?"

"Yes." Jonas' jaw tensed. Walking away might have once been an option, but not anymore. "We both know that it will take bloodshed to get what is ours."

"Except they will never give it to us. Eventually, they will slice our throats or leave us rotting in prison before they give in to our demands. They know it is only a matter of time before our resources run out and we are forced to —"

"Give up?" Jonas kicked over the wooden chair beside him, then pulled out his gun. The nozzle of his weapon brushed against Ngozi's cheek. He winced at the sudden movement of his injured arm, but bit back the pain. He didn't need anyone that bad. "I'm in charge now and I say we will not give up. Besides, you talk as a fool and make the death of those we've lost in this fight worth nothing. Is that what you want? Because if it is, walk away now and take the rest of your followers with you."

Ngozi's jaw trembled, and he dropped his gaze. "What are you suggesting?"

"That you have forgotten they used every one of us to do their dirty work, then spit us out like vomit onto the African soil. If a few more people die, then so be it, but you are a coward if you walk away now."

Jonas shot his rifle into the air, then

stepped into the center of the compound, looking one by one at each of the men who'd been drawn into the commotion. "Anyone else ready to walk away from this, or have you already forgotten how our government was quick to place all the blame on us while they spent the profits made from the slave camps like rich men?"

When no one responded, Jonas righted the chair he'd kicked over and sat back down, still grasping his weapon. Most of the men had already lost interest in the discussion and had gone back to sleeping in the afternoon heat.

One of his men approached, his left brow twitching. "I know where we can get supplies."

"Weapons?"

"Mainly food and communication devices."

Jonas wiped the sweat from his forehead with the back of his hand and considered the offer. He'd be the first to admit that weapons were a priority, but it was food that would sustain the fight. "Where?"

"There is a convoy of trucks headed from the capital to the refugee camp twenty kilometers north of us."

A plan began to form as Jonas mulled over the idea. "The government's not listening, so maybe you're right. Maybe it's time to take things a step further."

EIGHT

Paige gazed out the window of the Cessna at the hundreds of white tents dotting the flat landscape in the distance. Beyond them, billowy clouds met the blue-gray mountains rising from the earth in the east. The plane banked to the left in preparation for landing her and her team.

She took in a deep breath, then let it out slowly. In the past three months, her emotions had been pulled in more directions than she'd ever imagined possible. Lack of basic resources had showed her up close the heartbreaking struggle her patients faced daily. Tayla's image surfaced, reminding her how quickly situations became personal. Day-to-day living was difficult for most in the best of circumstances, but with the rebels slaughtering villagers and cholera ravaging the camp, survival would take a

74

miracle.

Paige grasped the armrests as the plane banked to the left and the majestic peaks of Mt. Maja came into view. She'd spent the past seven years since graduating from med school dealing with emergency medical situations, but here, limited resources called for creative responses for needs that never seemed to wane. With long hours and a steep learning curve, the work was draining both physically and emotionally. Which was why she was ready to go home. She searched for the extra reserve of energy it was going to take to deal with the situation and came up empty.

I don't want to do this any more, God. There are so many needs, and all I can see is suffering . . .

"Are you ready for this?" Nick's question from the pilot's seat brought her back to the present.

"I'm worried that what we have isn't going to be enough." She avoided answering his question. "A handful of nurses, a couple of lab technicians, plus a planeload of supplies . . . and over ten thousand people."

"If Jesus could feed a crowd of over five thousand with five loaves and two fishes, then I expect we can trust him to give us what we need today."

The analogy struck a cord. "Trust has come in spurts lately. We're going to need a few miracles in the coming days to get the mortality rate back under control."

"I know I'm praying for a miracle." Nick shot her a smile, then tugged on his ball cap. "Make sure you're buckled up. We'll be landing in another couple minutes."

Paige stared out across the flat plateau as they began their descent and took in the scene. They were low enough that she could make out the colorful clothes of the women standing between the white igloo-type tents that had become home for the thousands forced to leave their own land and way of life.

Two minutes later, the plane landed on the grassy field on the western edge of the camp that to Paige seemed to stretch on forever. Mt. Maja rose in the background, its icy cap hovering in the distance, a sharp contrast to the hot and humid temperatures on the ground.

She stepped down from the plane and tried to take in the familiar collage of sights, smells, and sounds engulfing her. Photos she'd seen of refugee camps before her arrival in the RD had only been able to convey sterilized stills of the scene. Their thousands of pixels had been unable to transfer the smells of cooking fires and dirty latrines. Or the desperation filling the air that these innocent men, women, and children were forced to deal with on a daily basis. Or the scent of death lingering in the air.

"Dr. Ryan?" A tall, lanky man wearing a safari hat stopped in front of their small group. "I'm Taz Michaels, and we're glad you're here. I'm the logistician for the camp."

"It's nice to meet you." Paige shook his hand, then introduced the rest of the team. "I can see that you've accomplished a lot in the short time you've been here, but Digane told us that the situation is deteriorating rapidly."

"We've already started removing the bodies, disinfecting and burying them."

"How many?"

"I lost count after the first fifty or sixty." He pointed to the other end of the camp where dozens of freshly dug graves marked the landscape. "We're digging new graves every day."

Paige's stomach cinched. The sting of death never lessened. "It looks like we've got a lot of work ahead of us."

"And number one on my list is to finish setting up your cholera treatment center." He picked up one of the bags and pulled the strap across his shoulder. "We've already constructed an isolation tent with the help of some of the locals."

"We'll need to train some of them to chlorinate the water sources and help keep the area inside the tent disinfected as well."

Nick handed her a medical bag, then quickly distributed the rest of the equipment.

"If you'll follow me, I'll show you where you'll be working." Taz started for the cluster of large tents set at the southern entrance of the camp. "Beside the cholera epidemic, we're dealing with typical refugee-camp issues. We have eight local nurses working in the newly set up clinic. As soon as the rest of the supplies arrive, there are also plans for a malnutrition center. Anything you need to know from me before we get going?"

"Several things." Paige had her own list of questions she needed to ask to get a complete feel of the situation. "I understand there're currently about ten thousand refugees?"

"At least two thousand have registered in the past seventy-two hours, which brings our total to just over ten thousand. We've set up twelve hundred tents with another five hundred on the way, but even that isn't going to be enough."

Paige gazed out across the sea of white tents — constructed to keep out the rain and reflect the sun's rays in the heat of the day — and prayed again for that miracle. From her vantage point, it was going to take more than five loaves of bread, or even five stones, to slay this giant.

Women carrying bright-yellow jerricans were lined up for as far as she could see at one of the water points, the skirts of their colorful dresses fluttering in the afternoon breeze. Toddlers clung to their legs or played beside them on the muddy paths.

A group of children ran up to them, waving and smiling in welcome. Despite the scent of death lingering in the air, life still went on. Paige waved back, wishing there was something she could do to make their lives normal again. No child deserved to live in these kinds of conditions.

Paige turned back to Taz, knowing that behind the bright smiles often lurked the dark realities of something even more serious. Those with the AIDS virus would be especially vulnerable to cholera. "What about the prevalence of HIV/AIDS?"

"We haven't had the time or resources to find out, but it's suspected to be high in the area, along with tuberculosis."

"Which will only fuel the cholera." Concern began chipping away at her desire to leave. "How much clean water is available?"

"About two-and-a-half liters per person per day."

Paige quickly calculated the substantive shortage. Even if the weather cooled, it wouldn't be nearly enough. "The recognized minimum standard is fifteen to twenty liters per person per day."

"With the fuel truck that's on its way we'll be able to dig a couple of boreholes. That should supply us with most of the water we need."

Clean water was only one of the logistical issues that would have to be tackled. The higher the influx of people arriving at the camp, the higher the need for sanitation — something hard to achieve in an emergency situation.

"What about latrines?"

"So far we've had two hundred latrines dug using the local labor, but as the numbers increase, we're going to need to dig more."

Paige shook her head, though this time she wasn't surprised with the answer. The international standard was twenty people per latrine, making this setup again far below minimum standards. She'd never get used to working against the odds.

Taz stopped in front of her. "What do I need to do to help get you started?"

"As soon as we get the supplies unloaded, we'll need to get the isolation tent set up so we can start registering and rehydrating patients."

She followed the team past a row of tents, stopping when Taz excused himself to talk with one of the refugees. A group of old men sat playing cards. Barefooted children laughed, seemingly oblivious to the drama taking place around them. A generator buzzed in the background, competing with music playing from a radio. A young mother cooked over a fire, its smoky scent filling Paige's nostrils. But she didn't miss the exhaustion that filled the woman's expression or her dehydrated form and sunken eyes. Cholera.

God, they're like prisoners with nowhere to run.

The scene triggered a verse she'd read a few months ago in which God had told Zechariah that he would free the prisoners from the waterless pit.

The now familiar feeling of helplessness that had haunted her since her arrival in the RD returned. They needed freedom. How many of these families had been displaced not once, but two and three times? They'd escaped their homes with no way to get food; they'd been separated from their families, vulnerable to the elements, and caught up as victims in someone else's war.

She patted the head of a small toddler with a yellow band around his ankle that signaled that he suffered from moderate malnutrition and needed to be watched by the medical team. Why was it that there were never enough latrines, water, and food? Even here she'd never be able to give them everything they needed.

Paige crouched down in front of the small group of children that had gathered around her. She pulled one of the square pieces of paper she'd brought with her out of her pocket and waved it slowly in front of her. Eyes wide, the children waited to see what she was going to do.

With the same dramatic flair her father had used when teaching her the art of origami, Paige began systematically folding and refolding the sheet of green paper. By now, several of the adults had joined the circle to see what she was doing. Two front legs emerged from the diamond-shaped folded paper, then two back legs. She held up the frog's body so everyone could see it, then gently blew up the main body of the small figure.

Giggles erupted from the group as she handed the frog to one of the little boys.

"You're good." Nick, who'd hung back beside her while the others stood talking, laughed. "Good enough to think about changing careers if you ever get tired of the medical side."

"I'll have to think about that." She glanced up at him, taken in by the toffee-brown eyes that conveyed a sense of calm she needed at the moment. "I have to admit that all this is overwhelming."

Nick held out his hand and one of the little girls grasped his fingers and grinned up at him. "Yes, but that's why you're here. And I'm already convinced that there's a certain doctor standing beside me who can handle the task ahead. All you have to worry about is one person at a time."

One person at a time.

Paige drew in a deep breath. She could do this.

"Dr. Ryan?" Taz walked back to her. The carefree smile he'd worn earlier had vanished.

Paige pressed her shoulders back. "What's wrong?"

"We have a potential problem on our hands. The truck that's on its way here with

83

fuel for the boreholes is stuck in the mud five kilometers down the road. There's already a crowd trying to take advantage of the situation and siphon the fuel."

Paige put her hand up to block the sun and gazed down the empty road. Digane might have put her in charge, but she wasn't ready for them to look to her for answers. From the short briefing she'd received before she left, she knew that the road leading from the camp was lightly populated. It wouldn't take long before word spread, and if the rebels got their hands on that fuel, the situation could quickly spiral out of control. It could take days before another truck arrived. Which meant they had to act fast.

"We need that fuel." She looked Taz in the eye. "Have the rest of the supplies unloaded from the plane. And in the meantime, we'll need a car and a driver to assess the situation."

Taz nodded. "Give me five minutes."

NINE

Monday, February 21, 3:52 p.m.
Kingani Road

Samson held onto the hand of his son, Asim, who tried to pull him toward the open market lining the opposite side of the road. Women sat on the ground beneath the blistering afternoon sun with their piles of tomatoes and onions in front of them. Behind them, dozens more vendors displayed fish, bowls of rice and sugar, and other wares on rickety tables, where they'd barter with customers until the moon rose high against the black sky.

Asim tugged harder. "I'm hungry."

"Not now. There is no time to stop, Asim."

Samson caught the sting he'd inflicted in his son's eyes and wished he could take back his sharp reply. He stepped over a deep rut slicing the dirt road. A week ago he would have pulled a coin from his pocket and given it to Asim to buy a treat from one of the vendors, even though Valina always reprimanded him for spoiling the child. He glanced down at his son's wide brown eyes and dark, curly hair and replayed the moment, six years ago, when he'd been told his wife had given birth to a son. After three girls, the appearance of a son had filled him with pride. And, at that time, had renewed his hope that the ancestors still smiled on him.

But today his pockets were empty. He had no money to buy a handful of dried fish and sauce from one of the plump mamas minding her stall, let alone purchase a small piece of candy for his son.

He maneuvered Asim around a flock of caged roosters. All that remained was the prevailing feeling of an empty stomach — and a haunting taste of life without Valina and his girls. If he was lucky, he'd find his family waiting for him at the camp. But their disappearance, and the brutal murder of many of his neighbors, had revealed to him the horrid truth: his village, and perhaps his family itself, was cursed.

Samson gripped Asim's hand tighter as he breathed in the smell of *goza* and fish sauce emanating from the small shop beside them, angry he couldn't give his son what his swollen belly craved. Their only hope was to make it to the camp, where he'd been told aid workers were giving out food packets. He'd also heard rumors that humanitarian workers would hire anyone willing to dig latrines and bore holes.

He pressed past a group of old men hiding from the late afternoon sun beneath the shade of a tree and wondered how much further to the refugee camp. His feet ached and his head pounded, but with the constant rumors of more attacks, he didn't dare spend another night on the road. When darkness had finally left them this morning, he'd been grateful for another day. But if they didn't make it to the camp within the next couple hours, they'd face another night with little to shelter them from the winds once the sun dropped below the horizon. And nothing to protect them from the rebels.

Asim pointed to a man carrying a green parrot along the other side of the road. "I want to see it."

The boy's keen sense of curiosity, it seemed, had for the moment overcome his desire to eat. The man, holding onto the handmade cage housing the bird, disappeared into the market.

"I'm sorry, Asim, but we must get to the camp."

"No!" Asim jerked away from him, and in an instant the boy had crossed the street to follow the man with the bird into the crowded market. Samson pushed back the panic enveloping him as he searched behind piles of fruits and vegetables for a glimpse of his son's red shirt. He ran down the narrow aisle his son had entered, but there was no sign of him.

"Asim!"

He stopped to ask the vendors one after another if they'd seen his son, but none had noticed the scrawny six-year-old chasing the green parrot. Most dozed in the heat of the late afternoon or fanned away the constant swarms of flies on their piles of dried fish.

Samson stopped at the far edge of the market. Jagged breaths stabbed at his chest as he caught sight of a tanker that lay off the road fifty meters ahead. Its front tires had dropped off into the sandy ditch on the far side. A crowd had gathered. He knew his son. Asim's curiosity would lead him to the center of the attraction.

The driver jumped down from the truck and yelled at the onlookers. Samson's mind spun. His work as a carpenter had given him the strength of two, even three, men. If they would hire him to help pull the vehicle back on the road, he might be able to buy food for another day.

But first he had to find Asim.

Samson ran toward the truck and scanned the crowd for his son. The pungent smell of petrol filled his nostrils. He quickened his speed when he caught sight of the boy's shirt. Asim stood a few meters from the truck while villagers filled containers with siphoned fuel from the tanker. Someone grabbed the driver and shoved him against the vehicle.

Samson caught the orange glow of a cigarette.

The explosion was deafening. The ground shook. Flashes of orange and yellow jumped from the fuel truck. The forest on the other side of the truck erupted into flames that leapt toward the sky.

Asim vanished behind a wall of black smoke.

TEN

Monday, February 21, 4:01 p.m.
Kingani Road

Paige felt the impact of the explosion from the backseat of the jeep. Black flumes billowed above the tree line a half mile ahead. If it was the tanker . . .

She leaned forward toward Taz, who drove the vehicle. "What's going on up there?"

"It's got to have something to do with the tanker."

Nick sat beside her, the same worry she felt gnawing on his expression. They both knew what would happen if they lost the fuel. Without it, there would be no way to get the water they needed to control the cholera epidemic. And with the way logistical things moved here, it could be days before they got another supply truck to the camp.

The afternoon breeze whipped across her face, bringing with it the smell of burning fuel. But it wasn't simply the loss of resources that frightened her. Anyone near the tanker during the explosion would have been injured. She'd read about the horrid explosion in Kenya where over a hundred people were killed and others seriously burned when a tanker exploded. Dozens of victims had been airlifted out of the area by the country's air force, but with the RD's military already stretched to the limit, an evacuation of that scale was out of the question here. Which could leave her and the limited facilities of the camp as their only option.

Paige held on to the door handle as their driver flew down the potholed road, bridging the distance between them and the explosion. Already she could see orange flames licking the truck while thick smoke rose from the surrounding vegetation along the road.

Rebels had ravaged and burned down villages. What if they were here?

The thought punched through her gut. She turned to Nick, thankful he'd agreed to her request to come with her. "Do you think this has something to do with the rebels?"

He shook his head. "It's hard to say, but I'd think the rebels would be out there siphoning off the gas for their own use

91

rather than blowing it up. They're short on resources and a tanker of gas would probably come in pretty handy."

"So they hijacked the tanker, then something went wrong?"

"That's a valid possibility."

And one she didn't like. They'd been told that the rebels had set up their base camp in the Mponi region, but in order to stay hidden it was assumed they moved often. Which meant there was no way to be certain where they were.

The jeep skidded to a stop a hundred feet from the truck. The air smelled like burning fuel. Paige choked, and a sick feeling washed over her. Bodies lay in the ditch, the remains charred from the blast. Her stomach churned at the stench of burning flesh. The explosion had turned them into human torches.

"We've got to move any survivors away from the truck and get them out of here."

Paige grabbed her medical bag and jumped from the jeep. The heavy smoke filled her lungs. She pressed her hand against her mouth and nose.

"Where are we going to take the victims?" Nick stood in front of her. "Besides the camp, the nearest hospital is over almost three hours away by car."

Paige hollered above the confusion. "Find the driver of that truck across the street. We can use the flatbed to transport people back to the camp."

"I've got my plane, but I'd only have room for three patients. Maybe four at the most."

"We'll leave it open as a possibility, but I'm not sure how I can afford to send any of my medical personnel with you." Paige began pulling what she needed from her bag. "I don't think we have any other choice but to make do with what we have with the supplies in the camp. If it becomes necessary, you can transport some to the hospital."

"We could contact the air force," Taz suggested. "They could airlift anyone with serious injuries to the nearest hospital."

Military assistance would be the best-case scenario in this mess. Kingani Hospital might not have everything to treat the victims, but their resources far outweighed those of the camp. Paige nodded. "It's worth a try."

Taz pulled out his cell phone and started walking away from the commotion. Paige turned to Nick. Lives would be lost if they didn't hurry.

"You worry about stabilizing people." Nick seemed to read her mind. "The police have just shown up. I'll work with them to get this mess organized and arrange the transport to the camp."

Paige dropped to the ground beside a man whose right side was burnt, thankful for Nick's ability to handle the situation.

A burly black man ran past her toward the tanker and the flames, but Nick blocked his route. "I need you to stay back, sir. There is a chance that the truck could explode again."

The man broke away from Nick's grasp and moved closer to the truck. "My son's here somewhere. I can't find him."

"Sir, I understand. There's a lot of chaos, but he must be here somewhere. I need you to move away from the truck."

Leaving Nick to deal with the man, Paige signaled to one of the policemen to carry an injured man to the truck, then rushed to the next patient. At least a dozen were dead; another three wouldn't make it through the night. A woman with burns across her face lay on the ground with a baby in her arms. Paige stabilized her as best she could, then watched as two men carried her and the child to the flatbed.

A flash of red caught her eye on the far side of the ditch. Someone was still out there. Ignoring the danger of the burning truck, Paige ran across the blackened grass toward the figure. Heat radiated across her face. Another loud pop exploded and sent a flame shooting up her arm, burning the flesh. Paige glanced at the red welt rising on her forearm and forced herself to ignore the searing pain.

Halfway down the blackened ditch, she realized that the small form, saved partly from its position behind a blackened tree stump, was a child. She lifted the limp figure and carried him to a patch of grass at a safe distance from the burning truck. She scanned the small boy for injuries. Keeping his body aligned and his head supported, she laid him on his back. A faint pulse beat beneath his jawline, but he wasn't breathing.

She yelled at him and shook him gently. No response.

"That's my son!" The man Nick had blocked earlier ran up to her and grabbed for the boy.

"Stop." Paige moved between the boy and his father. "I'm a doctor. If you want him to live, you're going to have to stay back and let me work." She grabbed the CPR mouthpiece from her bag and tilted the boy's head to check for anything in his mouth. Nothing. She breathed two small breaths, then brought her ear against his open mouth. His chest lay flat and unresponsive.

"Come on . . ." Vaguely aware that Nick had arrived, she breathed for him again.

The boy arched his back and started coughing as Paige turned him onto his side, relief flooding through her. Burns crisscrossed his small body, but at least he was alive. The burn on her own arm ached, but all she could think about was the dead bodies, burned victims, and the fact that no fuel could mean days without clean drinking water for the refugees. And that the man crouched beside her might lose his son.

God help me . . . help all of us.

"Please tell me what's going on." The man rocked on his knees beside her.

"He's breathing, but his pulse is weak." Paige continued her assessment, understanding the need to keep the father distracted. "What's his name?"

"Asim."

"How old is he?"

"Six." Disbelief shown in the father's eyes. "Is he going to live?"

Paige watched Asim's small chest rise and fall. "I don't know."

If he didn't succumb to the injuries, it would be a miracle, but she was even more concerned about the chance of infection.

Keeping wounds and burns clean in a disaster situation wasn't going to be easy.

She turned back to the father. "What's your name?"

"Samson."

"Samson, I'm Dr. Ryan. I've just started working in the refugee camp."

"We were on our way there."

"I want to take your son there now. I don't have the means to transport everyone to the hospital in Kingani, but I promise to do everything I can to help your son."

Paige moved aside and let Samson pick up his son.

Nick signaled to Paige. "We've got the injured in the truck. I think you need to get back to the camp with them now so you can treat them. I'll be right behind you with anyone else we find."

Paige nodded and climbed up into the truck. Resources in the camp might be limited, but it was still better than treating the victims here.

"Wait a minute." Nick's hand grasped her shoulder. "What happened to your arm?"

Paige looked down at the raised red welts across her forearm. "It's nothing."

"Nothing, Paige? Stop!"

She stepped back down onto the dusty road. Concern showed in Nick's eyes, but there wasn't time to deal with her burns. She'd make it through the next twenty-four hours with a few Tylenol. Half of those lying in the back of the truck would be lucky to still be alive by then.

"Nick, I —"

"You and I both know that you can't treat these people if you don't take care of yourself."

Paige frowned. Apparently Nick could be as stubborn as she.

"I'm only saying what you already know."

"What I know is that if I don't get these people back to the camp, someone's going to die. I can't let that happen."

"All I'm suggesting is that you let me fly you to the hospital and have your arm treated properly. We can be back within a couple hours."

"You know we don't have time for that." Paige jumped into the back of the truck and signaled to the driver, ignoring Nick's protests. "I'll see you back at the camp."

ELEVEN

A burst of adrenaline shot through Paige's chest, giving her the extra amount of energy she needed. She was back in the ER with its hectic waiting rooms, shiny tile floors, crash carts, and equipment. Saving lives was what she'd been trained to do, and treating patients was where she felt the most in her element . . .

She caught sight of the naked bulb dangling above her, and the scene in her mind vanished. She squinted in the dull yellow light, barely enough to aid her in stabilizing one of the burn victims. Tennessee and the high-tech hospital she'd left behind three months ago were both thousands of miles away.

Here, semipermanent tents assembled with wooden poles and white plastic sheeting surrounded her, along with the constant

99

backdrop of crying babies from the crowded waiting room of the main medical tent. Raindrops from a rare late afternoon shower pinged on the metal sheeting above her, adding to the constant noise.

The young woman in front of her moaned, snapping Paige back to reality. She had to keep her rampant emotions focused. She gave the woman an injection of morphine, wishing she could take away the discomfort. The third-degree burns caused nerve death, meaning she'd feel little in those areas. It was the second-degree burns, where the raw nerve cells were still alive, that would cause the most pain.

Despite the severity of the explosion and its consequences, she'd still been right about the miracle. With an explosion of that magnitude, the number of victims could have been far worse. Nick had transported the three most serious burn victims to the hospital in Kingani. Four other patients, including Asim, lay hooked up to IVs, their burns already rinsed to stop the skin from cooking.

Adding the explosion to the equation had created an even more volatile situation and had forced a number of quick decisions. Local nurses with experience in dealing with cholera had already begun registering and rehydrating patients. But as fast as they were working to process and isolate the cholera victims, there still remained an unending line of patients.

Taking a deep breath, she glanced across the dirt floor, covered with more plastic sheeting, to the noisy waiting room. She'd assigned five of the nurses to work a triage among the patients in the main clinic, referring the more serious cholera cases to the isolation tent. There, the rest of the medical staff monitored the already large number of patients with IV bags to ensure none of them ran dry.

Near the door, a baby lay still in his mother's arms, the sunken soft spots on his head signaling dehydration. Beside the boy's tired-looking mother, an old woman sat hunched forward, pain reflecting in her eyes. A couple of teenage girls huddled in the corner while a middle-aged man, probably dealing with tuberculosis, coughed continuously into a cloth.

She looked at her watch. Over an hour-and-a-half had passed since Nick had left, promising to return with the list of additional supplies she'd requested. But she needed him now. For some crazy reason, he'd become an anchor in the midst of a storm that was raging out of control.

A man entered the building and strode through the crowded waiting room without stopping. She squinted in the dim light and recognized the father of the young boy she'd pulled out of the ditch. While all the victims from the explosion had been transported to the camp, family members had walked.

He stopped at the foot of the bed. "I'm looking for my son, Asim?"

Paige signaled for one of the nurses to take over for her before motioning the father to follow her toward one of the metal cots set up at the far end of the room. "You can sit down and talk to him if you'd like, though don't expect him to respond. He'll probably sleep a lot during the next couple days."

Samson sat down beside his son and grasped his hand. The boy stirred, but didn't wake. "Tell me he will live."

Paige bit her lip, wishing she could, but it was a promise she knew she wouldn't be able to keep. "I gave him something to help him sleep, so for now he's doing okay. But you need to know that there is always the chance for infection to set in. And we don't have all the resources of a hospital, nor a way to transport him right now."

Deciding which patients to send on the plane with Nick had churned the guilt already raging inside her. She hated feeling as if she was playing God, but the situation had left her no choice. No landing lights at the camp meant that if Nick didn't make it back before the sunset, he wouldn't be able to return until tomorrow. Which also meant that this late in the day, transporting a second group of patients by air was no longer an option. Those left at the camp who still needed transportation were also the ones who weren't stable enough to make the difficult three-hour trip on the pot-holed Kingani road. And after dark, the trip became even more dangerous.

Nor would she mention to his father that Asim's malnourishment was a negative factor in his recovery. Samson was no doubt already facing his own guilt over the situation.

The man's dark eyes pleaded with her. "You cannot let him die."

Paige shoved every ounce of courage she could find into her voice. "The God I serve is a God of miracles, and I'm praying for one for your son tonight."

"My wife never misses a Sunday at church." Samson dropped his gaze. "But her faith — or her God — did nothing to save her when the rebels raided our camp."

Paige pressed her palms together. How did she respond to someone who'd just lost everything? And why did the truths of a peace that passed all understanding and God working things together for good seem suddenly hollow at the moment?

I know you're there, Lord. Increase my faith and give this man a miracle so He can see you working in his life. "Where is your wife?"

"I don't know." Tears welled in the big man's eyes as his gaze dropped to the floor. "My wife . . . my three girls . . . They all disappeared that night. You . . . you must know what they do to the women they capture . . ."

He broke off, and Paige felt the sickening reality of the situation intensify. She knew enough to realize that a high percentage of the women and girls who'd arrived here had been raped, many of them more than once. And even the safety measures put into place within the camp were not enough to completely stop the violence.

"I am so sorry. I honestly can't imagine facing what you're going through, but for now, you and your son should be safe. And we can pray that the rest of your family makes it here soon. I heard that there have already been several reunions of family members here." Paige cleared her throat. Nothing she could say would change what this man was facing. Or ease the stark pain of his loss. "There is a reception center you need to go to and register yourself and your son. You'll be given a document to prove that you're a resident of the camp." She studied the man's sullen expression. He had nothing but the clothes on his back and probably hadn't eaten much for days. "They'll give you a food package with rice, beans, oil, and other things along with blankets and clothing if you need it."

He started to turn away, then stopped. He motioned to her burnt arm, now medicated and wrapped with gaze. "You were injured?"

"I was burned during the second explosion, but it's nothing."

Samson's eyes widened as realization struck. "When you were trying to save my son's life —"

"Your son's life is what I'm worried about right now." Paige brushed off his concern. Worrying about her own injury seemed trivial with the child's life on the line.

"But you risked your life for him. A man in debt always dies the coward."

Paige shook her head. "What does that mean?"

"That I am now in your debt. And no debt of mine has ever gone unpaid."

Paige watched the broad-shouldered African step from the tent without another word. She was the one who was supposed to find answers to his problems. To bring hope to those who had lost everything. Yet she felt as if she'd done little for this man tonight. Even her attempt at spiritual encouragement had fallen flat.

She felt Asim's forehead. No fever meant that so far they were in the clear from infection. But she also knew that everything could change in an instant.

TWELVE

Nick crossed the edge of the camp, the fatigue of the day threatening to overcome him. Dozens of tents lay scattered across the vast landscape as dusk settled in, reminding him that his own problems were small compared to those who had fled the horrors of the rebel attacks. The camp was supposed to be a place of refuge, but he'd seen enough tragedy to know that, sometimes, nowhere was really safe. He could only pray that the desperation didn't turn into violence.

As he passed one of the guards who was paid to stop any unruly behavior before things got out of hand, he couldn't help but wonder if their presence really deterred anyone intent on causing trouble. With the country in a recently declared state of emergency, adding the army to their limited security would have been the ideal solution. But life was rarely ideal here. Rapes and beatings inside the camp were common, and while possession of a gun might be rare, a bit of cash on the side could easily turn the heads of those willing to smuggle weapons for the rebels.

He entered the health clinic, praying Paige didn't expect him to transport any more patients. Between a thunderstorm in the distance and the unlit runway of the camp, another takeoff simply wasn't an option. Hopefully, the planeload of medical supplies he'd managed to bring — along with the dinner he'd grabbed for her — would be enough for tonight.

From the far end of the tent Paige caught his gaze and waved. "Hey. You made it back."

He strode past the long line of beds, surprised at how glad he was to see her — and how relieved he was that she was okay. "I'm not sure who you're more happy to see. Me, or the supplies I promised."

"How about both?"

"I guess that response will have to do." He matched her smile. "Taz is having everything unloaded into the locked storage unit. I was able to get most of what you needed."

"Perfect."

He set the bag of food he carried on the edge of her desk, which had become her make-shift office. "How's your arm?"

"Still painful, but it could have been worse. I think the scarring will be minimal, if any."

"And how are you doing?"

"It's a bit like my residency days. Between supervising both the regular clinic and the cholera center I'm exhausted and running on adrenaline, but I think I'm going to make it." She scribbled a few notes on a file and handed it to one of the nurses. "Two more cases of severe cholera. I've lost track of how many we've placed in the isolation ward. The seventy-five beds we have aren't going to be near enough."

Nick frowned. Another confirmed case of cholera wasn't the thing that had him the most worried at the moment. Fatigue registered in Paige's eyes as she turned back to him. She was going to have to find a way to pace herself and get some rest, or in a day or two she wouldn't be able to function, let alone meet all the demands placed on her. And after all they'd experienced today, there was no telling what the future might hold. Twelve hours ago he'd left on a routine medical staff transport expecting to be home by supper. Instead, they'd lost a colleague and found themselves stuck in the middle of some godforsaken refugee camp. He could only pray that tomorrow would be better.

He tapped his fingers beside the pile of charts she'd started working through. "How late do you plan to work tonight?"

She rubbed her eyes and looked up at him. "I was told that they typically close the clinic at six, but because of the epidemic there are too many critical patients to leave with the night staff. I'll stay here instead of the hotel all the volunteers are booked into."

"Ahh, the Hilton." Nick chuckled. While the nearby location was a convenient place to house both local and foreign staff, he'd hardly call the shabby line of rooms a hotel — a designation that had made it a running joke. "From what I've heard, the conditions there are about as far away from a four-star hotel as this camp."

Paige set down the pen and smiled. "I was told that the hotel has a bit of a reputation for, shall I say, a mixture of sordid activities. And by the way, Taz told me he'd be happy to set up a cot for you in the registration tent if you'd like. It should be a bit more quiet than in here."

"I'm glad someone's looking out for me."

Nick watched as she grabbed the clip from her head and retied her shoulder-length hair. Even at this hour, the humidity still hung in the air, making loose wisps of hair stick to her neck. Truth was it had been a long time since a woman had captivated his attention, but he'd found it impossible to put her out of his mind on the flight to Kingani and back. Nor had he wanted to.

In the short time he'd known her, he'd already been impressed with her spunk and sense of humor. And he hadn't missed the fact that she was beautiful, with those blue-gray eyes and full lips.

He dropped his gaze before she accused him of staring and focused instead on the wood-grain pattern of the desk. Something that didn't interest him in the least. But the bottom line was that the convoy would arrive with all the supplies from the capital on Wednesday and then they wouldn't need him here anymore. She was leaving the country on Friday. He'd be lucky if he ever saw her again.

"Nick?"

He looked and caught her gaze. "Sorry. I'm feeling a bit . . . distracted tonight."

She pointed to the bag he'd brought and cocked her head. "I smell something other than the ever-persistent smell of chlorine that I'm quite sure wasn't on my supplies list."

"You finally noticed?" Nick opened up the sack and let the scent of grilled chicken fill the room. "I thought you might be hungry."

Her smile reached her eyes. "I honestly haven't had much time to think about eating, but now that you mention it . . ." Her stomach growled on cue.

"Then someone needs to help our doctor keep up her strength." He thumped the large stack of files with his thumb. "Can you sit outside for a few minutes and catch your breath? Not only are the stars beautiful, but a fifteen-minute break will go a long way toward recharging your batteries. And if you're worried about all this, I can assure you that it will still be here when you get back."

"It does tend to work that way, doesn't it? Along with the nagging guilt that won't go away." She pushed the paperwork aside and pulled over another chair. "Will this do? I've got a few minutes, but there are still several patients I want to keep my eye on."

Nick plopped down beside her and pulled out the containers. "I suppose I can understand your not being able to enjoy a perfect night sky with a somewhat dashing gentleman, but why the guilt?"

Her smile faded. "Most of these people have eaten hardly anything the past few days, which means I'm not sure I can justify filling my stomach. And that's not the only problem. Even a run-down hotel room is better than sharing a tent with eight or nine other people. And they don't have anywhere else to go."

"I'll make a deal with you." He held up a pair of plastic forks. "If I promise not to cater your dinner every night, will you at least eat this plate?"

She hesitated for a moment, then nodded. "Thank you."

"You're welcome." He handed her one of the forks along with a bowlful of the chicken and rice. "Digane confirmed that the rest of the team should be arriving early Wednesday. If you end up with a patient that needs to be transferred to the hospital, I'll be able to transport them for you in the morning."

She dug into her food. "I'm glad you're staying."

He caught her softened expression and wondered if her gratitude was because of the logistical help he was offering, or if there was something more to her response. He tried to dismiss the thought, but knew he didn't want to. Maybe he'd find a way to ask her out for a proper dinner before she left the country. They could talk about baseball and apple pie and get to know each other better.

He took another bite and smiled at the idea, as improbable as it seemed at the moment. Only God knew what the future held, but who was he to slam a door shut before finding out exactly what was on the other side?

THIRTEEN

Monday, February 21, 6:53 p.m.
Kingani Refugee Camp

Paige took another bite of the chicken and closed her eyes. For a moment, she could almost forget that they were sitting in the busy health clinic of a refugee camp, because she was sure she hadn't eaten anything this good since the last meal her mom cooked for her before leaving Nashville. The chicken was tender, the vegetables crisp and flavorful. She knew enough not to ask Nick where he'd bought dinner. It would spoil the illusion that it had been prepared by some master chef, not picked up at one of the country's back-alley restaurants. In this case, ignorance no doubt helped make everything taste better.

She peeked up at him, wishing those brown eyes of his weren't so darn mesmerizing. She dropped her gaze to study the prominent veins running across the back of his tanned hands and the calluses on his fingers . . . "This is delicious."

"Only because you haven't eaten all day. And I have something else for you as well. Dessert." He dug into his pants' pocket, pulled out two small bags of M&M's, and dropped them onto the table. "Now, I don't know what you think, but my sister insists that chocolate helps take the sting off of rotten days. I'm sure there's some medical reason you could explain to me."

She couldn't help but giggle, even though she'd definitely classify today at the top of her list of bad days. Besides, Casanova couldn't have come up with a better way of winning her over. At least when it came to her appetite. "Where did you get M&M's?"

He finished up the last bite of his rice. "My sister."

She eyed the candy. Surely three months didn't qualify as long enough to earn the right to crave things she couldn't find here, but chocolate, found only in mediocre-tasting candy bars here, had quickly scooted to the head of her list.

Nick slid his dish away from him and grabbed one of the bags of candy. "I heard a rumor about this good-looking new doctor who actually brought pizzas with her from Paris."

She felt a blush creep up her cheeks and hoped the room was dim enough that he didn't notice. "You heard right. At least the part about her bringing pizzas from Paris."

He ripped open the bag and popped a candy into his mouth. "You're crazy, you know."

"The other volunteers back in Jonga didn't think so." She pointed at her dinner with her fork before taking another bite. "This is great, but my mouth waters every time I imagine a deep-dish pizza with all the toppings."

"Craving anything else yet?"

"Beside pizza?" She nodded. "The oddest things. Like brie, black bean dip, and sour cream, for starters."

She leaned back in the chair, surprised at how at ease she felt with him, considering they'd practically been strangers twenty-four hours ago. What was it about bringing two expats together that magically erased all the formalities of the typical "boy meets girl" scenario and made her feel like they were long-lost friends? She pushed aside the notion that he was simply flirting with her to pass the time and forced her mind back to his question.

"And in three months you've probably faced more changes than at any other time in your life."

She nodded at his observation. Even med school hadn't seemed this foreign.

"Cultural differences," he continued, "language barriers, primitive living conditions, strange food, crazy hours —"

"And death."

That thought jerked her back to the reality of all that had happened today. Was it possible that only this morning she'd set off on her presumably last day on the field . . . met Tayla . . . watched Simon die? How could a life be snuffed out so quickly and unexpectedly?

Nick sat quietly beside her, seemingly content to allow the silence to hang between them. He obviously knew as well as she did that a listening ear could never take away the trauma of what she'd experienced, but tonight it somehow helped ease the frustration she'd felt all day. For as many patients as they'd been able to treat in the clinic, she knew there were dozens more out there who needed her. Sometimes what she had to give seemed so small and momentary.

She cleared her throat and struggled for what to say. "Back in Tennessee, I only saw one case of tuberculosis in all my years of practice there. Now I've seen more than I can count in the time I've been here, along with malaria, HIV, and children suffering from malnutrition." She looked up at him, her package of M&M's still untouched. Even chocolate had lost its normal anti-depressive effect. "How long have you been here?"

"Almost a year."

"Have you ever questioned your decision to come?"

"There have been quite a few times when I've wondered what in the world I'm doing here."

"But you stayed. Why?"

He rolled one of the M&M's in the palm of his hand. "We're not all here for selfless reasons."

"Then why'd you come?" She read his hesitation and regretted her question. "I'm sorry. That's none of my business —"

"It's okay, just . . . complicated. I came to Africa looking for myself, I guess you might say."

Apparently she wasn't the only one looking for answers tonight. "And have you discovered what you needed to find?"

"Some days." He popped the candy into his mouth. "What about you? Why did you come?"

She pulled the worn photo she always carried from her pocket and showed it to him.

"I used to keep this photo taped to my computer. Her name's Marila. She's an orphan I sponsored from Bogama."

"She's beautiful."

"Her father died from AIDS about two years ago. Then her mother died four months later. One day, I decided I wanted to do more than just send in a check every month. Six months later, I joined Volunteers for Hope."

"Just like that?"

"Pretty much, though it wasn't as spur of the moment as it sounds. I have this . . ." Paige shoved the photo back into her pocket, then hesitated. Not even her family understood the real reason she'd chosen to come.

"What?"

"It has to do partly with this silly list I made."

Nick's brow rose. The guy might seem focused, but he obviously wasn't the make-a-list-and-check-it-twice type of guy. "So you're a list maker."

She glanced up at him. "A list maker?"

"Like my mother. She made lists for everything. Shopping lists, dinner lists, appointments . . . everything."

Paige felt her cheeks flush again. "Yeah, that actually does sound like me, but this list is different. It's a list of a hundred things I want to do before I die. You know, a way to make sure I live life without any regrets."

"A hundred things?"

"You think it's crazy."

"Not at all. I guess I'm just not quite as . . . goal oriented as you are. What's on your list?"

Her eyelashes fluttered. "Eat sushi in Japan, plan a family reunion, learn to play the piano, and make soap, to name a few. Then there are others that are a bit more life changing."

"Like Africa? How did that make it onto your list?"

"Number twenty-four: visit Africa as a part of a relief effort." She reached for the M&M's and tore open the bag. "My mother's partly responsible for my adding that one to the list. She helped instill this desire in me to fix everything, so with me being a news junkie, Africa always managed to land at the top of my list. I just wasn't sure for a long time how I should reach that goal."

"That's a hard thing to do here, because you'll never fix everything."

"I think that's what's hit me the hardest. Sometimes the good I do seems so small and insignificant compared to all that needs to be done."

"It's like I said earlier. Don't focus on the bigger picture. Look at the person you're dealing with at the moment."

"Wisdom from a seasoned field worker?"

"Not me, my father. He always used to tell me that when we're called by God we need to go, then leave the outcome to Him."

"That's way easier said than done."

"No kidding. Which leads me to yet another serious issue we need to discuss." He pointed to his empty dinner bowl. "My bringing you dinner was on the condition that you'd forget about what's going on here for the next fifteen minutes."

"Hmm . . . already setting conditions on our friendship?"

His laugh was drowned out by screams echoing outside the tent. Nick jumped to his feet with her following right behind him. Three men gripping automatic rifles burst through the clinic's entrance and into the empty waiting room.

FOURTEEN

Monday, February 21, 7:17 p.m.
Kingani Refugee Camp

Paige's knees buckled. The packet of M&M's Nick had given her fell to the floor, spilling the candy across the clinic floor as she grasped onto the edge of a metal storage unit to regain her balance. The three men holding weapons shouted in Dha, and while she knew nothing beyond a few basic greetings in their language, the intent of the commands were clear. These men were not here seeking medical help or looking for a place of refuge. They'd carried their reign of terror into the camp.

Cold eyes stared back at her beneath the pale light of the bulb hanging above her head. She struggled to breathe. The handful of underpaid security guards they'd hired would be no match against the rebels.

One of the nurses screamed as Paige started toward a woman who'd ripped off her IV in an attempt to escape.

"Enzami!" One of the men held up his weapon.

Paige froze. The tone of his voice made clear his command to halt. She glanced at Nick out of the corner of her eye. His body language appeared alert and calm, but what were the odds that he'd be able to overpower a group of armed rebels?

This isn't what I signed up for, God . . .

"What do you want?" Nick took a step forward.

"Don't move." The tallest one pointed the gun at him and spoke in English. "We have a truck out front, and we plan to leave with it full. We want food and any communication devices you have."

Screams from the camp continued to fill the night air. A shot of nausea washed through Paige as she glanced toward the open doorway. There was no way of knowing how many men had invaded the camp — or what they'd do before they left.

Paige felt for the cell phone in her front pocket that had become her lifeline to her parents and sisters since her arrival. Even if she were able to contact someone in the country, any source of help would take hours to get here.

The men began rummaging through the

supply cabinets that lined one of the walls. For security reasons, the clinic's supplies were typically locked up in the metal shed by six every evening, but because of the cholera epidemic and working long hours they'd decided to lock up only nonessential items. She couldn't afford to lose any of her medical supplies.

"Please, there's nothing in here you need." She stepped in front of the nearest bed. "All we have in here are patients who need medical attention and supplies that are useless to you."

"Who are you?" His hand reached out and gripped her arm.

Paige winced and tried to bite back the sharp pain that shot through her injured arm. "I'm a doctor. These . . . these are my patients. They have nothing you need."

"We could use a doctor."

Nick took a step forward. "Leave her alone."

"Shut up." The man beside Nick swung his rifle across the side of Nick's head, knocking him to the ground.

Fear enveloped her as Nick groaned on the floor eight feet away. Her nurses stood against the wall of the waiting room, helpless — just like she was.

The foul smell of alcohol permeated the

room. "Maybe we should take her with us."

"Please, I —"

He dragged her toward the entrance while his men continued to ransack their medical supplies. She looked back to Nick, who'd managed to stand. Blood trickled down his forehead.

The explosion of a gun sounded in the doorway and the man holding her released his grip and slumped to the ground. Paige pushed him off her foot, then stumbled out of his reach.

Samson stood in the doorway holding an automatic rifle.

"Paige, get away from the door." Nick took advantage of the distraction. "Everyone else drop to the ground!"

Grabbing the fallen man's gun, Nick backed one of the rebels against the wall before he could react. Samson had the other on his knees. "What have you got to tie them up with?"

"I don't know." Shaking, Paige dug through one of the supply drawers that the rebels hadn't gotten to yet. While much of what she needed was on its way, the initial setup of the camp had provided the basics. Antiseptic, gauze, scissors . . . Her hand touched a pile of nylon cable ties. She pulled them from the drawer and handed them to Nick.

"I want you to stay here while we help get things under control in the camp." He wiped away the trail of blood from his head, then handed her a gun from one of the rebels.

"I can't do this." The gun trembled in her hands. "I've never shot a gun."

Nick took the weapon from her, aimed, and shot at the ground, missing one of the men by a couple inches. Paige jumped. "Point and shoot. You'll do fine. And if any of the other rebels come in here . . . shoot them."

"Shoot them?"

"And call Digane at the hospital and let him know what's going on."

The room spun as Nick rushed from the clinic behind Samson. He couldn't be serious. She hadn't come here to take lives. She was a doctor who'd made a vow to save people, not shoot them — even if they were rebels.

Something creaked behind her. She spun toward the front of the clinic.

It's just the wind, Paige.

One of the patients whimpered and she drew in a staggered breath. She could do this. There was too much at stake for her to fall apart now, and it was up to her to ensure the safety of those in the camp. She fished her phone from her pocket. She'd call Digane, who would send them help. Which meant everything would be okay by morning.

She flipped open her phone and fumbled with the keypad in the dim light.

No signal.

She held up the phone, but not even one bar registered. *No . . . no . . . no . . .* It had to work. She'd called home early this morning, catching her mom before she went to bed to wish her happy birthday. Her parents had gone to eat at Nana Rosa's, then spent the rest of the day shopping for a Jacuzzi tub for the master bathroom. Her dad had always spoiled her mom, something she'd added to her wish list in a man years ago.

One of the rebels stirred. She aimed the weapon at him and stepped backward, his glaring expression jarring her senses away from the normality of life half a world away.

He wiggled his way to a sitting position. "There is no use trying to call for help."

Paige steadied the gun in her hands. "Don't move. I will shoot."

"And then what? All the cell towers in this area have been sabotaged."

She shook her head. He couldn't be right. She had to get through to Kingani . . . "I don't understand."

"The cell phone towers are all down."

The room began to spin again. He couldn't be serious. This was a refugee camp, not the battleground for a war she wanted nothing to do with. Hopes of being rescued tonight, along with any remaining courage, vanished into the black night.

FIFTEEN

Monday, February 21, 9:47 p.m.
Mt. Maja, Senganie Route, 7,800 Feet
Brandon stared up at the enormous sky hovering above him and breathed in a lungful of the crisp night air. The view of the snow-capped mountain they'd chased after today was incredible, but it was still hard to beat the cloudless, black African sky. After the orange glow of the sunset vanished beneath the horizon, the Milky Way had appeared and now hung like a huge band of lights surrounded by thousands of tiny jewels. It almost made him want to believe there really was a God who'd created all of this.

Jodi sat perched on the edge of the boulder beside him, sipping tea while the fire the porters had built after dinner crackled in front of them. For months before their wedding, they'd discussed cruises, Paris, and the Caribbean as options for their honeymoon, but they'd never been able to let go of the idea to trek across Africa. So they'd spent the past six weeks wandering through the magical cities of Morocco and the sand dunes of the Sahara by 4×4 before cruising the waterways of Senegal. And at this moment he couldn't imagine being anywhere else. With anyone else.

He took a sip of his coffee. "How's your headache?"

Her left brow arched at his question. "I never said I had a headache."

"You didn't have to." He nudged her side with his elbow. She'd never been a good liar. "Taking a couple of pain pills twice in the past eight hours kind of gave it away."

She dipped her chin, but held his gaze. "You're far too observant."

"There are serious issues with climbing, Jodi. You can't mess around with altitude sickness —"

"I know all the signs and symptoms and will be careful." She leaned in against him. "All I need is a good night's sleep and time to adjust to the altitude."

He frowned, fearing her stubbornness would get in the way of common sense. Higher altitude meant lower oxygen in the air, and while there were medicines that helped prevent the symptoms, there were no guarantees. And in severe cases, illness could even cause death if the person didn't descend quickly enough. "Tomorrow's supposed to be rougher, with eight hours of climbing."

"I'll be ready."

The fire popped, and Jodi jumped.

Brandon's gaze jerked to the tree line surrounding them, looking for signs of movement, but he couldn't see anything beyond the wind blowing the tree limbs. Neither could he erase Robert's words of caution replaying in his mind.

While most of their group had already retired to their tents for the evening, several of the men were still up, their laughter mingling with the hushed voices of their guide and porters floating across the breeze from the other side of the camp.

"How serious do you think we should take the threat of an attack?"

"I think Robert's right, and there's nothing to worry about."

Jodi took a sip of her tea. "Maybe, but the thought of rebels attacking the camp . . . Well, it gives me the creeps."

Brandon wrapped his arm around her and pulled her closer. "Think about it. We're at almost eight thousand feet. They'd be crazy to trek all this way just for what we have in our packs."

"On the other hand, it might be worth it." Jodi nodded toward Ashley's tent, which housed every modern electronic invention known to trekkers. "That girl's got a bigger selection than Sportsman's Warehouse."

Brandon chuckled, then kissed the top of her nose. "Forget about Ashley James and the rebels for now. This trip is supposed to be about us and this endless night sky above us."

"It is beautiful." Jodi snuggled up against him and leaned her head into his shoulder.

Something snapped behind them. Brandon froze. This time it wasn't the fire. He stood slowly, blocking Jodi with his body.

She tugged on the edge of his jacket. "What is it?"

"I don't know."

Their guide, Mosi, appeared beside them. "Please, go to your tents."

"Did you see something?"

"It's probably nothing, but I don't want to take any chances."

"Jodi, go to the tent. I'll stay here in case I'm needed."

She grabbed his arm. "I'm not leaving you here —"

"Please."

She hesitated, then slipped into the misty

darkness toward their tent. A light flashed fifty yards away. Brandon fumbled in his pockets for something to defend himself with if it came to that and found a flashlight, a Swiss army knife, and an energy bar. Nothing that would save him against an armed rebel.

Something crashed through the dark shadows of the surrounding forest.

Instinctively, Brandon jumped up as five men entered the clearing holding guns.

"Everyone on the ground, now!"

Brandon felt the punch to his gut before he had time to respond. Unable to breathe, he dropped to the ground. He bit back the pain and glanced toward their darkened tent. Jodi was in there, waiting for him to do something . . . anything.

Robert jumped from his tent, flashlight in hand, then stopped short. The air rushed from Brandon's lungs. One of the rebels had Ashley. Robert swung at her attacker.

A gun went off and Robert dropped to the ground. Ashley screamed. A shot fired from the other side of the camp, then another. If they hurt Jodi . . .

Brandon started to stand, but the butt of a rifle cracked against his head. The threatening figure hovered above him in the dark. Brandon dropped back to the ground, clenching his fists together until his nails bit into his palm. Robert lay motionless in front of his tent. He should have stayed with Jodi.

One by one, tent zippers ripped open. All Jodi needed to do was give them what they wanted and she'd be okay. Once they had what they'd come for they'd leave them alone. They'd be all right. They had to be.

With the cold ground next to his face, he listened to the sounds of men shouting orders and tried to come up with a plan of attack against half a dozen armed men. His only defense was brute force and the anger they'd triggered, but the odds of him taking out armed rebels were still impossible. Instead, he crouched motionless on the ground and waited for an opportunity to move.

Two minutes later it was over as they left as silently as they'd come.

"You okay?" One of the other hikers crept up beside him.

"Robert was hit."

Brandon shined his flashlight toward Ashley's tent and quickly bridged the short distance between him and the older man. He'd insisted on a guide who was prepared to deal with medical issues, but no one had expected this.

He dropped down beside Robert. "Where

was he hit, Ashley?"

Ashley sat on the ground, rocking back and forth, her eyes wide with terror.

"Ashley?" Brandon felt for a pulse in Robert's neck.

Ashley gripped his wrist. "It's too late. He's dead."

Mosi stood over them. "What's happened?"

"He's dead."

"One of my porters is dead as well."

Brandon looked up. Light from the fire caught the alarm on Mosi's face. By now the four Canadians who made up the rest of their group had gathered at the center of the camp. Someone whimpered in the background. No one, it seemed, knew what to say to the young woman who'd just witnessed the murder of her father.

Mosi turned to address them. "I'm sending a runner down the mountain to the base camp for help, but it's going to take time. In the meantime, I need everyone to try and stay calm. There is no reason for them to return."

Brandon shone his flashlight into the crowd. Where was Jodi? "I've got to find my wife." He crossed the cold ground and flipped back the door of his tent.

"Jodi, we've got to . . ." He paused in the

doorway and shined the light inside the tent. It was empty. "Jodi?"

A cold rain had started, sending drops of water down the back of his neck. He ran to the makeshift bathroom. Nothing. Spinning around, he swung his flashlight back toward the group. The white beam caught the figure of Ashley's dad. Blood stained the ground and Ashley's hands, but there was no sign of Jodi.

A wave of panic surged through him. He'd heard what the rebels had done in other parts of the country, and he'd somehow fooled himself into thinking that as tourists they were immune. But these people had burned down villages, killed people, and raped their women.

His lungs constricted.

"Brandon?"

Brandon looked up at their guide. "Jodi's gone."

Sixteen

Monday, February 21, 10:12 p.m.
Mt. Maja, Senganie Route, 7,800 Feet

Brandon smacked his flashlight against his hand, then tilted the waning beam into the thick brush. Six of them had spread out in opposite directions, but so far there was no sign of Jodi. She'd simply vanished. Trudging through the underbrush, he weighed his limited options as the panic mounted. If they didn't find her soon, he'd have to head down the mountain toward the base camp. But even that route would more than likely be another dead end. If the rebels had kidnapped her, wouldn't they take her to their nearest hideout rather than to the mountain's base camp where they'd started their climb?

Stepping over a fallen log, he tried to comprehend the mind of the rebels. What sort of motivation drove a person to burn down villages and murder their own people?

Greed? Revenge? Desperation? Whatever the reason, it didn't matter now. He should have listened to the voice of common sense and insisted on cruising the Mediterranean for their honeymoon. Living life on the edge — if it cost him Jodi — wasn't worth it.

He stumbled over a fallen log and tried to recount how many shots he'd heard. One had killed Robert. A second, one of the porters. He'd heard three shots, maybe four. His jaw clinched, grinding his teeth together. There was no way to know. No way to know for sure if Jodi had been one of their victims.

But that didn't stop his mind from playing out the apparent scenario. Rebels had entered the tent, shot her, and she'd tried to escape. She wouldn't have been able to find the trail in the dark, so she'd simply run . . .

A rodent skittered across the white beam of his flashlight. No. His mind refused to accept that possibility. People died from altitude sickness and heart attacks on this mountain. No one was supposed to die from a gunshot wound.

Something rustled in the bush behind him. His nerves tensed. Slowly, he turned toward the noise, trying to differentiate between the night sounds of monkeys and insects as well as the dark shadows swaying in the moonlight.

He took a step forward, then froze. A branch snapped. "Jodi?"

Holding his breath, he moved in a slow circle. The beam of the flashlight cut through the darkness. Something — someone — was out there, waiting, watching —

A bushbuck scampered into the brush. Brandon let out the lungful of air he'd been holding and cursed. She had to be here somewhere, but nothing but the rustling sounds of the disappearing animal answered him.

He stomped through another ten feet of heavy bush and mud, straining to see what the darkness held. His mind worked to focus. If she'd tried to run from the rebels, she could have ended up off the path with a sprained ankle. Besides the rebels, there were plenty of dangers lurking in the surrounding dense forest. Snake and even leopard sightings weren't uncommon on the lower altitudes of the mountain.

"Jodi?"

His shoulder scraped against the rough bark of a tree. The darkness of the forest closed around him. He couldn't see more than half a dozen feet ahead of him, and she could be anywhere. Continuing would only end up with him lost . . . and do nothing to find Jodi. But if Jodi had taught him anything, it was persistence. He'd never met a woman with so much perseverance. It had carried her through eight months of painful physical therapy, and it would get her through whatever she was facing at this moment.

He turned back toward the camp, doing his best to retrace his steps in case he'd missed a clue that she'd been here.

The only explanation that made sense was that someone from among the rebels had seen Ashley and decided her stash of electronics was worth the climb. But if they'd wanted a hostage as well, why risk taking Jodi when there were dozens of hikers at the base camp who were far more accessible than those eight thousand feet up the surface of the mountain?

Entering the camp, he made his way back to his tent and began shoving items into his pack. Someone had dumped Jodi's things across her sleeping bag. He grabbed for the headlight and flicked on the strong beam. If they'd forced her to leave the tent, she wouldn't have had time to grab her things, but her cell phone and camera were gone. Which helped substantiate what he already believed to be true: the rebels had been here. But what had they done with Jodi?

Brandon grabbed his backpack and stood, scraping the top of the tent with his head as he exited.

Mosi approached him from the other side of the camp. "Anything?"

Brandon shook his head. "Her cell phone and camera are gone, as are mine, but there is no sign of where she might have gone. What about you and your men?"

"We can't communicate without radios, but three have just checked in having found nothing. We'll keep looking until we find her."

Brandon slung the backpack onto his shoulder and headed past the flickering fire toward the main trail that led toward the base camp. "I'm heading down the mountain. If they did take her and I hurry, I might be able to catch up with them."

"And then what?" Mosi moved to block his way. "No. You cannot leave."

"I can and I will."

"You do not understand the risks."

Mosi grasped his shoulder, but Brandon pulled away from the older man's grasp. "What I do understand is that my wife is missing and I have to find her."

"How? By running down the mountain in the dark? You will never find her that way."

"I will if you send one of the porters with me. They know the way better than anyone, which means we can catch up with them."

"We don't even know if that is where they have taken her. And then what do you do if you find them? You have no weapons. Nothing to fight against them. It is better to simply wait here until help arrives."

Brandon shook his head. Waiting here was not an option. "If I go, I'll be able to alert the authorities at the base camp."

Mosi didn't look convinced. "This is not the United States. Resources are scarce in my country, especially now. How much time do you think our army can spend searching for one missing woman when they're not even able to control the armed rebels murdering their own people?"

Brandon dropped his arms to his sides. "So you want me to just give up."

"Of course not. I am only suggesting that we wait until the porter I am sending down the mountain returns with help. Besides, finding her in the dark will be almost impossible."

Brandon didn't agree. Jodi could be out there bleeding to death for all they knew. And in a situation like that, every minute counted. If she was out there, he was going to find her. "I'm not willing to sit here and just wait. And the fact that no one has found her, means that more than likely they've taken her —"

"We have no way of knowing that they took her."

"Then where is she?" Brandon's booming voice split the quiet night air.

Mosi dropped his gaze. "I do not know where she is, but I still believe it is best to remain here."

"No." Brandon brushed past Mosi before stopping and turning back to face him. "I might not have any idea where she is, but I do intend to find her. And I'll never find her standing here arguing with you."

Ashley ran up beside him as he started for the trail, her fancy backpack bouncing on her back. "You're going down to the base camp."

Brandon grimaced. He didn't have time to deal with her. "News travels fast, but I don't have time to babysit."

"You don't understand." Panic laced Ashley's voice. "I can't stay on this mountain another second."

Her eyes still swollen from crying, Ashley looked anything but the stuck-up actress who'd joined them twenty-four hours ago. He felt sorry for how she'd lost her father in such a brutal way, but even her desolate expression did little to erase his irritation. The bottom line was that she'd slow him down, which wasn't a risk he was willing to take. Wherever Jodi was, she was in trouble and the more time that passed, the more difficult it was going to be to locate her.

"Please?"

"I said no."

"They murdered my father —"

"They took my wife." He stopped and caught her gaze. Her eyes pleaded with him to reconsider, but being saddled with someone who would just slow him down wasn't an option. "Listen, I understand what you're going through, but I can't be responsible for your well-being."

"Please —"

Something crashed through the brush on the far side of the camp. Brandon swung around, ready to attack if need be. If the rebels had returned . . .

One of the porters emerged from the trees, his dark face lit up by the yellow flicker of the dying fire. "We found her."

SEVENTEEN

Monday, February 21, 10:38 p.m.
Mt. Maja, Senganie Route, 7,800 Feet

Brandon snapped on his flashlight and ran toward the porter, his thoughts gnawing holes in his conscience. They never should have come here. Not with all the unrest in the country. And he never should have let Jodi return to their tent alone. If she'd stayed with him, they'd have both been fine. All the men had wanted were radios and phones. Robert had died because they'd felt threatened. They would have let Ashley go. Would have left Jodi alone if he'd been with her.

His boots crunched on the coarse gravel. Branches whipped at his pant legs. They were off the main trail and into the bush where spindly tree limbs and the black night sky hovered above them. But the stars had vanished behind clouds that now settled in above them, masking the earlier brilliant skies and making it harder to navigate through the thick brush. The forest around him blurred as he tried to keep up with the guide; the beam of the flashlight was too focused to offer him the light he needed.

His lungs screamed at the lack of air from the high altitude, but he pushed himself to keep up with the porter, who seemed to move effortlessly in the darkness. "Where is she?"

"Over here!"

Finally, his flashlight caught the edge of Jodi's red jacket. She lay on her back, head to the side, her face ghostly white. He dropped beside her and took her hand. "Jodi?"

The porter who had remained with her stood above them. "We were afraid to move her."

Air whooshed from his lungs. "Jodi."

Her eyes fluttered open and she groaned before closing them again. Blood had run down her face and dried on her cheek. He felt along her temple where blood matted her hair.

"Jodi, what happened?"

"I don't . . . know." Her eyes opened again. "They came with guns . . . I ran . . ."

He wiped away the blood with his shirt, but all he found was a cut along her hairline.

There had to be something else. "Were you shot?"

"I . . . ran."

"Were you shot?"

"My arm . . . hurts."

Frantically, he began looking for holes in her clothes — anything that might signify the entryway of a bullet. Blood seeped from her left shoulder. He told the porters where to aim their flashlights, then, after gently slipping off her jacket, ripped her shirt sleeve, exposing the wound. He'd seen enough scars from gunshot wounds to know that both entrance and exit wounds were not always easy to distinguish, and that he couldn't dismiss the possibility that she'd been hit twice.

He pulled off his own jacket and pressed it against the wound to stop the bleeding as his mind scrambled to deal with the emergency situation. He was used to working with patients who'd been seriously injured — but in physical therapy, long after they'd been patched up by ER doctors and surgeons. He reached for her wrist and took her pulse. It was fast, but steady. Breathing seemed normal, with no signs of a blocked airway.

What else?

"Do you hurt anywhere beside your shoulder?"

She shook her head. "Just my ankle, but that's to be expected."

If she was right, the metal pin was the least of their problems at the moment.

"We've got to get her out of here." He felt her forehead. Beside the gunshot wound, she was burning up with fever. He looked up the incline toward the camp. "Can you walk?"

Her chin quivered. "I don't know."

Brandon helped her to her feet. Even with Jodi's slight frame, he wasn't sure how far he could carry her down the mountain. But without a stretcher, any other options began to fade. "I've got to get her off this mountain and down to the base camp so she can be evacuated."

With the help of the porters he hoisted her onto his back, careful not to jar her shoulder. Ten minutes later they were at the camp, where he laid her on their sleeping bag in the tent and began to pack their water and supplies. He'd pay whatever it took for two of the porters to help get her down the mountain.

Mosi appeared outside the tent, holding one of the high-frequency radios. "It's a miracle the rebels missed this after tearing everything apart, but we found this in one of the tents. I've been in touch with the base camp."

"What did they say?"

"They will arrange for medical personnel to be waiting for us at the base camp, along with a plane so Jodi can be medivaced to the nearest hospital."

Brandon's mind swam with the daunting task ahead of them. Even going downhill, at a much quicker pace, it would take at least two or three hours to get to the base camp in the daytime. At night it could take them twice that long. And carrying Jodi . . .

"How do we get there?"

"Porters from the base camp are on the way up with stretchers right now."

"How long until they arrive?"

"Another five or six hours."

Which meant it would be almost dawn before they made it. "Forget it. I'm going to go now. I'll meet them halfway."

That would cut the time in half.

Ashley stood at the entrance of his tent. "I'm coming with you."

He threw his bag over his shoulder. "I meant what I said. I can't be responsible for you. I've got to get my wife the help she needs."

"I'll get down the mountain on my own."

150

Her voice rose a notch. "But there's no way I'm staying here another second."

Determination shone in Ashley's eyes, but he couldn't deal with both Jodi and a hysterical woman. "Listen to me, Ashley. As soon as it's daylight, one of the porters will take you back, but not now."

Mosi's chin dipped. "He's right. They'll bring a stretcher for your father as well and take him down the mountain in the morning."

Brandon glanced to where her father's body now lay bundled up in a sleeping bag ready for transport down the mountain. When had their excursion to the summit turned into a fight for their very survival?

"I'm going now —"

"You'll never make it in the dark." Fatigue washed over Brandon. "Wait until morning and go down with one of the porters."

The calculations were simple. It would take them half the time to get down the mountain if they met the porters climbing up. And once they got the stretcher, they could move Jodi even faster. Ashley would only slow them down.

Ashley turned to the group of porters listening to the exchange. "I'll pay a thousand dollars for two of you to guide me down the mountain and carry my father's body."

Two men stepped forward and hoisted the body of her father onto their shoulders.

"Fine." He was finished arguing with her. "Radio the base camp and tell them that we're headed down the mountain now and will meet the other porters along the trail. Because as far as Jodi is concerned, tomorrow morning might be too late."

EIGHTEEN

Monday, February 21, 11:02 p.m.
Kingani Refugee Camp

Paige shoved her stethoscope into her medical bag, ignoring the mess the rebels had strewn across the clinic floor. She yanked on the zipper. It snagged, breaking her fingernail in the process. Fine. She grabbed the bag by the bottom and stalked toward the door of the clinic. She didn't need to shut the dumb thing anyway. What did it matter? What did anything matter at this point? Anger seared her senses, managing to erase all the guilt she felt over her decision.

At least fourteen had been found dead in the camp after the raid, beaten to death by the Ghost Soldiers, and there had been nothing she could do to save any of them. If Samson hadn't managed to confiscate one of their guns and scatter the rebels, the bloody death toll would have been higher.

The three rebels they'd managed to capture were tied up and under guard, but they'd only postponed the inevitable. More rebels would be back.

"Paige?" Nick stood between her and the doorway. "I just wanted to check and see how you're doing."

Her nostrils flared. Great. He was the last person she wanted to see — because he was the one person who would try to talk some sense into her. And she was way past any rational thinking.

He stepped in front of her. "Where are you going?"

She brushed past him. "Home."

His hand grasped her forearm, stopping her at the edge of the empty bed where they'd just taken away the body of another one of the burn victims. "What are you talking about?"

She pulled away. She never should have told Digane she'd come. No matter what she did, the patients would keep coming. Babies would keep crying. IVs would keep dripping in the isolation ward. People would keep dying . . . like Marila.

"I'm going back to Nashville where it's thirty degrees cooler and they have plenty of water, electricity, and deep-dish pizza."

"You can't be serious. You're responsible

154

for getting this cholera treatment center up and running, and if that isn't enough, perhaps you forgot that there are rebels out there who would be happy to use you to make a point."

She rubbed the bruise the rebel had left on her arm. "I haven't forgotten anything."

"I can fly you out of here tomorrow if you insist, but as for right now, how in the world do you plan to get around them?"

Her free hand shook. She stuck it into the pocket of her lab coat and hoped he hadn't noticed. "I figure I can outrun them in the jeep."

"In the dark, on a road you don't know, past armed rebel soldiers? You're not thinking straight."

She groaned. Of course she wasn't thinking straight. If she had been, she wouldn't have come here in the first place. She'd be packing for her trip back to the States. And it wasn't as if she'd worked out all the details of her escape. She just knew she wasn't staying. She started again for the door. At least if she left she'd be in control of the situation. "You can say what you want, but I've already made my decision."

"You know, I thought you were different. The Paige Ryan I got to know today wouldn't up and run away because things got tough."

Man, she really didn't like this guy. She turned to face him. "Then obviously you don't really know me."

"Oh, I think I do, because I've met plenty who went home because they couldn't stick it out. They get tired of the living conditions. The constant rain during the rainy season where nothing gets dry and all your clothes end up smelling like a pile of damp socks. They get tired of the lack of sleep, the stress, and especially they get tired of the death. But I don't think you're really like them."

"That's where you're wrong. I'm sick and tired of all these things." She shoved the medical bag under her other arm. "And if that wasn't enough, I have a feeling that the going rate for an American doctor is pretty high and would have pulled some weight with their negotiations."

"Being fearful is normal."

"Oh, I'm way past fear. I'm completely terrified. But I'm also furious. Furious that we buried twenty more people today. And that . . ." She shook her head. "They've knocked out the cell towers so I can't even call my family and let them know I'm alive."

Something about losing that link to the real world had turned into the final straw.

Nick grabbed two chairs from against the wall and pushed them into the middle of the empty waiting room. "Give me five minutes."

"Why?" She spun around to face him. "So you can give me a pep talk and I'll change my mind?"

"Sit down. You're not the only one who's had to face a life-and-death situation and come up short. I just don't want you to one day hate your decision."

She hesitated, then plopped down onto one of the chairs, knowing she was going to regret the action. No matter what he'd used to be, there was no way he could understand what the past three months had done to her, let alone the past twenty-four hours. And there wasn't anything she could do to stop what was happening. In the process, she'd tried to dig down deep to find that deeper dose of faith so she could come out triumphant despite the circumstances. Instead, all she'd found was the intense desire to run. Which was exactly what she intended to do when his five minutes were up.

He slid onto the chair across from her and tugged on his ball cap, looking as uncomfortable as she felt. "I want you to listen to me. I know you're scared, but you know as well as I do that running isn't the answer.

You go out there and they will kill you. We'll wait until morning, then I'll fly back to Kingani and get help."

She wasn't ready to admit there was wisdom in what he said. She wanted to be back home in her one-bedroom apartment now, working twelve-hour shifts at the hospital and hanging out with her friends on her time off. Because the rebels were still out there, and it was only a matter of time before they returned and she and the others would be forced to go through tonight all over again.

She sucked in a sharp breath. "This is supposed to be a place of refuge, but not only can't I promise them that, there's nothing I can do to change things."

"You weren't brought here to save the world. You were brought here as a temporary field director to set up the cholera treatment center and get this epidemic under control. And this isn't a place where you can make out a list and neatly check things off. This is the real world where sometimes you've got to go with the punches, suck it up, be creative, and do things even when you want to run in the opposite direction."

She folded her arms across her chest and crossed her legs, resisting the urge to stand up and slug him. Her lists might not work here, but laying on the guilt wasn't going to work either. "And what would you know about the real world? You fly chartered planes for doctors and their patients."

Nick's expression darkened. "So that makes me, what? A glorified tour guide?"

"That's not what I said."

"That's what you implied."

"What I implied was that I'm the one who is supposed to be in charge of all of this, and —"

"And you're also the one who's leaving."

Her jaw tensed. He infuriated her. "This is a ridiculous conversation that's never going to get us anywhere, because you don't understand —"

"Yeah, I do." He slapped his hands against his thighs and leaned forward. "You're not the only person who's had to face situations that made you question what in the world you were doing."

Paige swallowed hard. The situation was clouding her judgment. Maybe she had been too quick to judge. "What are you talking about?"

"I . . ." Nick drew in a deep breath. "I joined the military when I was twenty-one. After a few years as an officer, I made it into the pilot training program. Fifteen months ago, I walked away from it all."

Paige's mind worked to put the pieces together. Nick was the last person she'd imagine running away from something. "Why'd you quit?"

"I'd been deployed to Iraq where I served as a medivac pilot." He shifted in his chair, clearly uncomfortable with telling his story. "We spent our days waiting for calls to evacuate wounded soldiers and transferring patients and supplies. One day, I was ordered to fly with a crew to a specific location in the desert in order to evacuate four wounded soldiers whose plane had gone down." Nick stared at the ground. "The whole mission began as a routine flight and rescue across the desert. But it didn't end that way."

NINETEEN

Fifteen Months Earlier
Tallil, Iraq

The boom of a Patriot missile going supersonic sounded overhead as Nick popped the last chewy mass of waffle fries into his mouth. Even the ketchup gravy, jokingly named for its thin consistency, failed to improve the taste.

Glancing at his watch, he ditched his tray and headed for the plywood "coffee shop." If his luck held, there wouldn't be any major emergencies tonight. But chances of that were slim. Last night he'd met a plane on the flight line at 0200 hours. One of the fighter pilots had come down with a case of appendicitis during his flight. Not exactly the way one expected to end a busy day of surveillance, flying over some of the most dangerous borders in the world.

A maze of tan tents used as barracks spread out before him. Beyond them, herds of sheep grazed the flat, sandy desert that was sprinkled with dry tufts of grass. The lack of color never failed to impact him. Except for the blue sky above and certain assigned military garb such as the bright yellow belt and purple gloves he'd worn on the flight line last night in order to be seen, everything was a variant of the color brown.

The radio hanging from his pocket burped. "Medivac . . . Medivac . . . Medivac . . ."

Thoughts of downtime vanished as Nick sprinted past the coffee shop toward the operations center while his crew chiefs and medics grabbed their gear and ran toward the twin Black Hawks. Other units might have the luxury of time to plan for a mission, but with his team every minute counted when they were dealing with injured soldiers. He had just enough time to receive the details of the injureds' location, then join the team at the flight line.

Within ten minutes his company was strapped in and ready to take off. Taking the lead, with a second Black Hawk trailing right behind him in case of a mechanical problem or hostile fire, they headed toward the downed plane. Beneath them lay a sea of brown dirt, broken only by a sparse scattering of oil wells and, ahead, the Ziggurat of Ur. Yesterday he'd visited the site with a group of fellow soldiers dressed in their Airman Battle Uniforms, guns, and body armor while their Iraqi tour guide explained the history of the ancient pyramid. Today there was no sign of the Humvees or army trucks that had filled the parking lot.

Minutes later, amongst the continual buzz of information from the operations center, he caught a glimpse of the crash. The left wing had broken off on impact. A body lay ten feet from the wreckage, but at this point it was impossible to tell if the fallen man was dead or alive.

Adrenaline soared through Nick's veins. *God, protect the lives of these four men. They have wives and children . . .*

His men rushed from the chopper while he waited, ready to move once the injured were in place in the carousel. With any luck, they'd be out of here in a matter of minutes.

Someone screamed.

"Ambush!"

Nick heard the volley of bullets crackle behind the aircraft and watched the crew chief take a bullet to the head. He tried to swallow the overwhelming wave of fear that encompassed him. One of the medics shouted for everyone to take cover, then dropped to the ground as another explosion sliced through the night air.

This was no typical extraction. Five no-mads, dressed in desert garb, appeared facing them thirty yards away at the top of a slight rise, machine guns in hand. They fired off another round, this time hitting the second helicopter. Nick moved to the side of the Black Hawk. He had to get his crew and the injured out of here.

He recognized Captain Lopez from the downed crew in the fading light, lying in a shallow ravine fifteen feet from the chopper, his right leg twisted at an odd angle. Twenty-eight years old. Married to his high school sweetheart. Father of three. The man was an open target.

Nick shouted at Captain Westbrook, the other pilot. "Stay here. I want your chopper up and flying at my command."

With a band of rebels still shooting at them, he made his way toward Lopez. Picking up the man, he ran as low to the ground as possible. A bullet whizzed past his ear and he quickly weighed his options. The downed plane had become the closest cover. Inside, Nick could smell the stench of blood. The victims from the crash were going to die if they didn't get them out of here soon. They had to get them to the helicopter.

"There are women and children out there," one of his crew spat out from inside the fallen craft. "To your right."

Nick glanced out one of the shattered windows of the plane. Seconds ticked off. Was this simply a group of nomads defending their land? Or were they insurgents using civilians as their cover?

He hated war. Hated the killing and the waste of life it left behind. He'd seen more death in the past four months than most people ever saw in a lifetime. Today, it was just too much. How was he supposed to deal with both evacuating his men and saving a bunch of civilians while the enemy shot them down like skeet targets?

A woman ran toward the plane, carrying a small boy. The wind pulled at her long black tunic. She tripped, almost dropping the boy, but somehow caught her balance and continued.

"Hold your fire, men!" Nick screamed out the order above the chaos of bullets striking metal.

The following silence sent chills up his spine. A blanket of evil permeated the air. Tears streaked through the dirt covering the woman's face. The boy had been shot, his clothes marked with crimson. Nick fell against the door of the plane, cutting his lip. Ignoring the bitter taste of blood in his mouth, he stepped out of the plane. The sharp sting of sand hit him as he took the boy into his arms.

Medics from the rescue crew began treating the wounded in the plane. Maybe taking care of this young boy would prove to the Iraqis they weren't here to fight. They simply wanted to take their own wounded home. For the moment, all firings of weapons had ceased. He could only pray to God that the cease-fire would last.

"How are the others?" Nick asked.

Westbrook shook his head. "Lopez was shot in the leg, but he's a tough codger. I don't think Johnson's going to make it. At least three others are dead. We've got to get out of here."

A flash of light penetrated the darkness. Westbrook was thrown against the side of the plane from the impact of the grenade. Nick felt a searing pain in his arm. Reaching up with his good hand, he felt warm liquid run down his fingers. There was nothing left to do now, but pray.

TWENTY

Monday, February 21, 11:34 p.m.
Kingani Refugee Camp

Paige studied Nick's eyes. His expression held a mixture of pain, regret, and sadness that made her bad day pale in comparison. And made her realize the shallowness of her earlier argument. She'd never save the world by running away.

She leaned forward. "What happened? Obviously you made it out alive."

Nick rested his hands against his thighs. "Somehow, we managed to get out of there after taking down three of the rebels, one of whom shot me in the arm. But I was one of the lucky ones. The boy died in my arms right before we left."

Any remaining irritation — justified or not — melted away. "I'm so sorry."

"After I got through with the physical therapy, I decided to take an honorable discharge, because on top of everything else, the local government ended up blaming us for their loss of innocent civilians that night."

Her eyes narrowed. "Even though it wasn't your fault?"

"That depends on whose side you were on. They say we fired against them first, an innocent group of nomads herding their flocks. No matter how many times I replay the events of that night, I'm at a loss to know what I could have done differently to save the lives of my comrades." He stared past her. "I still have nightmares about that day."

"Maybe there's nothing else you could have done. You couldn't exactly walk up to them through a volley of bullets and ask them what they wanted."

"According to their government? Yeah, I should have."

"But it still wasn't your fault."

"No matter whose fault, losing men on my watch — and watching them die along with innocent civilians — it's not exactly something that's easy to forgive yourself for."

Paige let out a slow breath while anger flared over the injustices that seemed to prevail in this world. And how hard it had become to try and make them right. Nick had experienced injustice in the middle of war. And now they were both on the front-lines of a different kind of war. One where people were killed to make a point and too often life held little value.

How do we change that, God?

Maybe sometimes there simply wasn't a black-and-white solution. Or maybe sometimes there wasn't a solution at all.

Paige shifted her focus back to Nick. "So why Africa?"

"A friend of mine from college worked as an instructor at a school that trained pilots to work with mission organizations. And since I wasn't ready to give up on flying, it seemed like the perfect solution. At first it was just a place where I could disappear. Then I realized I could actually help people using my skills."

"Do you ever regret your decision?" Paige's own doubts swirled in her head.

"I don't regret coming here, only that I ran away from the situation. I don't think I'll ever stop wondering what might have happened if I'd handled things differently." He leaned forward. "That's why you need to finish this assignment, for your own sake. I know what it's like to run and then try to redeem yourself."

"Are you still running?"

"There are nights when I can't sleep because all I see is the face of that little boy dying."

Paige stared at a black bug working its way across the bottom of her pants. She'd been haunted by her own images of what she'd seen the past few weeks. She pulled out the warm photo from her pocket. "I didn't tell you everything about Marila."

"What do you mean?"

"I visited her last November when I first arrived at the capital. It didn't take me long to realize that something was wrong." A range of emotions surged at the memory. "A week later, an Australian surgeon diagnosed her with a sarcoma, a life-threatening childhood cancer that affected her legs. There was no chemo or radiation here to treat this sweet child and by the time she was diagnosed it was too late. There was nothing the surgeon, or any of us, could do."

"I'm sorry."

"I was sent on to Jonga and a few weeks later received word that Marila died. I guess that's when everything started falling apart. I did my best to keep up with the workload, but for every one I saved, I felt as if I lost two."

"Overwhelming, isn't it?"

"Very. When we arrived here, I stopped on

one of the ridges and looked at the masses of people living in tents. It made me remember a verse out of Zechariah the pastor at our church read a few months ago. It said something about the blood covenant God had made with them, and how He would free the prisoners from the waterless pit." She flicked the bug off her knee and looked up at him. "And that's how I see them. Not prisoners in the traditional sense of the word, but prisoners all the same to their physical circumstances. And there's only so much I can do."

"Which is why the only thing left to do is admit our fear and hurts and continue on God's strength."

"But beneath all of the injustices in this world there has to be a ray of hope somewhere. Sometimes, like right now, I just don't see the freedom He promises."

Nick stared past her at the long row of patients. "Maybe freedom doesn't always mean physical freedom. Christ brought us spiritual freedom."

"Because he was poured out like a sacrifice to forgive the sins of many." Paige fiddled with her broken nail. Christ was their only hope, but even that knowledge didn't always make things easy. "I suppose it's easy for us to twist God's promise of eternal life in heaven to where we expect a heaven here on earth. We forget that sin destroyed that possibility in the Garden of Eden."

"Which means that while I don't know if I'll ever be able to stop second-guessing myself for what happened that day in Iraq or even understand why God allowed it to happen, maybe it's time we both found hope in the greater-reaching eternal promise."

She looked up at Nick. "What if I'm still not sure I can do this?"

The door to the clinic swung open and banged against the wall. A man stumbled through the doorway.

Nick jumped to his feet, blocking Paige.

"I'm sorry." The man held up his hands. "I'm looking for Dr. Ryan. I was told I could find her here."

Paige moved from behind Nick. If this was one of the rebels, she'd probably be dead by now. "I'm Dr. Ryan."

"My name is Prosper." He struggled to catch his breath. "I have just come from the base camp at Mt. Maja."

"You walked here?"

"I ran most of the way. Our phones are down. I need to arrange an emergency evacuation."

Lightning struck in the distance. "What's

the emergency?"

"Rebels raided Mt. Maja's base camp and a second camp on the Senganie Route where they shot and killed an American tourist along with one of the porters. Another woman was badly injured and needs to be transported to Kingani. We were told you have access to a plane."

Paige looked to Nick, who shook his head. "Even if I wanted to, there's no way I can fly to the base camp tonight. No one can in the dark and in these weather conditions."

"Then when?"

"In the morning. I can fly to the base camp once it's light, then on to the hospital in Kingani."

Paige wrapped her arms around her waist as the feelings of helplessness returned. "So what do we do now?"

"We try to sleep. And pray tomorrow is a better day."

TWENTY-ONE

Tuesday, February 22, 6:04 a.m.
2,500 Feet Above The Bensi Region

Sunlight peeked over the darkened horizon and lit the morning sky with a pale orange glow. Paige stared out of the glass cockpit at the stunning view of Mt. Maja in the distance. The summit's glistening peaks had replaced the web of white tents that stretched out below them on their ascent from the refugee camp. Whether they'd caught the rebels off guard with their early-morning takeoff, or if they simply didn't have the weapons to try and take down a small aircraft, she didn't know, but either way there had thankfully been no sign of rebel activity on the ground.

She leaned back against the seat, then adjusted the headphones Nick had given her at takeoff to combat the noise of the cockpit. "It's beautiful from up here, isn't it?"

"Now you know why I love to fly. Africa is this never-ending stretch of savannahs; thick, green forests; lazy, winding rivers; and wild animals." Nick blew out a deep breath. "It's like a drug I don't know if I'll ever be able to shake. Or want to shake, for that matter."

He reached for the water bottle propped between them. The back of his hand brushed against her elbow. "Sorry."

A shiver ran down her spine.

She glanced at his profile and took in his grin along with those dreamy, toffee-brown eyes of his. She tried to stop the flutter of her heart, because she knew what was happening. Intense situations tended to bond people who wouldn't otherwise choose to be together. Which meant if they both worked the lunch shift back home at the local pizza parlor, she'd never have given him a second glance.

Except she knew that wasn't true.

She'd have noticed Nick Gilbert anywhere. There was something about his laidback southern charm that had her stomach doing somersaults — a reaction she knew had nothing to do with the occasional drop in altitude of the plane, or even her apprehension over leaving the camp. No, if she was honest with herself, it had everything to do with the fact that he was sitting beside her, smelling of Old Spice and smoke from hundreds of cooking fires. And making her heart do things she hadn't felt for a long time.

She looked away, hoping that small gesture meant he wouldn't be able to read the open expression she knew she displayed. She'd always worn her heart for the world to see.

She needed a distraction and the Cessna 206 they were flying in seemed like the perfect place to start. "I have to admit that the first time I flew in one of these planes I was a bit nervous."

He caught her gaze, his brow raising in question. "Why's that?"

"While I've always loved to fly, I'd never flown in a small plane before."

"That's understandable. And this time?"

Paige ran her fingers along the bottom of the window frame. "Well, you have to admit this plane has seen better days. If you haven't noticed, there are what look like bullet holes along the belly and a definite need for a new coat of paint."

Nick laughed. "Our mission organization might run on a strict budget, meaning our aircrafts won't win any beauty contest, but our mechanics are the best and would never let any of our fleet go airborne without the engine and body being in top condition."

Paige glanced at the endless yellow grasses spotted with miniature trees below them. "That's good to know."

"One of these days, though, we're hoping to replace this baby with a Kodiak 100."

She turned back to Nick. "What's that?"

"It's been called a mountain rocket and was manufactured specifically for flying in a mission situation. It uses jet fuel, which is cheaper than Avgas, carries more cargo, is more cost effective, and can cruise at two hundred and twelve miles per hour . . ." He shook his head. "Sorry. You're probably not interested in all of that, are you?"

Her smile widened. "Actually, I meant it when I said that I've always loved flying. And learning to fly is number twenty-seven on my to-do list."

"Ahh, the to-do list. One of these days I want to see that entire list."

He winked at her, making her suddenly wonder which was more unsettling: flying in his dilapidated plane or those eyes of his that seemed to see right through her.

"Oh, no. I've never shown anyone the entire list." She felt her face heat up again. How did he always manage to do that to her?

"Now I'm even more intrigued."

For the first time she wished she'd never mentioned the list. But just because Nick Gilbert had managed to get her saying — and feeling — things she hadn't intended on didn't mean he needed to know about number fifty-seven (meet and marry Mr. Right) or sixty-two (honeymoon in the Seychelles) or —

"Personally," Nick continued, "I like the fact that you know what you want and go after it, and that in the process you're willing to get out of the box and do something crazy once in a while, like . . . like eating sushi in Japan or, for that matter, spending three months in the RD."

Paige laced her hands together and forced herself to stop dwelling on the list. While thinking out of the box might have its advantages, currently it had her mixed up in the path of a rebel takeover. Which meant in this case, staying inside the box — and heading home — would have been the far safer option.

The terrain below changed from open savannah to thick forest as they climbed in altitude toward the mountain's base camp. It was time to change the subject. Again. "So when did you start flying?"

"Believe it or not, flying was never on my to-do list. I planned to be a high school science teacher."

"So then how'd you become a pilot?"

"Do you want the short version or the long version?"

"I'm smart enough to leave that answer up to you." She turned and shot him a grin, but the pinched expression on his face told her she'd hit a nerve. "Or if it's too personal . . ."

"Iraq wasn't the first time I ran." Nick drummed his fingers against his leg. "I was twenty-one, one of those kids who think they know everything. My father expected me to take over the family landscaping business that had been started by my grandfather, but I'd mowed enough lawns in high school to know that wasn't what I wanted. Which was only one of many arguments we had starting in my teenage years up into early adulthood."

"So you didn't get along?"

"Nope." He flipped a couple switches and they banked slightly to the left as the flaming ball of sun spilt over the horizon like a liquid pot of gold. "I got a degree in chemistry with plans to become a high school science teacher. After graduation, I managed to get a position at a private high school where I made barely enough to afford boxed macaroni and cheese for dinner."

Paige chuckled. "Ouch."

"It was definitely a blow to my pride, and my father wasn't one to let me forget. During the first semester that I taught, and probably due to my mother's nagging, my father planned a hunting trip for the two of us over a long weekend. We hunted for two days and while my dad shot a deer, I couldn't even manage to get a prairie dog."

"Which reinforced those same feelings of never being good enough for him?"

"You should have been a counselor." Nick's smile broadened as they changed direction and headed north, then faded. "On the third day, he woke up not feeling well, but I was determined to show him I could hunt as well as he could, so I managed to talk him into going out for a couple more hours before we headed home."

Nick scratched the back of his neck, his gaze locked onto the view of the mountain ahead of them. "It was rainy and cold that day, and I should have listened to him. He had a heart attack that morning while we were out in the woods. By the time I got him to the hospital, it was too late."

"So you think that if you hadn't insisted on going out that morning, he'd still be alive today?"

"I'll always wonder. Mainly, I wonder if we could have ever repaired our relationship."

His confession struck too close to home. "Just like you'll always wonder if you could have saved that boy in Iraq, or what would have happened if I'd found out about Marila's illness sooner . . . They're all things we'll never know."

"You're not the only one who holds on to photos." Nick pulled out an envelope from his logbook beside him, hesitated for a moment, then handed it to her. "I've never shown this to anyone."

Paige glanced at the flowery writing on the front. It was addressed to Nick and postmarked October of last year. "What is it?"

"My mother sent it to me." He jutted his chin toward the envelope. "She and my sister found a few boxes of my father's personal things that my mother had shoved in the top of a closet when he died, then forgot about until she moved last fall. They found the photo tucked inside the jacket he always wore. It was taken on my twelfth birthday."

Paige opened the envelope and pulled out a worn photo of a younger version of Nick and a man smiling down at him who shared his same eyes and strong chin. "Your father?"

Nick nodded. "He never told me he loved me, but he carried this photo with him."

"He loved you. You can see it in his eyes."

"I just wish I'd had a chance to hear him say it. After he died, I quit my job and joined the air force."

"Any regrets?"

"At the time? Lots. But today, no. It forced me to finally grow up." Nick's features had finally relaxed some as he turned to her. "What about you? Did you always have your life planned out from the beginning?"

"In a sense. I remember one summer when I was six or seven bandaging up my best friend's busted-up knee and deciding then that I wanted to become a doctor. I never lost the desire to be able to help people."

"No regrets?"

"Overall? No, though I'm certainly not done working through my list."

Nick chuckled. "You're different, Paige, and I like how you think beyond the status quo."

Paige wondered when the feeling had become mutual. "Even after my meltdown last night?"

"Trust me, you're not the only one capable of losing it from time to time. And considering the circumstances . . ." Something on the instrument panel beeped and Nick flipped a switch. "The base camp is up ahead, so I'm starting our descent. We'll land in a few minutes."

Reality shot through her. They'd pick up the injured climber, along with the dead body, then take them to Kingani before heading back to the camp. Stopping at the hospital would give them a chance to insist that military help be sent to secure the volatile situation at the camp.

She caught sight of the small runway sitting at the base of the mountain and felt her anticipation grow. She'd fulfill her commitment to Digane by ensuring the treatment center was fully functional and the staff competent to handle the situation, but by Friday she was going to be on a flight out of the country and all of this was going to be behind her.

TWENTY-TWO

Brandon gasped for air. With his lungs constricting from both the cold and exertion, he forced himself to quicken his pace through the dense forest in order to keep up with Jodi and the four porters they'd met halfway down the mountain. They'd bundled up Jodi in a sleeping bag for the descent, then placed her on a unicycle-type stretcher. It clearly hadn't been made for comfort, but at least it was faster than carrying her.

The porters shouted to each other as they'd done the entire decent. Five hundred feet from the base camp, the narrow path finally leveled out, but even here they were close to three thousand feet above sea level. After hours of carrying Jodi, then running beside the porters the remaining distance, his fatigued body screamed for oxygen.

The pale-blue morning sky was just light enough that he could see his breath. All he could do now was pray that a rescue party and plane were waiting for them at the base camp.

He glanced behind them. A headlamp bobbed in the distance. Apparently he'd been wrong about Ashley slowing them down. Her motivation to get off the mountain had obviously pumped in the needed adrenalin to give her the energy to make the descent.

Painted green shacks strung out along the clearing in front of them. Beyond them was forest. After less than twenty-four hours on the mountain, it suddenly seemed a lifetime since he'd seen civilization. And yet they were still close to two hundred miles from the nearest hospital.

He scanned the flat expanse to the east where they'd landed Sunday night. A plane sat parked on the runway.

Ignoring the burning pain, Brandon headed for the plane with the porters right behind him. "Thank God . . . you're here."

The pilot and doctor quickly introduced themselves before Dr. Ryan started assessing Jodi. She glanced at him briefly, the concern clear in her expression. "I know your wife is the one injured, but are you okay?"

"I'm . . . I'm fine, Dr. Ryan."

"Skip the formalities. You can call me Paige."

"Okay." Brandon worked to catch his breath. "I'm just . . . winded. It took four hours to run down the mountain."

"What's her name?"

"Jodi. She's . . . my wife."

"Jodi?" Paige shook Jodi gently. "Can you hear me?"

Jodi let out a low groan. Her eyes fluttered open momentarily before closing again. Four hours of bumpy terrain down the side of the mountain had to be exhausting for Jodi, even though she'd been carried. And with her injuries . . .

"Brandon, I need you to tell me exactly what happened."

"The rebels invaded our camp last night. I . . . I didn't see what happened to her, but after they shot her, she must have tried to run, then fell and hit her head. We couldn't find any signs of any other injuries."

Paige felt Jodi's forehead. "She's burning up with fever. Did she have the fever before the attack?"

"No . . . She . . . she told me she was a little tired when we arrived at the first camp

186

around lunchtime, but insisted she would be fine. I made the comment that she felt warm, but it wasn't a fever. I thought . . . I thought she was just wearing too many clothes."

Paige gently peeled off a makeshift bandage to get a better look at the injury. A large patch of blood had seeped through the cloth.

Brandon pressed against the stretcher. "Why isn't she responding?"

"I don't know." Paige turned to the pilot. "I don't think we have time to go to the hospital in Kingani. We need to get her to the camp so I can stabilize her. She's lost too much blood."

"What camp?"

"It's a refugee camp. We have a clinic set up there."

Brandon shook his head, wondering when he'd wake up from the nightmare he'd fallen into. What had he been thinking when they'd decided to come here? "And you have what you need to help her there?"

"Initially. We're a twenty-minute flight from the refugee camp, but it's another hour past that to the nearest hospital. She needs to be properly assessed and stabilized as soon as possible. If we were in a flight ambulance things would be different. The refugee camp is her best option for the moment."

"Okay." Brandon stepped back from the plane as they loaded Ashley's father's body, followed by his daughter. Jodi was next to be transferred onto the plane. He choked back the emotion. She was lucky she wasn't the one lying in a body bag.

"Brandon?" Paige nodded at him from the door of the plane. "We need to go."

"I'm sorry." He stepped up into the plane, but the image of the body bag wouldn't leave.

Within five minutes, they were in the air. Brandon started praying. Something he rarely did. But facing life without Jodi wasn't something he was ready to contemplate. She'd make it. She had to.

The plane rose until the camp and surrounding trees were nothing more than dots along the horizon. Behind them Mt. Maja, with its ice-capped top, touched the clouds. Today they would have reached the third camp. By Thursday, they'd planned to drink champagne at the summit. Instead the flattened savannah spilled out beneath them, edged by thick forests to the south and a river that snaked across the terrain to the west.

The airplane rocked to the left. Brandon

felt the seatbelt jerk at his middle. He glanced back at Jodi, who lay on a stretcher beside Paige. If there'd have been room, he'd be sitting back there with her right now.

Ashley sat beside him, her face pale. "What's going on?"

"It's probably nothing more than a storm coming. Looks like clouds are gathering quickly to the east. I'm sure Nick's a great pilot."

She didn't smile at his attempt to defuse her fear. "I hate to fly."

"Then why choose to vacation halfway around the world?"

Ashley stared out the window. "You wouldn't understand."

"Try me. I need a distraction."

Ashley let out a deep breath and for a moment he thought she was going to ignore his request. "My father and I were close. He was the outdoor type, loving everything from motorcycle riding to rafting to climbing."

Brandon took in her manicured nails and shaped brows and wondered how her father had ever gotten her to join him. "And you?"

"I'll admit, I'm not exactly the outdoor type."

Really. He smiled and suppressed a chuckle.

"I'm not sure why he always insisted I come with him. Maybe it was simply because he never had the son he'd always wanted. But whatever the reason, even though these trips weren't exactly my thing, I really did love being with him."

A seed of sympathy took root. "I'm truly sorry for what happened."

"I just can't believe he's gone."

The plane rocked again.

"I need everyone to check their seatbelts." Their pilot spoke from the front of the plane. "Looks like it's going to be rough the next few minutes."

Brandon tugged on his seatbelt and looked out the window. Darkening storm clouds gathered behind them. Ahead, the flat expanse was dotted with a few trees and further on, the white tents of the refugee camp glistened in the rays of morning sunlight that managed to escape the cloud covering.

Something along a narrow ridge caught his eye. Before his mind could register what it was, a trail of fire whizzed from the ground toward them, followed by an explosion that rocked the left wing. Brandon grabbed the armrest. Beside him Ashley screamed.

The plane dove downward diagonally.

Panic swept through Brandon. They'd been shot.

"Engine two is down. Everyone hold on."

Brandon's mind struggled to grasp what was happening. Things like this weren't supposed to happen in remote, off-the-map places like the RD. He was just a tourist who'd come for a few days of adventure, with no interest in the politics of the country.

The ground rushed toward them, and the belly of the plane somehow managed to slide horizontally across the flat terrain. Pain shot through Brandon's knees as they smashed against the seat in front of him. Mud splashed across the windows, obscuring the view from the pilot's seat. Brandon's head smacked against the seat in front of him. Metal screeched. The wheels snapped from underneath the plane.

Then all was quiet.

Twenty-Three

Tuesday, February 22, 7:25 a.m.
American Embassy, RD

Paul pulled open the top drawer of his desk and dug for one of the Snicker bars he'd brought back with him from his last trip to DC six months ago. It was probably the last thing he needed, what with the persistent cough he'd developed overnight, but healthy or not, he was running on empty. He glanced at his phone and mentally calculated the time in Colorado. It was almost eleven-thirty. He should call Maggie. The kids would have gone to bed hours ago, but she was probably either watching a movie or reading one of her cheap romance novels. So much for the fatherly advice he'd given Isaac about family and priorities. So much for his own marriage.

His phone rang, and he answered it on the second ring. "Deputy Chief of Mission Paul Hayes, speaking."

"Paul? Is that you? You sound horrid."

"It's nice to hear your voice as well, sis." While Sarah was good at sending occasional e-mails, his middle sister rarely used the phone. Which had him worried.

"Are you sick?"

"Just some nasty cold I picked up." Paul shoved the drawer shut, ripped open the wrapper, and took a bite of his breakfast. "You're up late. Is anything wrong?"

"The twins went to bed early, so Maggie and I decided to watch a chick flick."

He smiled at the image of Maggie in her slippers and her red, satiny pajamas watching movies with his sister. Give her a happily-ever-after fairytale and she was content. Which had to make their life together look like some cheesy B-rated horror movie. "How are the kids?"

"The twins are fine."

"And Maggie?"

"She misses you. We all miss you."

Having three younger sisters had always complicated life. "That's not what Maggie said on the message she left me yesterday."

He stood to look out the open window overlooking the embassy lawns, lined by a row of mango trees. Even at this early hour of the morning it was already hot. Man, he wished he were in Colorado with Maggie right now. "E-mail me some more photos of the kids, will you? I know they're growing up too fast."

"That's because Maggie doesn't let them live on Snickers and Dr Pepper."

He dropped what was left of his candy bar onto the desk and eyed his drink. Maggie would have his hide if she saw him. "How'd you know?"

"For one, I'm your sister and know you pretty well. And that telltale ripping of a candy-bar wrapper was a pretty good give-away." Her voice caught. "You're going to have a heart attack if you don't take better care of yourself."

He scowled at the reprimand, but his sister was always right. And if Maggie was here, she'd tell him the same thing. Even his secretary complained about his eating habits. But none of them understood the stress he was under. Or the twinges of guilt that kept surfacing, reminding him of everything he should be doing. Like making up with Maggie, seeing his daughters, find-ing time for a proper meal —

"Paul?"

"Yeah, I . . . I'm sorry." He sat back down in his chair. "I've been a bit distracted lately. There are some things we're dealing with right now at the office."

"I watched CNN tonight. They mentioned outbreaks of fighting in the north."

"Nothing for you to worry about." He glanced at his watch. He'd called a short meeting with his team, and now he was the one who was going to be late. "I really need to go —"

"And your family really needs you. What happened between you and Maggie?"

Her question took him off guard. It wasn't the subject he wanted to be discussing with his sister right now.

"She told me she's here because the two of you decided that I needed some extra help with Tucker and the new baby, but I don't believe her."

He wanted to sound as if it really wasn't a big deal. That Maggie really had left because his sister needed someone to help her out around the house, but that excuse wasn't true and they both knew it.

Paul took another bite of his candy bar. He'd picked up the phone to call Maggie a dozen times in the past twenty-four hours, and each time he'd hung up before dialing. He knew she was hurt, but when this was all over and he was able to return to the States, he'd find a way to make it up to her. Dinner, tickets to the opera, or maybe a weekend at the bed and breakfast in Breckenridge where they'd spent their honeymoon. Except he was afraid that this time, any attempts to make things right would end up being too little too late.

"Don't try to pretend that this has something to do with me," Sarah said. "You need to ask her to come home."

He swallowed hard. "That's not my choice to make."

"So that's it, then? You just let your wife walk away after twenty-five years of marriage without a second glance at all you've gone through together?"

"Sarah." His jaw tensed. She had no right to accuse him. "Now's really not the time."

"That's the problem. It's never the right time, is it? Your work has always come first, and Paul —"

"What I do is important. You know that."

"Paul." There was a pause on the line. "Maggie's older sister went to the doctor yesterday. They've diagnosed her with breast cancer."

"She . . . what? I don't understand. She never mentioned a problem."

"She had a mammogram two weeks ago, and they found a lump."

Why hadn't Maggie told him? "It's cancer?"

"They caught it early, so her prognosis is

good. But she'll still have to go through treatment."

"Meaning?"

"They've scheduled surgery for next week. Then she's looking at radiation."

The walls pressed in around him. "I still don't understand — why didn't she tell me?"

"Because you weren't here."

Paul slumped in his chair and tried to digest the news. How had he spent his entire life playing the role of the good guy for his country, but when it came to his own family he'd become the villain?

You should have been there.

"Call her. Twenty-five years is too much time to simply throw away. And she needs you now."

He wasn't sure it would make a difference.

"Promise me, Paul. Just call her."

The white-tiled floor blurred beneath him. "I'll call her."

"Promise?"

"Yeah." He glanced down at the open door of the conference room, feeling torn.

"Don't lose her."

He hung up the phone, then held his head in his hands. How had he ever let things get this far out of control? This never should have happened.

Isaac stood in the doorway. "You ready to start?"

Paul waved his hand. "Yeah, I'm coming."

For now, he was going to have to go in there and do what he'd always done. Shove aside any family issues and focus on the problem at hand. Years of experience should make it easy.

The team he'd called in, both Dhambizao nationals and U.S. government employees posted at the embassy, was already set up around the oval table in the conference room when he arrived a minute-and-a-half later. He dumped what was left of his breakfast on the table and sat down. "Who's got an update of the situations with the rebels?"

Carl Williams, one of the consular officers, originally from Virginia, stiffened in his chair. "We're still getting mixed reports from our government sources. They claim the army has everything under control, while the rebels are reporting that they are now in control of the whole Mponi region."

"What else?"

Isaac leaned forward. "The rebels also have threatened that if amnesty is not granted they will advance to the capital. But Carl's correct — the government continues to maintain that there is no substance to their threats."

"Carl, what's the death toll in that region?"

"It depends on who you are talking to. The government is still reporting the toll at less than thirty, but there are rumors circulating that make it closer to four, maybe five, hundred."

Paul whistled under his breath. "That's a significant difference. What about the airport? Any delays reported?"

"Commercial flights continue to operate from the capital's international airport." His assistant, Mercy, spoke up for the first time. "But that is subject to change depending on the rebel activity."

"And the evacuation process?" Paul asked.

Mercy tapped her pen against the table. "All Americans registered with the embassy and living in the Mponi region have been informed of the order to evacuate. We also have ensured that all humanitarian groups and U.S. citizens outside that region have an evacuation plan ready to implement in case a countrywide warning is issued for them to leave."

Paul frowned. He needed something new. How hard could it be to get cold, hard facts? "We've got rebels on the loose, which puts American lives at stake, and yet everything you've just given me I could have read — and did read, by the way — in this morning's paper. I need to know why I'm receiving information — and unconfirmed information at that — from the newspaper and not the local authorities."

Isaac cleared his throat. "I've . . . I've had some issues in getting detailed information from my contacts."

"Which brings up several problems." Paul folded his arms across his chest. "One, I've got dozens of family members of expats living in this country and they are looking to us for answers. So what do you propose I tell them? That everything's fine and there's nothing to worry about despite the fact that CNN just reported that people are being slaughtered in their beds?"

"I —"

"I'm not finished." Paul cut Isaac off. "Second, you were hired for this position because as a former senior law enforcement officer of the RD, you are supposed to have contacts in this government. Which means you should be able to drag the chief of police, or the deputy of foreign affairs, or anyone else out of bed in the middle of the night and get the information out of them that I want."

"Yes, sir."

Paul caught the irritation in Isaac's voice and briefly regretted his sharp response, but the weight of the situation hung heavy in the air. If the man couldn't do his job, he didn't belong on his team. Because if they couldn't all do their jobs, more lives were going to be lost.

TWENTY-FOUR

Tuesday, February 22, 7:47 a.m.
Kingani Refugee Camp

Nick jumped from the plane and automatically began barking orders. It was a miracle they were all alive. He'd managed to come in for the landing at a fairly level position at the edge of the camp, which had lessened the impact, but he still shouldered the responsibility of getting his passengers to safety. Something he'd been unable to do in Iraq. He glanced at the bottom of the plane that lay against the red dirt. It was a miracle there wasn't more damage, but the threat hadn't passed. A leak in the fuselage could mean the chance of an explosion. Added to that, the rebels were out there. They needed to get to safety as quickly as possible.

Nick jimmied open the passenger door and helped Paige step down from the plane. The apprehension she had struggled with the night before had been replaced by a clear streak of determination. Whatever the inner turmoil she was coping with, she was in her element and it showed.

With the last of the group wrestled out of the plane, Nick took up the rear as the guards helped to carry Jodi and the body of Ashley's father to the camp. In the distance, the group of rebels stood along the ridge, too far away to cause any more damage, but they'd made their position clear: the refugee camp had just become a key player in the rebel's game to win amnesty for their colleagues. Which put at even greater risk the ten thousand plus people spread out before them across the flat terrain.

"Nick." Paige turned to face him. She blocked the sun with her hand while the breeze teased the back of her hair. "Aren't you coming?"

"I need to see what kind of damage we're looking at."

"Looks pretty final to me." Her gaze shifted from the plane to the rise behind him. "And the rebels . . ."

"I'll be okay. If they wanted to take live hostages, they'd be here by now."

She shot him a look of disapproval and for a moment he reconsidered going back to the camp with her, but he needed to know if there was any way this plane could fly them out of there.

"I won't stay long. I promise."

He watched her hurry toward the clinic, then turned back to the plane. If he could find a way to get it back in the air, it might be their only way out of the camp.

Twenty minutes later, Nick admitted defeat by kicking the tire, wincing at the pain that shot up his leg. There was no way this plane was flying again any time soon. He pulled out his logbook, the first-aid kit, and a couple of personal items he didn't want the rebels getting their hands on, then headed to the clinic.

You're going to have to show us another way out, God.

Inside the clinic, Paige stood beside one of the metal beds, adjusting Jodi Collin's IV while her husband, Brandon, sat beside her. At least the woman seemed to be sleeping comfortably for the time being.

Nick bridged the gap between them. "How is she?"

Paige dropped her hands to her side, fatigue clearly mixed with the determination he'd seen earlier. "Stable for now. I was able to remove the bullet, but her fever's increased, and I'm not sure what the source of the infection is. I've started her on a broad-spectrum antibiotic, but I don't know that it will be enough. Now I'm wondering if we should have risked going straight to the hospital in Kingani . . ."

Nick shook his head. He'd learned first-hand that when you started playing the what-if game, you always lost. "You had no way of knowing what was going to happen. You made the best judgment you could considering the circumstances. Don't second-guess your decision."

"What I'm concerned about is that she also has some strange symptoms that don't seem to be connected with the gunshot wound. You would think altitude sickness, perhaps, but instead her chest is congested."

"I don't see how we've got a choice. We've got to get her to a proper hospital." Brandon turned to Nick. "What about the plane? Is there any way it will fly?"

Nick shook his head. "It's not going anywhere. And with those rebels out there, neither are we."

Brandon held his wife's hand. "I need you both to tell me what's going on here. I just managed to survive a horrific experience on that mountain and now you say we're trapped here?"

"Unless something changes out there, that's a pretty good conclusion." As much as he hated to admit it, Brandon's assessment was on target. But that didn't mean he was ready to give in to the rebels. "We need to sit down and discuss our options."

"I agree." Paige turned to one of her nurses. "I need you to go find Taz. Tell him we need to speak to him immediately. Brandon, why don't you join us."

Five minutes later, the four of them sat in the back of the clinic while Samson stood guard outside, carrying one of the confiscated rebel weapons. But even though Samson was armed, if the rebels decided to attack, there was little anyone would be able to do about it.

Brandon stood and started pacing. "I still don't understand. We were told that the conflict was miles away from Mt. Maja and the camps."

Nick shrugged. "Rebels don't exactly play by the rules. From what I've seen, they are facing little resistance from President Tau's army, which means they're gaining ground quickly."

"Can't we fight them off?"

Taz tapped his safari hat against his knee. "We might outnumber them, but we've got a couple guns and a camp full of displaced people who are mainly women and children. We can't exactly raise up an army with our resources."

Brandon didn't look convinced. "So what happens in the meantime? I'm not willing to sit here and watch my wife's health deteriorate."

"I'm not sure we have any options until the rebels are neutralized. Flying's obviously out of the picture, and they've blocked the main roads."

"And sabotaged the cell-phone towers," Paige added.

Brandon smacked his hands against the table. "Surely someone will notice we're missing and call in the military before this goes any further."

"That's what I'm hoping happens, but it could still be several days before they realize something is wrong. Power outages are common and even with the satellite phones, they expect there to be times that we can't get through." Nick processed the situation like a military strategist, but with hundreds of civilians involved, their options were limited unless they could get past the rebels. "The bottom line is that with issues of logistics it could take several days before help arrives, and that's assuming they can get past the rebels."

"What if Jodi doesn't have days?" Brandon turned to Paige. "I appreciate your attempts to take care of my wife, but she needs to be in a hospital with proper medical care."

Nick watched the pain reflected in Paige's expression. And it wasn't just Jodi that they were all concerned about. No road access meant no fuel for boreholes and no more supplies. Samson's quick thinking had meant that while the rebels got away with their satellite phones and radios, they hadn't been able to touch their food supply. Of course, there were no guarantees that they wouldn't return with a larger group.

"Let's look at what we do have. What about the medical supplies?"

Paige thumbed the corner of the current inventory list. "We have basic supplies that should last another week if we're lucky. And we should have enough to keep the cholera treatment center running if the number of cases starts to drop, as it should within the next forty-eight hours or so. We need that convoy that's on its way, not with just medical supplies and food, but personnel as well. But with the rebels standing guard, I'm not sure we can count on them."

Taz shook his head. "Maybe not, but I saw how rapidly you were able to organize the isolation tent for the cholera victims. We can find a way to deal with this."

Paige didn't look convinced. "How? Round up volunteers who are willing to guard the perimeter of the camp?"

"That's not a bad idea," Nick said, "but if the rebels return, there is little we can do to stop them. They're armed, trained men who have a lot at stake."

"We have a lot at stake as well." The determination was back in Paige's eyes. "The lives of these refugees. Each one of them is here out of desperation, most of them with nothing more than the shirt on their back. They have little food, and their living conditions are anything but adequate. Which means if we're not careful we're going to have a whole different type of emergency."

"We're going to need to focus on one problem at a time and find a way to run the camp with what we have." Taz placed his hat back onto his head. "Thankfully, this standoff can't last forever. Give the army a day or two to organize themselves and get here. The rebels might have weapons, but there can't be that many of them."

"Dr. Ryan?" One of the nurses set a battery-operated radio on the table. "I'm sorry to interrupt, but you mentioned you wanted to hear the news updates."

"Yes. Thank you." Paige turned up the volume.

■ ■ ■ ■

. . . these same rebels, who were involved in the attempted assassination of President Tau in November, insist that their reign of terror will continue until their commanders are not only let go, but are granted amnesty from any charges related to the slave trade they ran deep inside the Dzambizan mountains.

But while rumors continue to spread regarding the burning of villages in the north and the slaughtering of innocent people, the government continues to maintain its position that while there has been isolated instances of the rebel's attempted uprising, the president's army is still in control of the situation and the country is under no threat from advancing rebel forces. In an interview with one of President Tau's spokesmen . . .

"Isolated instances?" Paige clicked off the radio. Surely there was someone out there who knew the truth about what was going on. "Are you telling me that they don't have a clue about what is happening here?"

Nick let out the breath he'd been holding. "More than likely they know exactly what's going on, but admitting the truth shows weakness in the government. And threatens things like humanitarian aid and tourism that bring in millions."

Paige stood and moved to the end of the row of beds. "So they keep up this crazy farce that everything's okay while people are either dying from cholera or being murdered?"

Nick shoved aside the wave of despair that threatened to overwhelm him. "Then it's up to us to stop them."

Twenty-Five

Paige stood at the far edge of the camp as
men lowered Robert and the victims from
last night's raid into the freshly dug graves.
With no refrigeration, they'd had no choice
but to bury the bodies as soon as possible.
The wind blew across her face, hot and dry,
making her long for the cooler temperatures
of Tennessee. And a place where the worst
stress, outside her job, was getting stuck in
afternoon traffic. Now she was looking at
the very real possibility of not even being
able to make her flight on Friday.

She pushed away the thought. In the
distance, the shadowy figures of the rebels
lined the slight rise where they'd taken up
position for the past few hours. She turned
back to the small crowd of people standing
beyond the loose piles of red earth. The
rebels' presence was a reminder of the

control they'd lost.

Already, those living in the camp were becoming restless. Reassurances that the army would come and take care of the rebels had done little to ease the marked fear on their faces. And now, instead of spending time in the surrounding forest searching for firewood or walking to one of the surrounding villages in search of work or a place to sell their remaining possessions, they stood in front of the registration tent with fear in their eyes, demanding answers to the appearance of the rebels.

Paige watched the wind blow the dirt as it dropped from the shovels. They were right. With little food, an inadequate water supply, and few, if any, weapons, the situation was spiraling out of control. In the end, all their promises would do little to stop the slow panic already snaking its way through the camp. And with the rebels surrounding the camp, there was nowhere for any of them to run.

The men continued shoveling dirt over the bodies as the onlookers slowly started walking back to their tents. Ashley remained beside her father's grave, her expression void as she watched the men drop the final shovels of dirt.

Paige looked away, unwilling to intrude

upon this painful, private moment.

Nick brushed up beside her, his hands jammed into his front pockets as he stared at the freshly dug graves. "How are you doing?"

Her eyes filled with tears, and she shrugged, wondering how to answer. "I don't know. The last twenty-four hours have seemed so surreal."

"It's okay."

"To cry?" She wrapped her arms around her waist, wishing she could just let the dam of emotion that had built up break, but there was too much at stake for her to fall apart. Too many people depending on her for strength. "I'm scared, Nick. If those supplies don't get here soon, we're going to have to keep digging more graves. We have more cholera patients than we have beds, I'm worried about one of the burn victims, and I can't get Jodi's fever under control."

"Complications from the gunshot?"

"I don't think so, but I'm not sure, and I don't have the equipment I need to test for the source of the infection. I don't have half of what I need." She rolled the hem of her shirt between her fingers while her mind searched for a solution. "The bottom line is that before long I'm going to have to start making judgments and choosing who is treated because there is simply not enough medicine to go around."

"Don't go there yet. All you can do is treat one person at a time and pray that God will stop what these men are doing before we get to the crisis point."

"And if we do get to that point?"

"How much time do we have?"

"Everyone who's registered received a food packet. Technically, it's supposed to last fifteen days, but I've been told that by day ten they are running low and often go hungry until the next ration is given out." The math — and the consequences — were easy to calculate. "For those who have already been here a week or more, they're going to need more of the rations soon. Taz said we might have enough food for half of them. We need those supply trucks."

Paige studied the endless rows of tents, their flaps blowing in the morning wind, where children and mothers fought to survive on a meager existence. Desperation had already caused dozens of fights throughout the camp in the past few hours, which, if allowed to continue, would in turn put them all in danger.

She looked up at Nick. "I'm not going home, am I?"

"Not without a miracle."

Desperation to leave vied with her compassion for these people. "How do we stop the rebels?"

The small crowd that had gathered to watch the burial had now left, leaving in their place an eerie silence. "I've been talking some more with Taz and several of the other men. As soon as we're done here, we're going to send four or five men to the nearest town, which is about five kilometers down the main road. There we should be able to get a call through and get some help."

Paige felt the haunting stare of the rebels behind them and tried to shake it off. "How are you going to get past them?"

"We don't think they have more than a couple dozen men guarding the camp, so getting past them shouldn't be too difficult. The problem is that could change quickly if reinforcements arrive."

Which meant any move they made would have to be now. The border lay to the north, and so far the neighboring government was refusing to allow anyone to enter the country. Dozens had attempted to cross, but most had been forced back to the camp. With the base of Mt. Maja to the east and heavy forests to the west, the rebels had essentially cut them off, giving the armed men the leverage they'd wanted.

"And if your plan doesn't work?"

"If we don't check in, somebody will eventually assume something's wrong."

"But even if the men get through and the government agrees to bring in the army, that will take time." Something they didn't have.

After little sleep the night before, exhaustion had settled over her body. Gathering any remaining threads of mental strength, she folded her arms tightly across her chest and stared at the row of fresh graves, serving as a poignant reminder of the severity of the situation.

Ashley walked past them toward the clinic, catching Paige's attention. The young woman's fancy designer boots left footprints in the soft soil and stood out in this place of poverty. And yet despite the outward differences, she, like many in this camp, had lost what she considered most important.

"Ashley?"

The young woman turned and stared at her.

Paige struggled to find the right words. "I'm so sorry about your father. If there's anything I can do for you . . ."

"Like what?" Ashley's features hardened. "Look at this place. If I stay here, I'll end up catching some horrid disease like leprosy or AIDS or . . . Ebola."

Paige's eyes widened. "Speaking as a doctor, the odds of you coming down with any of those diseases are pretty slim. Follow basic hygiene principles, and I'm sure you'll be okay."

" 'Okay'? You're kidding, right?" Ashley's voice cracked. "If the rebels don't massacre us all, we'll all be wiped out by some epidemic before help gets here."

Paige looked to Nick for help. Instead, he stood silent beside her, looking even more uncomfortable than she did. Apparently she wasn't the only one who found the girl disconcerting. She'd only been around her a few short hours, but already wondered why someone like her had ever decided to rough it and come to the middle of nowhere to climb a mountain.

Paige shook her head and tried to swallow her judgment. "The army will be here before long to neutralize the situation. They'll escort the supply trucks here for the people and take you back to the capital, where you can fly home."

"She's right." Nick nodded. "It might take a day or two, but even the rebels won't be able to stand up against an armed convoy."

"A day or two?" Ashley pulled her dark glasses from her posh backpack and slid them on, covering up her red eyes. "You don't understand. This . . . this place. I have no intention of staying another twenty-four hours. My family has money. I'll find a way out."

Paige watched Ashley start back toward the medical clinic. Beyond her, boys played soccer with a homemade ball, while some older kids lounged outside one of the tents, listening to a battery-operated radio. These kids deserved to be in school. Paige turned back toward the row of men lining the hills to the west and reminding her that all the rules had changed.

"She's kidding, right?"

"I wouldn't put it past her."

Paige turned and caught Nick's gaze. "But you don't think she'll really do something stupid, do you?"

"Like what?"

"I don't know. Try and pay off the rebels—"

The sound of a motor interrupted Paige midsentence. She turned around to see a jeep squeal to a stop twenty feet away. One of the men in it stood and dumped a body over the edge of the vehicle. Paige felt her legs give out beneath her. Two more bodies were thrown onto the dusty ground, then the jeep accelerated back toward the guarded ridge.

"Nick . . ."

"I saw two of them this morning." Taz stepped up beside them, the horror of what Paige felt mirrored on his face. "They said they were getting out of here."

Paige grabbed Nick's arm. It was a message. And if something didn't change, this place was going to turn into a death camp.

TWENTY-SIX

Tuesday, February 22, 11:52 a.m.
Downtown Bogama
Paul signaled for his driver to turn up the radio as they weaved in and out of traffic on their way to the deputy of foreign affairs' office.

. . . A tour group, including four Americans due to climb Mt. Maja in the Republic of Dhambizao, has not been heard from since February 21 and are feared by friends and family to be missing. Conflict in the north of the country has escalated in the past few days, leading to what many believe to be the start of a civil war. The U.S. Embassy reported that the four American and four Canadian tourists arrived in the country Friday night only hours before the embassy, along with diplomats from Canada, England, and Germany, issued warnings to its citizens to evacuate the northern region of the area. But with growing conflict and rumors of rebel raids at the base camp, it appears that the warning may have come too late . . .

Paul's cell phone rang as his driver pulled up in front of the four-story government building, drowning out the rest of the BBC's latest report on the country's situation. For a region that was already supposed to be evacuated, the count was now up to eight missing tourists, along with a handful of aid workers he hadn't been able to contact, making him wish he believed in miracles. Finding them all alive would be that miracle. Unfortunately, after twenty years in this business, he'd given up believing in those a long time ago.

"Wait for me here," he hollered to his driver, then flipped open his cell to answer the call. "Paul Hayes here."

"Mr. Hayes, finally. I've been trying to track you down for the past six hours."

The accent pegged the caller as an American, but whoever it was, he wasn't in the mood for another crisis. "I'm sorry, who are you?"

"This is Mitch Peterson. My fiancée, Ashley James, who has now been declared missing, was a part of the tour trekking Mt. Maja."

Mitch Peterson wasn't the first phone call he'd received this morning from worried family members. Paul mentally ran through the list of names he'd received an hour ago. Brandon and Jodi Collins from a small suburb outside St. Louis. Robert James, a Houston oil tycoon and his daughter, Ashley, who was a Hollywood actress . . . "Yes, her name was on the dossier I was given this morning, but we're still trying to verify both the original source and the fact that the group actually is missing, as we've yet to receive an official report of any problems from the base camp."

Or any report for that matter, which made him question the source of the rumors spreading through the news waves.

"I'm the source."

"You reported them missing? Where are you?"

"LA."

"LA?" Paul stopped in front of the government building, with its yellow lawns and over-grown bushes. "You're thousands of miles away, and yet you're somehow more aware of the situation than we are?"

"You don't understand. Ashley wasn't exactly keen on this trip. She had a satellite phone and when she wasn't calling me, she was sending text messages."

"There could be a dozen reasons why you haven't heard from her, but none of them are reasons to panic. Bad satellite reception, a dead battery —"

"The news is reporting intense fighting around the base of the mountain. I don't think all of this is a coincidence."

"I'm fully aware of what the news is reporting, but I'd prefer to verify the situation before spreading rumors."

"And how do you plan to do that?"

Paul didn't like the insinuations in the man's voice. "I'm on my way to a meeting with the deputy of foreign affairs right now to coordinate efforts to deal with the situation."

"And then?"

"I've got your number. I'll call you."

Paul shoved the phone into his back pocket, then took the front stairs of the government office two at a time, frustration burning a hole in his gut. Instead of chasing down information that should have automatically been handed to him, or dealing with rumors from unqualified sources, he should be sitting in front of the fire in Colorado on an extended leave with his family. Which was what he was going to demand once this was over. If Maggie would let him.

Twenty years ago, he'd joined the marines, intent on saving the world. Grabbing a diplomatic position with the State Department after leaving the service seemed like the perfect decision at the time. He could raise a family, see the world, and serve his country all at the same time. And now it had come to this.

He pushed aside his rambling thoughts of the twins and Maggie. He'd made his choice, which meant he was going to have to play this one out. Though, if he had his way, this would be the last time he put his family on the line for another country that refused to play ball with him. He was tired of the pointless games and receiving nothing more than unsubstantiated reports that left him with little, if any, information he could work with.

He popped a couple of Tums into his mouth and hurried down the long corridor. People were lined up along the chipped walls that hadn't been repainted for years. Why paint when there wasn't enough money to insure your people had proper medical care or clean water or even adequate food? The mountains in the north might hold countless resources, from coltan used in cell phones to diamonds, but despite promises by the government that the wealth would reach the people, he'd yet to see a single attempt to use the resources for the benefit of the people.

Paul turned a corner and entered the reception area that held the deputy's office. An air conditioner hummed quietly behind the secretary. A gold nameplate for James Ngani, deputy of foreign affairs, hung on his door. Paul didn't even stop at the secretary's desk to find out if the man was available. There wasn't time for formalities.

"You can't go in there. The deputy's in the middle of a meeting." The secretary jumped from her chair to block his entrance, but she was too slow.

"Then it looks as if he's going to have to postpone his meeting." Paul barreled through the unlocked door and stared at the pudgy man sitting behind the desk. He slammed the door behind him. "You're a difficult person to get a hold of, Deputy Ngani."

"Paul Hayes." The frown on the man's ebony face broadened, increasing the lines across his bald head. "I'm on the phone. Make an appointment."

"I'm sorry for the intrusion, but I've run out of time to play Mr. Nice Guy. I keep hearing rumors that this country's in a state of emergency, but for some reason, no one seems to have noticed."

Ngani mumbled something into the phone, then slammed down the receiver. "I suppose there's a reason for this outlandish behavior. I could have you and your entire staff kicked out of the country by nightfall for this."

"For stopping by for a friendly visit? Now that would go over real well with the UN and the dozens of humanitarian workers the world sends over every year, wouldn't it?"

"Don't threaten me."

Paul's jaw tensed. He was breaking every rule of diplomacy, but he was way past the slow dance required to tiptoe around matters of foreign affairs. He braced his hands against the table and leaned forward. "I want some answers."

"What's the question?"

Paul slid into the open chair across from the deputy. "According to the news, rebels raided Mt. Maja's base camp. So with one confirmed American death and now possibly more, I want to know why I've had little if any contact from your offices."

Ngani squirmed in his chair. "As you know, we have continued to keep your offices up to date with everything that is happening, but you have to understand that we also have to be extremely careful."

The deputy picked up his phone, but Paul grabbed the receiver and slammed it down.

"I'll call security and have you thrown out —"

"I don't have time for games. My people are in danger, and I want something done about it."

"What do you want to know? We've sent out updated information on a daily basis to your offices."

"That has told me nothing."

Ngani's gaze shifted down. "You must understand that while our army continues to hold back the rebels, they are both well armed and well organized. If we were to rush in there we could end up with a botched rescue attempt that leaves more dead than alive."

"So we just sit back and do nothing while the rebels take over the country?"

"You act as if we're at war, which we're not. Yes, there have been a number of mild skirmishes in the northern region, but I can assure you that the army is in control."

"So you keep telling me."

"Perhaps if you and your people would spend less time contacting our offices and demanding information, and more time letting us do our job, we could put an end to this unfortunate situation."

Paul forced back a laugh. So the blame now fell with him. Brilliant reasoning. "Does that statement include my inquiries regarding humanitarian workers who are here to help your country, or would you prefer they spent less time helping your people?"

"Of course not."

"Then what happens next? We wait while the rebels slaughter both your people and mine?"

"I told you; the situation is under control."

"Then tell me what measures you've taken so far and what risk my people are in."

"You know as well as I do that the government is already in talks with the rebels, but this is an internal affair that my government is more than capable of dealing with."

"Then why do you insist on keeping my office in the dark?" Paul's head began to spin. He was sick of going in circles and getting nowhere. "Either you're purposely downplaying what's going on out there, or you're out and out lying to me. Neither is an option I like."

Ngani rubbed the back of his neck. "I've told you I don't know anything about the raids involving Americans —"

"Then tell me something you do know. There have been dozens of reports of slaughtered villagers in the Mponi region in the past few days, by rebels who aren't happy with the way things are progressing in the so-called peace negotiations you've been holding. I have my men and every American citizen in the country poised to be evacuated, yet somehow all I hear from your office is that the army has everything under control."

"Because we do. Don't forget that fear tends to escalate the problem, which is what the rebels want —"

"As does naivety. Is that what you want? To insure the rest of the world doesn't see that you're incapable of handling this rebel onslaught?"

"I suggest that you don't talk about things you clearly know little about."

"Fine." Paul garnered a deep breath. Obviously, his tactics weren't working. "Then I'm formally informing your office that I will be contacting the State Department about pulling all foreign-aid workers upon my return to my office."

Paul stormed from the room before the deputy had a chance to respond. No doubt he'd just severed the already fragile relationship with the deputy, but he was past caring. He had a job to do, and he intended to do it.

His phone rang halfway down the stairs. He pulled it from his pocket and checked the caller ID. It was Mercy.

"Paul here."

"You need to return to the embassy as soon as possible. There's someone here you need to talk to."

Great. All he needed was another complication. "Who is it?"

"Her name's Leah Freeman. She's an American working with Volunteers for Hope International. She and several other Americans, Brits, an Aussie, and some RD nationals were on their way to the refugee camp up in Kingani with a convoy of trucks carrying supplies for the camp."

Paul stopped at the bottom of the stairs. "I knew about the convoy. What happened?"

"She can tell you her story, but the convoy was hijacked by the rebels."

"Where are the others?"

There was a long pause on the line. "They're all dead."

TWENTY-SEVEN

Tuesday, February 22, 2:47 p.m.
Kingani Refugee Camp

Paige helped move the unconscious woman onto one of the last empty cots in the isolation ward while she mentally shifted her thinking into emergency mode. Without treatment, fifty-percent of those infected with cholera would die. With treatment, the death rate dropped sharply to one percent. But those statistics meant nothing to the woman who'd just lost her husband and three small children. And now they were about to lose her.

One of the local nurses pulled off the blood-pressure cuff. "She has no palpable pulse and no blood pressure."

Paige nodded. "Her veins have collapsed. There's no way to get a line into her."

Which meant without a way to administer the oral rehydration treatment, the woman didn't have a chance. They only had one option left.

Paige tied on a surgical mask, then rolled the supply tray closer. "We're going to have to put in a nasogastic tube in order to re-hydrate her."

Marking the placement of the tube, she lubricated, then began inserting it. The woman started gagging. Paige checked to make sure it was placed properly, then suctioned. A moment later, she let out the lung-ful of air she'd been holding. With the tube in place, the woman now had a chance to live.

Paige finished giving instructions to the nurse on how to administer the oral re-hydration packet, then slid off her mask. It was the one ironic thing about cholera: as fast as the illness could take a life, with the proper rehydration therapy it only took a few hours of treatment and most were able to sit up and talk. After another day or two, they were able to leave the isolation tent.

Exhaustion mingled with a sense of relief. She needed some fresh air. Pulling off her gloves and surgical gown, she washed her hands and stepped outside, greeting Samson, who guarded both the isolation tent and the main medical clinic. He had been put in charge of organizing men to watch over both the clinics and the food distribution center, as well as the perimeter of the camp, and had refused to go off duty when his replacement came. As far as she knew, the only time he left his post was to check on the guards or the progress of his son.

She breathed in the smoke-tinged air, wishing she knew what the rebels wanted. They stood around the perimeter of the camp like Joshua and the Israelites, as if they were silently waiting for the order to attack. And if they did decide to sweep through the camp, stealing whatever medical supplies and equipment they had, or even take hostages, there was little she and the others would be able to do to stop them.

Brandon was crossing the dusty grounds toward the clinic. The anger that had first marked his expression had been replaced with a deep sense of resolve, and from his actions, a desire to do something about the situation.

Paige followed him into the main medical tent. "Any updates on what's going on out there?"

"Samson has done a good job in organizing extra guards, but I'm not sure if it will be enough. Gathering wood has become an issue, for one. There are still places around the edges of the camp that the rebels are not patrolling, but resources will not last long." He sat down beside his wife. "How is she?"

Paige toyed with the end of her ponytail, wishing she had answers. She needed to be in a hospital with a lab where she could order tests and pinpoint the source of Jodi's symptoms. "She's stable, and I'm thankful she's finally sleeping. The wound seems to be healing, but something else is attacking her body."

"And you don't have any idea what it is?"

"As of right now? No."

Brandon took his wife's hand. Jodi stirred, but didn't wake up. "Her hands are swollen."

"So are her feet, and now there's a rash there as well, like hives."

"I don't understand. She was fine up on the mountain."

"You told me she'd complained about a headache."

"Yes, but I really thought she was just tired. We weren't high enough yet for me to worry too much about altitude sickness. She tends to take on more than she can handle, so I'd planned to keep an eye on her. But she didn't complain of anything else."

"Did she have a cough?"

"No, why?"

Paige leaned against the end of the bed.

"She complained of abdominal pain and has been coughing, so I gave her something to help her sleep, which is why she's drowsy. But until I pinpoint what's wrong there's little I can do."

Without a lab that could isolate the illness, all she could do was treat the symptoms. At this point, it could be anything from Rocky Mountain spotted fever to pneumonia.

Brandon rubbed the stubble on his chin. "This was our honeymoon. Everyone thought we were crazy to come here, but we both love to travel and never were much at doing the traditional tourist thing."

"I'd have to agree that this part of Africa is an interesting location to choose for a romantic getaway."

Brandon laughed. "This trip was so important to her. She was in a serious car wreck a year-and-a-half ago and after a miraculous recovery, wanted to prove to herself — and to everyone she knew — that the Jodi who'd spent her life running marathons and rock climbing was back."

Paige worked to fit the pieces of the puzzle together. "You mentioned she'd been complaining of headaches. Do you think she was ready for this?"

"She's been fine. Or so I thought. A little

tired perhaps the last few days, but Jodi was never one to complain. She was used to pushing through the pain and keeping going."

Which meant she might have been experiencing symptoms she hadn't told Brandon about.

"I know this is hard on you, Brandon, but I'm praying for wisdom to know how to treat Jodi. And that this will be over soon — for all of us."

"You believe in God?"

She looked down at him. "Yeah, I do."

"Even after what's happened the past twenty-four hours?"

The long row of patients lined up in front of her seemed to mock her. She squeezed her eyes shut for a moment, wishing she could squeeze the doubts away as easily. What kind of God would allow thousands of people to be ripped from their homes, killed, and raped . . . Anything she said would ring hollow. Until the curse of sin was lifted, no one would have complete freedom in this world.

"What's happening isn't because of God, but because of sin in the world." She massaged her shoulder with her fingers. How could she convince him of something she didn't fully comprehend herself? She was the one whose only clear goal had been to get through this assignment alive so she could return home. "I won't say I always understand why God allows so much suffering, or that I don't question why He doesn't step in and stop things like this from happening, because I do. But you mentioned how it was miraculous Jodi survived the accident. Did you ever stop and think that God saved her for a purpose?"

"For what? For this? What would be the point of saving her from that wreck only to turn around and have her die by the hands of a rogue group of rebels?" Brandon shook his head. "It just seems like if there is a God, then He'd zap them like Sodom and Gomorrah instead of letting all these innocent people die."

"All I know is that there is a God, and He cares what happens to both you and Jodi. All this, the fighting, killing, and disease . . . it was never a part of His plan."

"Maybe." Brandon stood and shoved his hands into his pockets. "Listen. Taz is sending teams to check the chlorine levels in the water, and I told him I'd help. I can't just sit around and do nothing. I'll be back later to see how she's doing."

Paige glanced over his shoulder at Ashley who sat doing her nails on one of the cots.

"Would you mind waiting a minute? I've got someone who needs to join you."

He followed her gaze. "Ashley? I'm not sure I want that woman on my team." He lowered his voice. "I don't mean to be rude, but she's —"

"I'm sure I could come up with a few choice adjectives as well, but the girl's just lost her father and deserves some sympathy. Something to distract her, maybe?"

"Fine. I'll be outside. Tell her we're leaving in five minutes if she wants to come."

Paige crossed the room, stopping at Ashley's cot. "Hey, I thought —"

"I'm glad you're here." Ashley waved her fingernail file in the air. "I need to get some hot water. I went to the food tent, but all they would give me was a handful of . . . of packets."

"They're food packets for the next ten days."

"Ten days?" Ashley's laugh rang hollow. "It's a handful of dried beans and cornmeal. There's got to be something else to eat around here."

Paige folded her arms across her chest and shook her head. The woman might have given up on the idea of appealing to the rebels' sense of greed by offering them money, but she certainly hadn't come close to getting rid of her pompous attitude.

"You know, I'm really sorry you lost your father, and I honestly can't imagine what you're going through right now, but what I do know is that there are over ten thousand people out there who need our help. Most of them have lost people they love, along with their homes and everything except the clothes on their back."

"So what do you want me to do?"

"What do I want you to do?" Paige attempted to rein in her temper. "For starters, stop feeling sorry for yourself. You've sat on that cot since you arrived and all you've done is complain. I wish I could change the situation, but my nurses aren't here to wait on you. And if we're going to get out of this alive, we're going to all have to band together and do whatever we can to make sure we don't have to bury anymore bodies. So, in the meantime, it would help if you could make yourself useful."

Ashley's file dropped to the bed and tears filled her eyes.

Great. So much for a show of sympathy. "I'm sorry. I didn't mean to upset you."

"It doesn't matter, because I know what you think. I know what everyone thinks. I'm some spoiled rich girl who can't make it without her assistant in tow or her five-star accommodations."

"I don't know anything about you other than what I've seen on television." She had to give the woman some benefit of the doubt. "And I'm sure the media doesn't paint a realistic picture of who you really are."

"If you knew who I really was, you probably wouldn't want to know me. My family has more money than this country's yearly budget, and while I've worked hard to get where I am, I'm used to getting what I want, when I want it."

"Then why did you come here? The RD isn't exactly on the top-ten tourist destination list."

Ashley pulled her legs up beneath her on the cot. "Mainly because my father loved to hike and this was another challenge he could conquer. I wanted to try it with him. Believe it or not, he did pass on a few good traits to his spoiled daughter."

"He must have been a good man."

"He was, in spite of me."

Paige sat down beside her. "I'm sure that's not true."

"My father saw money as an opportunity to give to those in need. The RD was one of the places where he'd become involved the past few years. He helped to fund an orphanage in Bogama, and visited two, maybe three, times a year."

"I didn't know that."

"Most people don't. While I love being in the spotlight and in front of the camera, my father just liked to give stuff away."

"I truly am sorry for what happened up on that mountain."

"Most of what he did, along with my mother, revolved around charity work." She wiped away a tear. "But that doesn't matter anymore."

"I think it still does matter. I bet you take after him more than you think. There's a group headed out into the camp right now to test the chlorine at the various water sites. They could use some extra help."

TWENTY-EIGHT

Tuesday, February 22, 3:35 p.m.
Kingani Refugee Camp

Ashley slid her sunglasses up the bridge of her nose and hurried to catch up with Taz, whom she'd been assigned to work with for the rest of the afternoon. He whistled down the dusty path like he didn't have a care in the world. Something had to be wrong with a guy who was good-looking yet chose to live in this godforsaken wilderness. And what kind of name was Taz, anyway?

She wiped away a bead of sweat from her forehead and groaned. She never should have listened to Paige. The smell of cooking smoke, mingling with the foul odor of perspiration and filthy latrines, turned her stomach, reminding her that she was thousands of miles away from home. She'd pay anything for a hot shower, some decent coffee . . . and a chance to see her father one more time.

Instead, white tents flapped in the wind beneath a cloudless blue sky. Dozens of children ran past her with extended stomachs, runny noses, and smiles on their faces, as if this were nothing more than a weekend camping trip during summer vacation.

Ashley let out a sharp *humph.* She hated camping. The only time she ever wore trekking gear and slept in a sleeping bag had been to pacify her father on trips like this one, where she had porters at her beck and call to bring her what she needed. Here, entire families, with their passels of children, stood at the entrances of their tents, cooking and talking. She disliked cooking almost as much as she disliked children. Which was why she and Mitch had decided not to have any. It wasn't that she was a scrooge. Not really. It was simply that her priorities were set, and children tended to get in the way. She'd seen it in her best friend, who had started out like her, with dreams of hitting it big in Hollywood, until one day she fell in love. When Jordan came along a year later, Lucy went from aspiring actress to chief chef and diaper changer.

That wasn't going to happen to her.

A group of little children in tattered clothes scampered in front of Ashley. She took a step back to get out of their way while Taz pulled a digital camera from his pocket and started taking their pictures. The kids squealed with delight and pointed to the camera until Taz showed them their digital images on the view screen.

One of the girls walked up to Ashley and tugged on the hem of her shirt. Ashley took another step backward and ran into one of the tent posts in the process.

"They don't bite."

"Of course they don't bite." Ashley looked at Taz, then back to the little girl. She cleared her throat. "Hi."

The little girl beamed. *"Tsiko teyo."*

"Excuse me?"

"She said thank you," Taz translated.

Ashley's frown faded. "Thank you? For what?"

"For coming. She thinks you're one of the aid workers here to help."

The little girl waved, then ran off with the rest of the children to play in the hot sun. No frilly dresses or toys or televisions or PlayStations. Just homemade balls and piles of dirt instead of sandcastles. She buried the guilty sensation. She had her accountant write out large contributions to a dozen charities from Haiti to Sudan every year. Surely that was enough.

"Ashley?"

She moved away from the tent and brushed off the dusty fingerprints the girl had left on the bottom of her shirt. "Yeah."

"You know, when I asked for a volunteer to help me check the water, I was assuming that the volunteer would actually, you know, help me check the water."

Ashley rolled her eyes and started after him. In LA, she had a personal assistant who not only brought her a latte every morning, but kept her Porsche full of gas and her dry cleaning done. The woman's only job was to ensure she showed up for work with her lines memorized and enough energy after the day's shoot to attend whatever parties were being held that night. Manual labor wasn't exactly on her résumé, and from the look of things, Taz didn't even need her. No doubt they all felt sorry for the rich American who'd had her expensive holiday ruined.

They reached the water source where dozens of women, with babies wrapped tightly against their backs with pieces of colorful cloth, waited in a never-ending line with their yellow jerricans. She handed him the black test kit she'd been carrying. "What exactly is the point of this?"

"Right now we have a dozen points throughout the camp where the water comes in from the river and allows the people limited access. What we really need is a tank full of gas so we can run a borehole, but for now, we can treat the water we have." He held up the test to check the results. "If the chlorine is too low, then it's probably contaminated by bacteria. If it's too high, the taste is altered and the people won't drink it. Thankfully, this water is okay, because clean water can reduce diarrhea incidences in the camp by ninety percent and is the only way we're going to be able to stop this epidemic."

She raised her brow.

Taz chuckled and started walking again. "I suppose things like cholera and other related topics aren't exactly watercooler topics where you come from."

"Not exactly."

"So tell me, Ashley James. Where are you from?"

She glanced up at him, wondering if it was pity she saw in his green eyes or simply annoyance. She didn't want either. She couldn't help it if she wasn't like Dr. Paige Ryan, who was clearly capable of saving the world. She lowered her gaze and watched Taz work. He wasn't as handsome as Mitch by a long shot, with that silly safari hat he wore, scrawny, sunburned legs, and a strange, black bracelet made from who knows what. Of course, Mitch would never have come to such a remote place as Africa. He'd made it quite clear several times that she was nuts to agree to come with her father.

Maybe he'd been right. If they hadn't come, her father would still be alive.

She reeled her thoughts back to Taz's question. "Houston, originally, but I'm living in LA right now."

"Ahh . . . so you're a city girl."

Clearly he was mocking her. "Like you hadn't noticed?"

"What do you do there?"

"You don't know who I am?"

"Should I?"

"You've heard of *Casey's*, haven't you?" she asked.

Ashley skirted around a mud puddle, then walked through the thick throng of people behind Taz toward the next testing site, wondering how he didn't get lost in the sprawling maze of white tents and people. Every scene was the same. Women sat in front of the shelters either cooking beside fires that sent up wisps of gray smoke into the air or nursing infants, while the older children played in the long afternoon shadows of the tents.

"Casey's what?" he asked.

"It's not a what; it's the name of a sit-com."

"Sorry. I don't exactly watch much TV around here."

"We just finished shooting the second season after receiving an Emmy for best comedy and my nominee for best lead comedy actress."

"Then I guess congratulations are in order. I'm assuming you play the role of Casey?"

"Casey? No. Alexandra Mitchell. Alex for short." She couldn't remember the last time she'd had to explain to someone who she was, because over the course of the past two seasons, the show — and its cast — had become household names. "Casey's the name of the coffee shop where I work on the show. It's about a bunch of aspiring actors and comedians who live in LA and work at Casey's —"

"Can you hand me that second test?"

Ashley let out an unladylike *humph* as she handed it to him. Apparently Taz was no different from all the other volunteers here who'd apparently lost their minds — and given up any chance of a decent livelihood, she was sure, to tromp around taking care of the underprivileged without a clue as to what was happening in the rest of the world. It was time to change the subject.

"What about you?" Ashley stopped beside him at the pump where another unending line of women stood to get water. "What brought you out here in the middle of nowhere?"

"I went to school and got a degree in law." Taz started the second test without missing a beat. "But after five years of paperwork and meetings, I chucked it all for this."

"Why in the world would you do that?"

"Why?" Taz turned around and faced her, surprise clearly written on his expression. "I suppose I never quite got used to working sixty hours a week for a paycheck but no life. And like most of the volunteers here, I wanted to find a way to make a difference in the lives of people. For me that meant outside the courtroom."

She might not ever understand his reasoning, but she did know his type. He'd probably worked in some podunk town as a public defender to every lowlife who walked through the door. And to save some of his measly salary, he'd lived at home before coming here, because not only was it cheaper; it was also easier than living on his own. His girlfriend, if he even had one, was someone he met at church, who promised to wait for him, but that relationship wouldn't last because she'd probably . . .

Ashley froze.

A mangy dog sauntered up between her and Taz, then stopped in front of her, ripping her from her thoughts. Ribs protruding from his sides and his bared teeth and low growl told her he meant business.

Ashley took a step back and motioned. "Go away."

The dog didn't move. Instead, he lifted his lip and snarled at her.

"I said go away."

"Ashley?"

Ashley barely heard Taz's question. The dog snarled again and started coming toward her. She stepped backward until she was flat against the wall of one of the tents. A couple of children giggled.

"Taz . . . He's going to bite me."

"He's not going to bite you. He's just looking for food." Taz threw a stick at the dog. It yelped and ran off. "He's harmless."

"Harmless. Right." Like a case of dysentery.

Taz folded his arms across his chest, clearly unimpressed with her handling of the situation. "Listen, I'll understand if you would rather go back to the medical clinic and wait there until we're all rescued."

And give him the satisfaction of thinking she couldn't do her part? There was no way that was going to happen. "I'm fine."

"You look real fine. You're white as a sheet."

"I said I'm fine."

Ashley started down the trail toward the next water site, but Taz stopped in front of her, blocking her way.

"Listen, I understand that you prefer your fancy cars and high-profile parties, but at least what I do here makes a difference in the lives of people."

Ashley felt her jaw drop. What a self-serving ape. Like he had a monopoly on saving the world. "What I do makes a difference as well."

Taz folded his arms and chuckled. "Tell me, Ashley James. How do you save the world?"

She glanced at the group of children playing in the sand. Despite their tattered clothes and dirty faces, they were all laughing. She tugged on the bottom of her shirt. This wasn't exactly the place to be making her point. "People . . . people need people of influence like me."

"Why?"

"Why?" Since when did she have to spend her time defending her choices in life? This man was turning out to be more exasperating than an uncomfortable pair of stilettos. "Because . . . because while people like you are out here saving the world, you need someone to act as your spokesman. Someone like me who people listen to."

"A valid point. So what is the last charity organization you promoted?"

She strummed her fingers against the test kit. "I'm on the board of several charitable organizations and have been involved in their fund-raising dinners, champagne breakfasts —"

"Hmmm. And how many of these people here benefited?"

"That's not fair. Even in my position, I can't save everyone."

"Not much is fair in this part of the world." He shook his head. "You know, I'm honestly glad you have your Emmy nominee and fancy parties, but here we spend our days making sure people have enough clean water to drink so they don't die from a cholera outbreak. And, no, they don't wake up and decide which designer outfit they're going to wear into work or if they should grab a café au lait or perhaps a cinnamon dolce latte instead —"

Ashley's jaw tensed. "You have no right to judge me —"

"Oh, I don't? Then what have you been doing? Judging me because I decided to escape the corporate world for something that makes me happy. If you ask me, it took more courage for me to leave than you'll ever have."

"Now who's sounding self-righteous?" Ashley pressed her lips together. A small crowd had gathered, stopping her from lighting into him like she wanted to. Apparently they'd become the entertainment for the day. She, for one, wanted no part.

"Just forget it." She brushed through the crowd toward the next water point. As far as she was concerned the show was over.

"Forget what? That all these people have been ripped from their home and are now living in tents? Or forget that those who aren't sick with cholera are probably infected with HIV/AIDS and TB?"

"I mean it Taz." He wasn't going to shower her with a load of guilt. All she wanted was to get back home where she could forget about all of this. "Let's just check your blasted water system and get this over with."

"Fine." He hurried down the path, then stopped at the far edge of one of the tents. A little girl lay huddled on the ground in the shade of one of the tents. There were no adults or other children around. Instead, she lay alone in a fetal position.

Taz knelt down and felt her forehead.

"Taz?"

"She's burning up with fever." He picked up the girl and started running. "We've got to get her to the clinic. Now!"

Twenty-Nine

Tuesday, February 22, 4:08 p.m.
Kingani Refugee Camp

Samson stood beneath the umbrella of a gnarled acacia tree and gazed past the unending rows of white tents and groups of women gathered around small cooking fires. Beyond them, a billow of black smoke rose, marking the remnants of yet another village destroyed by the rebels. He'd listened to the radio reports where government spokesmen, speaking from their plush homes behind electric fences, assured the people that President Tau's army had crushed the rebels and that there was no need for panic.

But this was not what he'd seen when the rebels appeared in the darkness, shooting their automatic weapon and waving their machetes while burning down his family's huts. No doubt news traveled slowly to the ears of the fat government officials who seemed to care little about the precarious situation thousands now faced.

He shoved his hands into his pockets, wondering if there was a solution, or if this was simply how the rest of his life would play out. Perhaps his people had unknowingly angered the ancestors and were now cursed. What other explanation was there? Their own victory last night during the rebels' surprise raid had been nothing more than a fluke because they hadn't expected any resistance. It was only a matter of time before the rebels returned, and this time, they'd come with reinforcements.

He caught sight of a shadowy figure looming on the rise. He'd foolishly wanted to believe these Ghost Soldiers would disappear once they raided the camp, but instead camp guards had reported sightings of them everywhere. They lurked in the thick trees of the forest, stood guard along the banks of the river, and infested the nearby villages, turning this place of refuge into a prison.

He shifted his weight, wishing he could find relief from the hammering heat. He'd spent the past two hours circling the perimeter of the camp, ensuring that all volunteer guards stood in their place. Eight hadn't shown up and another three had come to their posts drunk.

No, he was fooling himself if he thought the guards surrounding the camp could do anything to stop the rebels if — when — they decided to attack again. Two years working as a security guard in the capital had taught him that. Without armed backup or trained forces who could control and monitor the situation they were no better off than a group of tethered goats. And the threat of violence wasn't limited to outside sources. He'd already dealt with clashes inside the camp as the stress of the refugees continued to rise.

And the stress had escalated when they'd watched the rebels dump the dead bodies onto the ground. Even the two dollars a day promised to those who volunteered to guard the camp wasn't enough to hold back the fear or keep the guards in their places. He started for the clinic to check on Asim. His official watch didn't start for another two hours, which meant Dr. Ryan would nag at him to rest until then, but sleep had become elusive. Instead he automatically scanned every shadow for Valina as he passed through the busy market where stalls had been set up in an attempt to create an economy. Goods were traded and temporary barber and sewing shops set up as people tried to supplement the provisions given to them by the aid organization. But how long could any of them continue living like this?

And how much time would pass before he discovered whether or not Valina was still alive? He studied the stacks of firewood lined up along the path, unable to bring himself to imagine what the Ghost Soldiers were doing to her. Better off that she had succumbed to the sharp edge of the machete the day he lost her than be alive and tortured in one of their camps. But he held onto hope, as small as it was, that he would see her again.

Familiar anger seared through him like hot coals. Like Dr. Ryan, Valina would tell him that God was still in control no matter what happened around them. But why hold onto the belief in a god who allowed such horror to occur?

A group of kids played soccer beside the line of women waiting for water. One woman walked by with a jerrican balanced on her head, her face partially hidden by a scarf that blocked the sun.

Samson paused, then turned back to look at her. There was something familiar about her gait, the swing of her hips, the curve of her waist . . . His heart pounded.

Valina.

He ran toward her, shouting her name,

before grasping the woman's shoulder and turning her around. Scared, brown, unfamiliar eyes looked up at him.

He jerked his arm back. "I'm sorry, I . . ."

The blue canopy of sky spun above him. He shook off the wave of dizziness. He had been so sure. Certain it had been his wife, and that tonight he'd hold her in his arms . . .

Samson shook his head as the woman walked away. Perhaps the doctor had been right and he needed to sleep. But how could he? A plan began to form in his mind. Staying here was doing nothing to find his family. If he could find the camp of the Ghost Soldiers, he might be able to find Valina and his girls. Then together they'd escape the terror of this place and start a new life.

He stood at the edge of the camp, his mind at odds with what he should do. Except he knew he couldn't leave. He'd made a covenant to help protect the doctor and the people of this camp, and he would not go back on his word.

A flutter of commotion caught his eye. Taz ran past him with a young girl in his arms, the American woman from the mountain trailing behind him. How many more would die, trapped in this camp?

Something snapped in the recesses of his

mind. He ran forward. "Wait, please."

Taz turned toward him. "What's wrong?"

He took in the familiar pink dress, bare feet, and long braids. There was no mistake this time. "Please, stop. That's my daughter."

THIRTY

Paige held up the finished origami for Asim and smiled. "Elephant."

"Elephant." Asim repeated the word in broken English, but his grin transcended all languages.

So far, no infection had set into the wounds. She prayed that the extra boost in calories she'd ordered for him would help quicken the healing process, because while his malnutrition wasn't severe, the high-energy peanut paste provided protein along with an antibiotic treatment and vitamins.

Scarce rains had translated into thin crops and less food for those living outside the cities. On top of everything else, they needed a therapeutic feeding center for the entire camp, but until supplies were trucked in, there was little she could do to fight the need.

Instead of worrying about what she couldn't do, she tried focusing her attention on Asim. She tousled his kinky black hair. "A few more days, and you'll be able to leave this tent."

And go where?

The question haunted her. Little boys didn't belong in refugee camps where there was nothing but long hot days and nights. But while most humanitarian agencies advocated maintaining education services in order to preserve a sense of normalcy, the resources simply weren't here. Which reminded her of the reality of her question. Until things were resolved with the rebels, no resources were coming in, none of them were leaving . . . and she wasn't going home.

A wave of homesickness torpedoed across her heart. But she wasn't the only one longing to go home. Or the only one wondering if she was going to survive this nightmare.

Brandon called to her, pulling her from her thoughts. "Do you have a minute?"

Paige patted Asim on the head and nodded. "Of course."

She followed him across the room, out of earshot of Jodi's bed.

"I've been sitting with Jodi. She's in a lot of pain."

"I've given her everything I can. Any more

and her respiratory status could be compromised."

"I don't understand what's wrong. You said the gunshot wound is healing, but she seems to be getting weaker by the hour."

"Her body is fighting something, and we're still trying to pinpoint what it is." Paige ran over Jodi's symptoms in her head for the dozenth time. So many of the diagnoses Paige was now being forced to make were nothing more than gut instinct. Even the lab technician who'd come with them on the plane was severely limited beyond anything but the basics. Which brought her back to Jodi. And the fact that she had no idea what was wrong with her.

While the gunshot wound seemed to be healing as expected, Jodi had developed other complications that seemed unrelated. The hives had spread from her ankles and wrists and her lungs were filling with fluids. Paige had already run through the list of possibilities with her nurses, covering every exotic disease she could think of, but nothing they'd discussed completely fit the symptoms.

Paige picked up Jodi's chart from her desk and tapped her finger against the top. There had to be something she was missing. "I don't know where else to look. She's not been sick until now?" They'd been over it all before, but it wouldn't hurt to go through it again.

"No."

"Anything that had symptoms of an amoeba or parasite-like diarrhea or flu?"

"No. The only thing she complained about was a couple headaches, and of course her leg bothers her some. She has a pin in her ankle, but it was something she never let slow her down."

"Where else did you visit before the RD?"

"Morocco for a couple days, then a cruise down the Atlantic Ocean along West Africa. When we were on land, we tended to skip the local tourist magnets and head for the bush, but we also tried to be smart as to where we went and what we ate. We arrived in the RD last Wednesday, spent a couple days at the game park outside of Ngamoli, then headed for the base camp."

Which meant it could be anything.

She pointed to Dayo, her local lab assistant, wishing he had the resources that would in turn make her job easier. But he was limited to testing for basic issues like pregnancy, malaria, TB, and HIV.

"As primitive as our lab might be, we're still able to diagnose a few things. Unfortunately, every test he's been able to run on

Jodi has come back negative."

Brandon blew out a sharp sigh. "I understand your position, but I need answers. I can't handle watching her suffer, especially when there is nothing I can do."

"For now, all I can do is treat the symptoms and try to make her comfortable, hoping her immune system and the antibiotics can fight off whatever this is."

"Could the lab in the hospital in the capital diagnose her?"

"I can't make any guarantees, but I would think so. Even in this part of the world, they'd have much greater access to supplies than I do."

Brandon's gaze shot to the door. "Then I've got to get her there."

"Brandon, wait. I realize your urgency to find answers, but leaving the camp carries with it its own risks. You saw what happened this morning to those three men who tried to leave. They'll do the same thing to you if they have the chance. And Jodi needs you alive."

"There's a jeep. If I could get past them, then outrun them —"

"Brandon, look at me." Somehow she had to convince him that running at this point wasn't the answer. "I know you're worried about Jodi, but right now she's in stable condition and isn't running the risk of dying. If you try and mess with the rebels, her odds of *not* making it out of here alive will rise substantially."

"I've got to at least consider the possibility."

"You've also got to consider the reality."

"My wife has run the Boston Marathon eight times. She's climbed the Canadian Rockies, Mount Whitney, and Mount Kilimanjaro. Coming here was a chance for her to prove that she hadn't lost everything important to her in the accident."

Her concern for Jodi ran deep, but her patient wasn't the only one she was worried about. "When's the last time you ate?"

Brandon shrugged. "I don't know."

"I want you to go to the food tent. They have beans and rice fixed for the staff. Get something to eat. Then go talk to Nick if you still think planning an escape is what you need to do."

Brandon hesitated, then nodded. "Okay."

Dayo set another stack of charts on her desk as Brandon left the clinic. "What did you tell him?"

"What could I tell him besides the truth? That I have no idea why his wife is sick. I've thought of every scenario I can, but whatever it is, it simply doesn't fit into any

267

normal pattern. I've looked at Rocky Mountain tick fever, meningococcal infection, even the measles."

Dayo tapped Jodi's chart. "Maybe you're on to something."

Paige shook her head. "What do you mean?"

"Measles. We know the typical symptoms of measles — fever, cough, red eyes, and eventually spots in the mouth. But what if this isn't a typical case of the measles?"

He had her attention. "Explain. Except for a handful of cases I've had to treat in the past couple of months, measles isn't exactly a disease I'm used to facing on a day-to-day basis."

"I worked with a Canadian volunteer three years ago who talked about a patient he'd treated with atypical measles. It occurs in people who are incompletely immunized against measles with a killed measles vaccine, then are exposed to a wild-type measles virus. That specific vaccine was only used from 1963 to 1969, and it sensitized the patient to the measles virus and didn't offer any real protection."

"What are the symptoms?"

"Exactly what we're looking at. Fever, the build-up of fluids, pneumonia, swelling of the extremities, with a rash that is atypical in measles."

"It's more like hives."

"Exactly. And it appeared first on her ankles and wrists."

Paige considered the diagnosis. Measles presented a new problem. In a perfect scenario, most people who contracted measles would recover with few, if any, complications. But with the cholera crisis, conditions in the camp were far from perfect. Which meant the disease could be a death sentence for dozens if allowed to spread.

"If you're right, we're going to need to set up a separate isolation tent. We can't handle an epidemic of measles going through the camp."

"Do you think it has spread?"

"We have no way of knowing at this point. But we better be prepared. Because if it does spread, we're going to have another disaster on our hands."

A commotion in the waiting room interrupted their conversation. Taz rushed through the crowded area, carrying a small child in his arms.

Paige grabbed her stethoscope and jumped into action.

"Put her there." She pointed to the only empty bed, then felt the child's forehead.

She was burning up with fever. "Where did you find her?"

"Out among the tents while we were checking the water."

"Do you have any idea where her parents are?"

This young girl wouldn't be the first child to have been separated from her family during the chaos of one of the raids, or to have lost parents due to the cholera. In the past twenty-four hours, she'd already treated a number of children who would carry emotional scars from their experiences. And no pink origami animal could bring a lasting smile to their lips after the horrors they'd witnessed.

Samson stepped forward. "Her name is Raina. She . . . she's my daughter. Which means my wife and other children are here."

A gnawing sense of worry stopped Paige from celebrating with Samson. The telltale marks were clear. Fever . . . red eyes . . . tiny spots on the inside of the mouth.

"Jodi can't be the source, but it's definitely measles." Paige glanced up at Dayo, who stood at the end of the bed. "And it's already started to spread."

THIRTY-ONE

Paul watched Leah from behind the glass pane of the conference-room door. She sat at the end of the long table, her hands tapping against the surface as she stared straight ahead. He'd only had to deal with a handful of civilian cases where American expats had experienced extreme personal trauma, but every time he'd prayed it would be the last. It was every embassy worker's worst nightmare to have to send home a dead body. He was already sending home six.

Mercy stepped in beside him, her gaze studying the young woman as well. "I feel so sorry for the girl. She seems so young and vulnerable."

"How old is she?"

"Twenty-two?"

Paul slid his thumb down the cold Coke

271

in his hand. "My baby sister's not too much older. They probably have a lot in common. Young, full of energy, ready to save the world . . ."

"I guess this is hitting a little too close to home."

"Way too close. If my sister asked my advice about coming here, I would have said no in a heartbeat. What kind of parents let their kid come over here?"

Mercy's expression darkened. "Tragedy can strike no matter where you live, from New York to Bogama."

"Maybe."

Paul walked into the room ahead of Mercy. Leah looked up at them. Her eyes were red. She was probably exhausted. Probably didn't want to sleep after what she'd seen.

Paul slid the Coke onto the table in front of her. "Thirsty?"

"Thanks." Leah took the offered drink, but didn't open it. Instead, she simply started running her finger round the rim.

He sat down across from her before dumping his pad of paper and pen onto the table. Mercy would take notes, but he always liked to write down his own impressions. "My name is Paul Hayes."

She glanced up again briefly. "It's . . . It's

nice to meet you."

"Mercy will be taking notes on what happened so I can file a complete report to my superiors. Is that okay?"

"Sure."

"First, let me say how sorry I am that you had to witness such a terrible tragedy. I know how hard it is to lose people you care about."

"Thank you."

There was no inflection in her voice. No emotion except for the red splotches on her face that showed she'd been crying. Once they were done here, he'd call in a friend he knew who specialized in counseling trauma victims. This girl was going to need all the help she could get.

"How are you feeling?"

Leah's gaze moved to her clinched fists, then back to the wall again. "Somebody gave me something for my headache, so I'm better now."

Hives had broken out across her neck. Another sign of trauma. This girl was far too young to have to deal with what had happened out there.

"How long have you been in the country?"

"Five months."

"You're young."

She looked up and caught his gaze for the

first time. "Twenty-two. I graduated from nursing school last summer."

"My sister, Lilly, graduated from college a couple years ago."

"What does she do now?"

"She manages a boutique in Denver and designs clothes on the side. She hopes to have her own line of clothing one day."

"Sounds safe."

"It is." Paul tapped his pencil on the table. "Tell me what brought you here."

"To the RD?"

Paul nodded, hoping he wasn't moving too fast. He'd never been good at engaging in small talk or being sympathetic. Or so Maggie had recently told him.

"I . . . I decided I wanted to do something important with my life." She stared at her chipped fingernail polish, then started picking at her thumbnail. "I looked at the Peace Corp, Mercy Ships, and even the military, but ended up signing with Volunteers for Hope for a year."

"Where were you headed when the rebels attacked?"

"We were to drive from the capital through Mbali and Kingani to the camp."

"Any military escorts?"

"Normally, no, but with the fighting going on in the north, we had one armed man for every truck." Her eyes filled with tears. "But that wasn't enough."

"And what was your specific assignment?"

"We were supposed to deliver medical supplies and food, then stay on to help run the camp."

"Who was on your team?"

"We . . . we had several nurses, a laboratory tech, a mental health officer, and a couple doctors."

"What exactly were you transporting?"

"We had forty-foot trailers full of everything you could think of. Besides medical supplies, there were plastic pipes and faucets for water wells, canvas tents, generators, high-protein foods for children, and basic ration packets that contained things like rice, beans, and sugar. There was also a bunch of electronic equipment like radios and a satellite phone."

"Most of those items were probably in the top ten on the rebels' wish list." Paul felt his stomach burn. Something didn't add up. Who had authorized sending a convoy into rebel territory without adequate military support? And how had the rebels known the convoy's route and schedule? He worked to push away his own personal feelings. "What happened next? How did the rebels gain control of the vehicles?"

She shook her head and closed her eyes for a moment as if she wanted to shut out the memories. "We were up north, about an hour or so out of Bomaja, when they appeared out of nowhere. We'd been driving nine, maybe ten, hours and everyone was tired. I remember cresting this hill . . ." Her voice broke. "Then we stopped."

"What happened next?"

"I . . . I'm not sure."

Tears poured down her cheeks and her breathing quickened. Paul squirmed in his chair and pulled on his buttoned collar, trying to form his next question.

Mercy dug in her purse and pulled out a tissue to hand to Leah. "Take your time."

Paul swallowed hard. "She's right, Leah. Whenever you're ready, go ahead."

Leah blew her nose, then wadded up the tissue in her hand. Mercy handed her another one.

"It all happened so fast." Leah breathed deeply. "I was riding in the last truck. The other trucks stopped ahead of us. Our driver radioed the truck ahead to see what was wrong, but there was no answer, so he climbed down from the cab. The next thing I knew . . ." She shook her head, her hands trembling.

Paul leaned forward. "Leah?"

"There . . . there were men with huge guns everywhere. They started shooting at us. The driver fell . . . there was blood . . . I saw Tommy get hit in the stomach. There was nothing I could do. They . . . they just kept shooting and shooting. I started to run. Someone screamed. The trees swallowed me, but I had to see what was happening. As I turned around, I saw the trucks speed over the next hill." Leah's gaze dropped. "All that was left was the dead bodies of my friends."

"How did they miss you?"

"I don't know." She shook her head. "I should be dead like them."

Mercy reached out and squeezed Leah's hand. "No. Don't ever believe that."

"Did they *let* you escape?" Paul asked.

"I don't think so. One of the other guys in my truck tried to fight back. He managed to knock the gun from one of the rebel's hands. Another one overpowered him before he was able to grab the gun. I guess it was enough of a distraction for me to get away."

"What happened next?"

"I hid in the bushes along the side of the road. Thirty minutes passed, maybe an hour, I don't know. I finally forced myself to get up, but I was so terrified they'd realize they'd missed someone, that they'd come back and kill me like the rest."

"But they didn't."

"No."

"So what did you do next?"

"I went to see if anybody was alive, but they . . . they were all dead. I didn't want to leave them lying there on the road, but I knew I had to go get help. I dragged their bodies into the bushes one at a time, Sheila, Tommy, Raúl . . . all of them. They needed to be protected and it was the only way I knew how. Eventually, I heard a car coming down the road. It was a couple who lived up north. They were leaving because of the fighting in the region and offered to give me a ride to the capital." She shook her head and shivered. "I never told them what happened."

"I'm so sorry." Mercy clasped the young girl's hand. "So sorry."

Her eyes flooded with tears again. "Maybe I should have tried to bring them with me, but the car was small and I didn't know what to do —"

"It's okay." Paul cleared his throat. "You did everything you could, and we've got someone taking care of them right now. We'll make sure that they are all sent home to their families so they can have proper burials."

"This wasn't supposed to happen."

Paul shook his head. "It never is."

"I'd like to talk to my family."

"Of course." Paul leaned back in his chair. "I'll have Mercy show you where you can call them in a few minutes, but I do have one other question. We've been trying to get a hold of Digane Olam in Kingani. Do you know if there was any communication with the refugee camp?"

"When our driver checked in with the office in Kingani to give them an update of our arrival time, Mr. Olam mentioned that he hadn't heard from the camp since last night."

Paul smacked the table. While the government denied that the rebels were a threat, American citizens and hundreds of Zambizans were being slaughtered. He had no doubt that the rebels knew about the camp, and it certainly wouldn't be the first time that rebels had used refugee camps as places not only to raid food and supplies, but to run guns and drugs, putting both aid workers and civilians at risk.

Paul leaned back in his chair. "Take Leah to call her parents, then I want you to try to get Olam on the phone again."

"Yes, sir."

He glanced at Leah and saw his sister Lilly again. It was time to put a stop to this.

THIRTY-TWO

Tuesday, February 22, 6:04 p.m.
Kingani Refugee Camp

Paige dug into the thick slice of pumpkin pie sitting in front of her and took a big bite. For as long as she could remember, her mother had skipped the convenience of store-bought desserts and created holiday meals by scratch. And while she might be accused by some of being partial, in her opinion, nobody made a better Christmas dinner with all the trimmings than her mother. The past hour held all the evidence anyone would ever need.

She swiped a dollop of whipped cream with her finger and stuck it into her mouth. "This is fantastic, Mom."

"You say that every year."

"Only because it's true." Paige dabbed her mouth with a napkin before taking another bite. Dorothy had been right. There was no place like home.

Christmas lights twinkled in the background on the eight-foot fresh pine tree that was framed by the tall window of her parents' Nashville home. Everything about the two-story house was familiar, because her mom had changed little in the past thirty years, which was fine with Paige. Family — and coming home for Christmas — had always been the one constant in the busy world they lived in.

Her mother had always managed to create the perfect setting for every occasion. Easter egg hunts with her cousins on the back lawn, her sweet-sixteen party, a high school graduation tea with her best friends . . . She, on the other hand, had been born without skills to make a crème brûlée or even a made-from-scratch pumpkin pie, for that matter, and had always felt much more at home in the emergency room than in the kitchen. Which was why she loved spending the holidays at home.

"Paige?"

Paige opened her eyes and smiled. Nick stood over her, with that lopsided grin he always wore and that stray lock of hair she was always tempted to reach up and touch . . . The foggy dream cleared as the white plastic walls of the medical tent closed in on her. She'd just crash-landed back in Oz.

She glanced at her watch, then jumped up from her chair. "I must have fallen asleep. I only meant to close my eyes for a minute."

"When is the last time you had a good night's sleep?"

"It doesn't matter. I —"

"Wait a minute." He grabbed her arm, stopping her from charging across the room. "At least you had a smile on your face. What were you dreaming about?"

Paige let out a long sigh, wishing she could capture the moment again. "I'm not sure what triggered it, but Christmas at my parents' home."

The reminder of her parents started her worrying again. No doubt they'd heard what was happening in the country, though information would no doubt be scarce. She'd purposely told them she'd call when she could, so they wouldn't worry. They knew that the phone service was far from reliable, even in the capital. But none of those excuses would stop them from worrying.

"What's your favorite part of the holiday season?"

She blinked. "My favorite part? My mom's homemade pumpkin pie." If she tried hard enough, she could almost smell the cinnamon. "Besides the fact that we're together as a family, the taste of nutmeg and cinnamon makes me feel like a kid again, with no worries beyond skinned knees and wondering if Billy Patterson is going to steal my lunch because he loves my mother's cookies."

Nick laughed. "At least it wasn't a nightmare."

She looked up and caught his gaze. "No, that's what today is."

"More bad news?"

She crossed her arms and tried to make sense of everything that was happening, but couldn't. Where were the baskets of fish and loaves of bread she'd prayed for? "Dayo and I have diagnosed Jodi with the measles."

"Measles?" She'd obviously caught Nick off guard. "How in the world did she pick that up? Wouldn't she have been immunized for that as a child?"

"Even if you're immunized, you can still get them. Brandon told me they've been traveling the past couple weeks throughout West Africa, plus they spent several days up north at the game park, which would have given her plenty of time to be exposed. And because she's not the only one infected I'm guessing she picked it up after she arrived in the country."

"Then brought it to the camp."

Paige nodded. "Exactly. Though at the moment, the source isn't my main concern."

"What is?" He followed her to her desk. "I mean, having the measles isn't that bad, is it? I thought most people were immune to the disease nowadays."

"There was a short period of time back in the sixties when some of those who received the vaccinations didn't become immune. Jodi fits right into that category."

"So she was never immune to the disease to begin with." Nick shook his head. "Maybe we'll still get lucky after all. With any luck, it won't spread much beyond these four walls."

"It's not a matter of luck." Paige lowered her chin and stared at the floor, wishing she could have stayed lost in her dream. But that would do little to move the massive mountain they were all facing. "I'm hoping that will be the case, but there are no guarantees. I've sent for everyone who was up on the mountain so I can examine them. I'm also making sure that the leaders of the different sections of the camp are aware of the symptoms so they can spread the word and be on the lookout."

"How serious is this?"

"Typically, the CDC reports less than a hundred cases of measles a year, but it's a whole different scenario here. Less than fifty percent of these people have been vaccinated in this part of the country." Paige wiped away the beads of perspiration from her forehead. Maybe along with a quick cure for measles she should pray for a drop in the soaring temperatures. "Which means that without any intervention, we could be looking at a significant number of deaths before the disease runs its course."

"How many?"

"Usually the death rate is low, but combined with a serious cholera epidemic and other health problems we find here, the fatality rate can easily jump to twenty-five percent. But even without any deaths, the disease can cause a number of serious side effects."

"Like?"

"Blindness, encephalitis, diarrhea, pneumonia . . ."

The situation was becoming clear to both of them. "All made worse when we're looking at dealing with this in the confines of a refugee camp."

She nodded. "Exactly."

"So in a best-case scenario, what would you be doing right now?"

"Taz is setting up a separate isolation tent for those infected. As with the cholera, that will help slow down the spread, but there are still few guarantees at this point."

"And next?"

"Well, while there have been numerous questions raised as to the effectiveness of an emergency vaccination campaign during an outbreak, I've seen enough evidence to support the fact that it can reduce both the number of actual cases and the deaths." Her fingernails dug into the palms of her hands. "The problem is, at this point, we both know this is impossible."

The determined look on Nick's face showed he wasn't ready to give up on the idea. "Take the rebels out of the equation. How long would it take to procure enough vaccines for this camp?"

Paige shrugged, wishing the scenario were possible. "VHI was already planning a vaccination campaign in the north in the next few weeks, so getting our hands on the vaccines that are currently in the capital would be fairly simple, but that isn't the biggest hurdle."

Nick's gaze narrowed. "What do you mean?"

"Even without the rebels, there are a number of logistical issues involved that makes the situation complex."

"Like?"

"You don't give up, do you?"

"Nope."

Paige smiled at his persistence, something they obviously had in common. "Some vaccines, like this one, require the use of a cold chain, because they have to be kept at a constant temperature. This necessitates the use of generator-powered refrigerators and ice to insure the vaccine's viability and makes transporting them challenging. We would also need extra teams and coordinators to help administer the shots, as well as equipment like syringes, vaccination cards, and tally sheets."

"Wow."

"The bottom line is that without the vaccine — and additional supplies to deal with the cholera — the crisis we are facing is only going to continue to get worse."

"Then there's no getting around it anymore." Nick folded his arms across his chest. "Someone's going to have to leave the camp."

The thought sent shivers up Paige's spine. "I've thought about that, but the rebels have made it quite clear that they're not playing games. How can I ask anyone to risk his life like that?"

"Do you have another suggestion?"

She glanced at Jodi and shook her head. "I think we're out of options."

THIRTY-THREE

Tuesday, February 22, 8:43 p.m.
Kingani Refugee Camp

Ashley squeezed the water out of the thin cloth she held, then placed it back on Raina's hot forehead. She wasn't sure what had happened between the time they spotted the young girl and now, but something — presumably a combination of guilt and sympathy — had propelled her to volunteer to sit with the young girl while her father searched the camp for the rest of his family. For some reason, the idea of Raina waking up alone amongst the long row of metal beds in the clinic was too much even for a scrooge like herself.

Something about Raina, though, had ripped through her heart and tugged on emotions she'd never felt before. Despite the girl's shoddy appearance and torn dress, there was something angelic about her round, ebony face and that peaceful expression as she slept. It almost made Ashley wish she could whisk her away from this place back to her apartment in LA . . .

The reality of where they were came crashing back, multiplying the panic in her chest. How had a simple eight-day adventure holiday with her father turned into such a nightmare?

She arched her back, wishing there was a way to take a long, hot shower. Life back home had been orderly and predictable, the way she liked it — including her upscale loft that had more square footage than a dozen refugee tents. She closed her eyes and envisioned the hardwood floors and granite countertops in the kitchen . . . Vivid pictures of women standing in line for water and the long row of latrines pressed into her thoughts.

No. She shoved aside the guilt. She'd worked hard to become who she was, despite her father's money and influence.

Raina stirred and let out a soft groan. The young girl's cheeks glistened with fever. Ashley glanced down the row of beds, looking for the nurse, not knowing what she should do.

"Ashley?"

A voice behind her pulled her from her thoughts. She glanced up at the tall frame beside her. Taz stood, hands in the pockets of his khaki shorts, wearing that horrid, ever-present safari hat and looking at her with those sappy, puppy-dog eyes of his.

Her jaw tensed. "How long have you been standing there?"

"I just got here."

"And . . ." She wasn't in the mood for another guilt trip. Her conscience seemed to be giving her enough of that lately. He'd just be the icing on a very bad day.

"I needed to speak to Paige. Is she around?"

"Nick went with her to one of the tents where there is another suspected case of measles."

He shifted his weight to his other foot and cocked his head. "Paige isn't the only reason I stopped by. I was hoping I might run into you."

"Me?"

"I . . . uh . . . I just wanted to make sure you were okay." He shot her a smile. "Well . . . and to apologize."

Her eyes widened. He had her attention now. "You want to apologize. To me?"

"Yeah, I realize I was a bit harsh on you earlier and said some things I shouldn't have. For one, people like you make it possible for people like me to be here. And two, you didn't sign up to work here, and being thrown into a situation where there are rebels and refugees . . . Well, all I'm saying is that I should have given you the benefit of the doubt and not been so judgmental."

She gave him and his dorky Indiana Jones hat a second look. Mitch wouldn't be caught dead dressed like that, but he probably wouldn't have apologized either. Which meant nothing. Mitch might not be quick to back down and admit his mistakes, but he had plenty of other outstanding qualities, which was why she'd fallen in love with him. He was a hard worker, well organized —

"Ashley?"

Her chin rose. "I'm sorry. I guess I wasn't expecting an apology."

"I'm a bit surprised to find you sitting with Raina."

"I was worried about her and . . . I don't know. Her father is out looking for her mother and I didn't want her to wake up and find no one here."

He did it again, the right-sided quirky smile that made her squirm.

She stared at the tarp-covered floor to avoid looking at him. She was used to ignoring what the tabloids said about her, so why did it matter what Taz thought? "What?"

"I was right. I knew you had a soft bone in your body."

"Yeah. I'm sure it's just a case of temporary insanity."

He sat down next to her on the bed — way too close. "How's she doing?"

Ashley skittered over a couple inches. "The doctor is hoping that the disease will run its course without any side effects, but we'll have to wait and see. It just . . . it all seems so unfair."

"Who said life was fair?"

"I'm sorry. I tend to . . . ramble when I'm upset."

"Don't worry about it. We all do."

"No, you don't. Not like me, anyway."

She pressed her hands together so they wouldn't shake. Apparently the urge to confess had been inadvertently activated along with her maternal instincts. What was it with this guy?

Taz shook his head. "What do you mean?"

"You all act like working in a refugee camp is comparable to working at some typical nine-to-five job. I don't know how you do it. To me, all I see is dirt, disease, long lines for water, smelly latrines, and crowded living conditions."

"Well, I wouldn't exactly say that the last two days have been typical for any of us."

"So tell me why you're really here?" Ashley looked up and caught his gaze. "Guilt? An unquenchable desire to save the world?"

Taz shoved his hands into his front pockets. "I'm here because I believe in what I'm doing, and know I'm making a difference."

She so didn't understand him. "Enough to leave your family and put your own life at risk in the hands of a bunch of crazy rebels?"

His smile was back. "You've got to admit that I'll never get bored."

"Maybe not, but I'd welcome some familiar routine at the moment." She jutted her chin toward the door. "Here I'm sleeping on a metal hospital bed and eating who knows what for breakfast. Let's just say this is all *way* out of my comfort zone."

"Don't be so hard on yourself. You lost your father up there on that mountain. None of us knows how we'd react to something like that happening."

"I still can't believe he's gone, but then I look at Raina and think about all she's lost. Her mother and sisters could be dead."

"It kind of puts things into perspective, doesn't it?"

"Don't get me wrong." She again dipped the cloth into the small bowl of water beside the bed and placed it back on Raina's forehead. "I'd still rather be in LA on the set or hanging out with my friends. I mean this isn't exactly the Hilton."

Taz chuckled. "Not exactly."

"But maybe that's what bothers me the most."

"What's that?"

"At least when all this is over I get to go home to my comfortable loft in the city. But these people . . . they have nowhere else to go."

"And now with a possible measles epidemic on the horizon . . ."

If she even managed to make it out alive. "I guess it does put things into a different perspective. Makes me thankful for what I have and even a bit nostalgic for people I miss, like my mother."

"Tell me about her."

"My mother?" Ashley smiled at the handful of memories that surfaced. "It's funny how I miss her. We're not exactly close. She's an ex-model, but still just as beautiful. She's also a terrible cook who can beat just about anyone at poker and who spends most of her time doing charity work. She tried to be a good mother, I suppose."

"That could probably be said for most parents. None of them are perfect, but they do what they can with what they have."

She clasped her hands in front of her, surprised at how at ease she felt talking to him. "You seemed to have turned out okay."

"Really? A couple hours ago I had the impression that you thought I was some lame mama's boy who couldn't make it in the real world."

"It was supposed to be a compliment."

He shot her a smile. "Then I'll take it as one."

He started for the door before she could think of a comeback. Three men in black blocked his exit.

Ashley's heart lodged in her throat. "Taz . . ."

Her scream was muffled as one of the men crossed the room and stuffed a rag into her mouth. The taste of fuel filled her lungs. They pulled her toward the door, easily subduing her efforts to escape. A moment later, she was shoved into the back of a jeep as the vehicle roared away, taking her with them into the darkness.

THIRTY-FOUR

Wednesday, February 23, 6:21 a.m.
Kingani Refugee Camp

Nick finished drawing the curve of the Dzambizi River that followed the western border of the country, then took a final look at his map. His rough sketch of the terrain surrounding the camp looked more like a game plan for a junior high game of Capture the Flag. Not a strategy for survival.

Five of them crowded around the rectangular table set up outside the medical clinic: Nick, Paige, Brandon, and two of the local leaders from the camp, Nigel and Philip. It was up to them to figure out how to send a team for help without anyone ending up in a body bag. The freshly dug graves of three young men in the distance, along with the abduction of Taz, Ashley, and four of the staff last night were enough of a reminder that the rebels weren't playing games.

The easiest and fastest way out would

have been by plane, but without parts and a month of major work, he — and his plane — were grounded. Which meant that the only remaining way out was across the rough terrain and past a couple dozen armed rebels.

Nick looked up at the group. "Where's Samson?"

Brandon shrugged. "He's not back yet."

Worry niggled at Nick as he gazed toward the forest where he'd last seen Samson two hours ago. The sun had finally made its entrance over the horizon, but they'd already sent out scouts with strict instructions to find out any information about the rebels' movements, hoping to gain some sort of sense as to their positions and numbers. If they were going to make it out alive, they were going to have to know their options.

Nick studied the map. The east side of the camp lay nestled against the base of Mt. Maja, and while the other side of the mountain held popular routes for tourists, the west side was too remote and rugged to cross quickly. Which left them with three viable options. The river, the main road to Kingani, and the forest to the west of the camp. Any hope of escape depended on the scouts finding vulnerabilities that offered the best chance of success.

"The sun's already up, so let's go over our options. Nigel. What did you and Philip find?"

A schoolteacher from Kinja, Nigel had been one of the first to join the security team after the first raid by the rebels. "As we all know, the river runs south on the west side of the camp toward the border. Crossing the river is not difficult, but rebels have men lined up every quarter kilometer for at least four kilometers in each direction. There is some bush along the riverbank, but for the most part it is open terrain, giving them the advantage. In my opinion, a small group would never get past them without traveling far up or down river from the camp."

"He is right." Philip, a mechanic who'd lost everything during the rebel attack of his village, pushed his heavy glasses up the bridge of his nose. "Which is why we think we need to fight them."

Nick's brow rose. "Fight them?"

"Think about it. We've got well over ten thousand people in this camp —"

"Of which three-fourths are women and children, and no seasoned soldiers."

Brandon nodded. "We only have a handful of weapons. They'd end up slaughtering us."

"And while I appreciate your resolve, Philip, at this point I strongly believe that an attack on our part isn't worth the risk." Nick shook his head. Military strategizing was something he'd purposely left behind months ago. "What did you find, Brandon?"

"I wish there was a way, but the main road to Kingani is lined with snipers, so it's out as well. We all know what happened the last time someone tried."

Nick felt their options vanish. "Which leaves the forest, but I'm not sure how good a choice that is. From what I understand, it's not much different from the eastern side of the camp. It's full of dense bush and rocky terrain, which makes it hard to negotiate."

"And snakes." Samson walked up to the table. "But we can do it."

Nick glanced up at Samson. "Snakes?"

"There is not much to worry about as long as you leave them alone."

Nick pressed his fingers against the edge of the table. He hated snakes.

"I agree the forest is the only way out of here." Samson sat down at the table. "I can lead you through the forest to the nearest town where, hopefully, the rebels have left communications intact."

Nick tapped his pencil against the map. "You know that's going to be the toughest route."

"Which is why it is not well guarded. They know how hard it is to navigate."

"But you can get us to a town that has a cell-phone tower?"

"I was born here and have lived at the base of these mountains most of my life."

"How far to the next town through the forest?" Nick asked.

"Twenty-five, thirty kilometers, but you were right when you said that it won't be easy."

"So we're looking at at least . . . four or five hours, if we're lucky."

Brandon didn't look convinced. "I think it's too great a risk. We're already limited on security in the camp. Who's going to ensure the safety of the camp if the rebels decide to strike again? And I'm not sure that Samson is the one to lead the group. You should stay here with your children. They need their father."

"I am not the only one here with family," Samson said. "Your wife is here, Philip has four children . . . Besides, you will never get through the forest without me."

Nick's temples pounded. This wasn't the

first time he'd held the lives of a team in his hands. Or the first time he'd take the brunt of the responsibility if something went wrong. "He's right, Brandon. I need both of you."

"There is a woman here from my village." Samson leaned forward. "She has offered to take care of my children while I am working. They will be fine."

"I think we're all hesitant to risk lives to get help, but more will die without help. And we've also got Ashley, Taz, and the staff that was taken to consider." Paige spoke up for the first time, making him wish he could read her thoughts. Despite his continual assurances to the contrary, he knew she blamed herself for Dayo and three of her local nurses' abduction. A feeling that hit far too close to home.

Her normal smile was absent as she continued. "Unless the rebels are openly asking for a ransom, it's up to us to inform the embassy where they are so the military can put together a rescue plan."

Brandon leaned forward. "We don't even know where they are."

Nick studied the layout of the map. "Maybe not, but I think we know enough to make an educated guess. Granted, there is a lot of territory to cover, but I don't think their base camp is far from here."

"Why do you say that?" Paige asked.

"Think about it. It's the only thing that makes sense. We know they seem to work in pairs. They take shifts with most of them on foot, and they arrive from the southwest."

Samson put an *X* on the map between the refugee camp and Kinja. "You're right, Nick, in that we're still looking at a large territory and it's fairly remote, but this area would give them easy access to the camp here and the dirt road that splits off east from the main Kingani road. It would also give them access to water, firewood, and cell-phone coverage."

Nick drew a line from the refugee camp to Samson's *X*. "From here, they could make it back to the rebel base in what . . . less than an hour on foot? And even less time by using one of their vehicles."

Brandon nodded. "And they are still close enough to have raided Mt. Maja's base camp, which would be about here on the map."

Nick listened to their dialogue. The risks were still there, but at least a plan was finally falling into place. "If we can give the military that information, hopefully, paired with satellite intel, they'll be able to track down both the rebels and Taz and the others, who we can assume were taken to the rebel base."

Brandon tapped on the map. "If your theory is correct, there's a chance we'd end up going pretty close to their base."

Nick tried to stay optimistic. "As long as we're in cell-phone range, we'll be able to communicate our situation and get the army to move in here."

"How long do you think it will take them to mobilize?" Brandon's concern for his wife reflected in his eyes.

"I don't know," Paige said. "While we're finally seeing fewer cases of cholera, if we don't do anything we're going to be seeing more and more symptoms of measles. And while vaccinating the population won't completely stop an epidemic, it has been proven to slow down the spread, which in this situation, I believe, is essential."

Nick leaned forward. "How soon do the vaccinations have to be given to be the most effective?"

"Ideally within three days of exposure, which at this point in the timeline gives us another forty-eight hours."

Forty-eight hours. Nick felt his stomach churn. Four hours to the nearest town, time to obtain the vaccine and set up a cold chain, plus find a way to deal with the rebels sitting at their back door . . . If they were going to pull this off, they didn't have a lot of time to spare.

Nick cleared his throat. "We can take a quick vote, but in my opinion we've run out of options."

Brandon nodded his agreement. "We're cut off from the world, and until we get the army in here, we'll continue to be vulnerable to attacks. I'm still not convinced we can do this without losing someone, but I'm in. Unfortunately, I have to agree that it's a chance we've got to take."

"Then are we all in favor that we go?"

He glanced at Paige, who nodded her head along with the rest. He was tempted to ask her to come with them, but he knew it was only an excuse to try and keep her safe. He hated leaving her here, but he knew she had patients she would never leave behind.

"We have men who will guard the camp while you're gone," Paige said. "We might not be able to stop the rebels, but we can slow them down."

Brandon glanced at his watch. "So when do we go?"

Nick's gaze flickered to Paige. "The sun's already up. I think we should try and be out of here in the next fifteen minutes."

306

THIRTY-FIVE

Wednesday, February 23, 6:56 a.m.
Kingani Refugee Camp

Paige started for the clinic that had already begun to fill up with patients, hating that she wouldn't have a chance to tell Nick good-bye. With the decision made to send out a team, the men now clamored for his attention as they worked out last-minute details. Which meant she wasn't needed anymore.

She glanced back at him, unsure of when her feelings had gone from simply enjoying the familiarity of a shared background to something deeper. But even if she couldn't define that moment, neither could she deny that it had happened. Or that something deep within her already missed him.

Postponing the inevitable onslaught of demands that would keep her running the next twelve-plus hours, she moved past the clinic to stand on the slight rise in the middle of the camp. To the east, the sun hovered above the horizon, its yellow glow already warming the air and glistening against the icy peaks of Mt. Maja in the distance. The now familiar white tents dotting the landscape contrasted with the brown-and-green earth, where hundreds of people milled about their campsites, getting ready for yet another day.

She slipped her hand into the pocket of her lab coat and fingered Marila's photo, hating the fact that sometimes there were no other options. Even if it meant that someone — or all of them — didn't make it back alive. She shuddered involuntarily. Had it really come to this?

Don't look at the bigger picture. Look at the person you're dealing with at the moment.

A young girl wearing a brown dress ran past the opening of one of the tents toward a pile of jerricans. She set one of the empty cans on her head, covering hair that had been braided in neat, short rows, and began gracefully moving toward the water.

All she had to do was look at one person at a time and leave the rest to God.

"Paige?"

"Brandon." She turned around and forced a smile, disappointed it wasn't Nick. Worry lines creased his forehead, and heavy bags framed his eyes. He'd aged in the past twenty-four hours. They probably all had. "Are you okay?"

"I don't know. I . . . I wanted to talk to you about Jodi before I leave. I saw her this morning, and I'm just . . . I can't help but worry. She doesn't seem to be getting any better."

Paige sighed. It was the conversation she'd been trying to avoid. Because while she hadn't lied to him, neither had she volunteered the entire truth. Which was that her hands were tied, and without a proper lab and the needed medicines, there was little else she could do. The real fight belonged to Jodi — and God.

"You know I'm doing everything I can, but there are still a lot of hurdles that she's going to have to get through before she's out of the woods."

"Like?"

"One of the biggest issues with measles is the complications that often come with it. We have the pneumonia pretty well under control, but because her immune system is compromised due to both the gunshot wound and the fact that she lost her spleen in a previous accident, she also runs the risk of catching other infections." Paige drew in a slow breath, wishing she had the answers he wanted. "The truth is that she needs to be in a hospital where they can fight the disease more aggressively."

"Which means my wife could die from a blasted case of measles. A disease that was supposedly eradicated in the States fifty years ago."

"Jodi's a fighter."

"I can't lose her."

"You know I'm doing everything I can, but you do have to realize that the next forty-eight hours are going to be crucial —"

"Hey, Brandon. Are you about ready to go?"

"Yeah, I'm coming." He glanced at Nick, who was slinging his backpack onto his shoulder, then turned back to Paige. "Take care of her for me. Please."

"You know I will."

"And . . ." His chin dipped slightly. "It's been a long time since I asked anyone this, but don't stop praying for us."

"I won't." Paige watched as Brandon turned to join the men; then she headed toward the clinic, trying to dismiss the turbulent emotions charging through her. What she thought she felt toward Nick would no doubt pass by the time all this was over. *Please God. Bring them back alive. All of them.*

"Paige, wait."

She turned at the sound of Nick's voice. Her heart pounded in her throat.

He stopped in front of her, his expression somber. "I hate leaving you here by yourself."

"I'm hardly by myself." Paige laughed, despite the tense undercurrents. He knew, as well as she did, that at any moment the situation could swing from bad to worse.

"Five loaves and two fish. That's all you need."

"I know. We'll be okay." She nodded and forced a smile, blinking back the tears threatening to come. So much was at stake. But she hadn't let herself cry the past three months, and she wasn't going to start now.

"You okay?" His hand brushed against her arm.

"Yeah, just worried."

"About me or the supplies?"

"How about both?"

She stared up into his toffee-brown eyes and felt her stomach quiver. How had this man managed to wind himself around her heart in such a short period of time? She took a step back, resisting the urge to throw herself into his arms and beg him to tell her everything was going to be okay. They both knew that everything might not be okay.

Which was what scared her most. If she lost him now, she'd never know what might have been between them.

He pulled his hand back slowly. "I want you to be careful."

"You . . ." Her voice caught. "You're the one having to tramp through the snake-infested forest."

"I'll be fine. Really." His expression darkened. "There is . . . there is one other thing. There are rumors that some of the rebels have infiltrated the camp and are holding valid registration cards."

A wave of panic swept through her. *How much more complicated is this going to get, God?* "Which means they've probably smuggled in weapons?"

"I don't know for sure. Just be careful."

Paige swallowed hard. "Then I guess I'll see you when you return."

He hesitated, then tipped her chin up so she had to look into his eyes. Her pulse quickened as she caught the intensity in his gaze. She had to tell him not to go. She wasn't ready to do this on her own and needed him here with her.

"Nick, I —"

His lips brushed against hers, catching her off guard. The fear that had tried to engulf her evaporated. All she could think of was that she needed him. All she could feel was the warmth of his nearness as their kiss intensified for one suspended moment.

He took a step back, then pressed his forehead to hers. "I'll be back. I promise."

Heart pounding, she watched him turn around without another word and walk away.

THIRTY-SIX

Wednesday, February 23, 10:37 a.m.
Bensari Forest, Kingani Region

The scent of rotting leaves filled his senses as Nick skidded down the steep ravine behind Samson, wondering how the burly man moved as fast as he did. The thick canopy of evergreen trees blocked most of the sunlight above them, lending an eerie feel to the already claustrophobic damp forest, while a layer of ferns and roots twisted and turned along the damp forest floor, slowing their progress.

He swatted at a mosquito — one of the hundreds that had discovered the new human feeding grounds — and quickened his steps. Brandon walked beside him in silence as they trampled through a seemingly never-ending narrow pathway of dark, hanging vines.

A monkey howled in the distance. A bird cawed. Another mosquito buzzed in his ear.

He swatted the back of his neck, where the welts of other bites swelled. For the past three-and-a-half hours they had tromped through the forest until mile after mile of tall trees and thick bush blurred together and looked strangely familiar.

Like they were going in circles.

Nick glanced behind him where Nigel and Philip struggled to keep up and blew out a sharp breath. They should have left those two back at the camp. At this pace, they'd be lucky if they made the village by nightfall. He shook off his suspicions. Everyone's nerves were on edge, and his mind had started to play tricks on him. Just because the same, unending canopy of green hovered above them didn't mean Samson was leading them into some sort of trap. Or that the schoolteacher and his friend were rebels plotting to murder them before they got to the village.

But innocent or not, deep inside the thick forest was the perfect place to make someone disappear. And somewhere, along the edges of this forest, the rebels had set up a camp. Which meant that at any moment they could stumble across the rebel base, leaving Paige and the refugees at the mercy of the Ghost Soldiers.

He forced his thoughts to something more

pleasant.

Paige.

No matter how hard he tried, he couldn't get her out of his mind. Maybe he shouldn't have kissed her, but there had been something irresistible about her as she'd looked up at him with those big, gray-blue eyes, full of both determination and vulnerability. She'd awakened something inside him he hadn't felt for a long time. And from her response, she'd felt the same thing.

He climbed up another steep ravine, his lungs hungry for air. He'd performed dozens of military ops where lives had hung in the balance and where death lingered around the corner. With Paige, he'd wanted more than anything else to take on the role of protector and tell her that everything was going to be okay. That he'd fight off the bad guys for her so she could save the world, then go home. But that hadn't been a promise he'd been able to make.

Brandon slowed down at the top of the rise, temporarily pulling Nick's thoughts back to the present.

"What's wrong?"

"I don't know." Brandon shrugged. "I think we're going in circles."

That nagging concern that something was wrong returned. "I agree. Everything looks the same, which means we have to trust Samson."

"Do you?"

"Trust him?" Nick weighed the question. Samson was just far enough ahead to be out of earshot. He might have entertained a few doubts, but at the moment, not trusting him wasn't really an option. "He's given me every reason to trust him, no reason not to."

"You've heard the rumors about rebel moles inside the refugee camp?"

"Yeah." There was no way to know how many of the rebels had infiltrated the camp or how many weapons they'd brought with them. Gun smuggling wasn't an uncommon practice in camps and had made the risk of them leaving even greater. Unfortunately it was a risk he'd felt he had to take.

They started walking again before they lost sight of their guide. If he was leading them in circles, there was no way they could know for sure.

"I can't shake the feeling that the mole could be one of them."

Nick glanced behind him. He caught a glimpse of Nigel's red shirt. Nigel and Philip had dropped further behind them. "The same thought has crossed my mind, though this isn't exactly the time to worry about who's on our team. Besides, I have a hard time believing those guys behind us are rebels. They can hardly keep up with us. The rebels we've seen have been trained by the military. They're certainly not school-teachers from Kinja."

"It wouldn't be the first time someone pretended to be someone they weren't." Brandon started walking again. "Then what about Samson? He volunteered to lead up the camp security, putting him in the perfect position if he was a rebel."

"He also shot one of the rebels and stopped them from kidnapping Paige." A rodent dashed into the deep undergrowth in front of them. As long as he didn't see a snake . . . He pushed the thought aside. "That kind of behavior doesn't exactly help the opposing side."

"It would if he was intent on keeping his cover, because think about it: what better place to be than to lead up the camp secu-rity?"

Samson held up his hand. They scurried to catch up with him. A vine snapped beneath Nick's foot. "What's wrong?"

"Nigel and Philip aren't behind us."

Nick turned around. "I just saw them —"

A gun fired.

Nick took off back up the ridge, careful to

stay behind the cover of the dense brush. Either the rebels had found them, or Brandon's fears of a mole among them had been on target.

Stopping at a small clearing, he scanned the underbrush, looking for something out of place. Nigel sat on a dead log, holding his hand. There was no sign of anyone else, including Philip. Where was he?

"Nigel, what's going on?"

Nigel held out his arm, his hand shaking. "He tried to kill me. Philip shot me."

Blood ran down his hand, staining his light-beige pants.

"I want you to slow down and take a deep breath." Nick stayed partially hidden behind one of the trees. "Where's Philip?"

"I don't know. It . . ." He shook his head. "It all happened so fast. I stopped to tie my shoe and the next thing I knew there . . . there was a gun in my face. I . . . pushed him. I think he slipped down the ravine."

"What about his weapon?"

"I don't know."

Nick made his way cautiously toward the incline, knowing an ambush wasn't out of the question. The five nomads and their desert garb flashed in front of him, machine guns in hand. Nick flinched, then shoved away the image. This was not the time for haunting images from his past. He had to stay focused. If Philip was one of the rebels, he would easily be able to pick them off one at a time.

He looked over the edge of the ravine. Philip lay prone at the bottom, no visible signs of blood, his neck oddly twisted.

Where was the gun?

Samson and Brandon appeared at the summit. "What happened?"

"Take care of Nigel — he's been shot." Nick pointed to his backpack. "I've got a first-aid kit in there. I think Philip's dead."

"Be careful."

Nick handed Brandon his bag, then slid down the ravine. There was no sign of blood or other signs of injury. He checked Philip's pulse. Nothing. "He's dead."

Brandon called from the top. "What about a weapon?"

Nick searched the forest floor for the gun, stepping over and around patches of mud. It lay partially hidden in the brush.

"I've got it."

Nick shoved the gun into his back pocket, then grabbed a gnarled vine and started climbing back up the steep slope. Brandon offered his hand at the top. "Did you see any signs of anyone else?"

"No one."

"Nigel. Did you see anyone else here?"

He shook his head. "He was one of them. One of the rebels."

Brandon had already ripped off a piece of Nigel's sleeve and started doctoring the wound. "Looks like it's just a flesh wound, with no bones broken. Do you need to stop for a few minutes —"

"No." Nigel glanced down the ravine to where Philip's body lay. "I'll be fine. I will not let that bastard win."

"Then we must hurry." Samson started back toward where they'd come from. "The sun is already high in the sky."

"What about his body?" Brandon asked.

"I say we leave it there for the vultures."

Nick wanted to dismiss Nigel's suggestion, but knew they had no choice.

Nigel took the lead with Samson. Maybe this time he'd do a better job of keeping up. He and Brandon followed. "Do you trust him?"

Brandon shook his head. "It was all too . . . too convenient. From the way he described what happened, Nigel is the one who should be d'ad, not Philip."

"Maybe." Nick stepped over a thick vine lacing the forest floor and landed in a pile of mud. He pulled his boot out of the muck. "But if Nigel is one of them, why not just

321

shoot us all and have it over?"

"I don't know. Because he's playing it safe? Or maybe it's because we're worth more to them alive."

Nick felt for the gun he'd slid into the back of his waistband. "Or maybe the mole is back there, lying dead at the bottom of the ravine."

Brandon shook his head. "Let's hope you're the one who's right."

THIRTY-SEVEN

Wednesday, February 23, 11:03 a.m.
Rebel Base Camp
. . . According to sources inside the Democratic Republic of Dhambizao, the notorious Ghost Soldiers continue to warn that there will be no peace in the country until international indictments for five of their leaders, arrested at the end of last year, are dropped. But there are conflicting reports as to exactly what this means.

Despite the continued government assurances, according to one reporter, the standoff between the rebel soldiers and President Tau's ground forces has already resulted in the deaths of at least four hundred men, women, and children throughout the region. And even as talks between both parties resumed in the capital on Monday after a two-week recess, many fear that talking will do nothing to change the volatile situation.

Reliable sources have also informed us that

one of the four Americans reported missing yesterday is Robert James, who is believed to have been in the country as a tourist. Mr. James, a high-profile oil executive from Houston, Texas, was climbing Mt. Maja with his daughter, actress Ashley James, who is best known for her role in the critically acclaimed American sitcom *Casey's.*

Families of the missing are asking for any information on the whereabouts of their loved ones. The U.S. Embassy said it would continue to coordinate their efforts with the State Department in Washington as well as the RD government.

In other news from the country . . .

Jonas switched off the radio and took a long drink of his beer, letting the cool liquid slide down his throat. His fingers tightened against the bottle.

He glanced at the half dozen hostages from the refugee camp who sat on woven reed mats, then settled his gaze on the woman on the end. There was fear in her eyes, and something had nagged at him ever since his men had brought her here. For a doctor, her mannerisms were polished, but she'd hesitated, relying heavily on the Dzambizan nurses. He moved his gaze from her face to her body. Clothes and boots new, not worn, nails polished . . .

Something wasn't right.

Jonas crossed the dusty courtyard, each lengthy step measured, and stopped in front of her. "Stand up."

His reason for the raid on the camp last night had been twofold. One, he needed a doctor to deliver his child, and two, he needed continued leverage against a government that continued its foolish and futile dismissal of his demands. Now he wondered if he might have failed at both attempts.

"Who are you?"

She stood slowly, her hands trembling at her sides. Coward. He should have known she'd lied to him.

Jonas reached out and slapped her hard across the face. She stumbled backward, landing hard against the cement wall and knocking the air from her lungs. She gasped for a breath.

"Leave her alone!" The man sitting beside her jumped up, but he was too slow.

Jonas slid his gun from the back of his pants and cocked the trigger. "I would not try and play hero." He waved the gun at the man. "Sit."

A trickle of blood ran down the corner of the woman's mouth. She pressed her fingers against her lips and whimpered.

Jonas was far from finished with her. "So you think I am a fool?"

Her eyes widened with terror. "Of course not, I . . .

"Then why did you lie to me? You are not a doctor, are you?"

"Yes . . . no . . ." Her eyes filled with tears as she shook her head. "I never said I was a doctor."

"But you implied as much."

He'd told Ngozi that he was willing to risk his life for revenge, but if he did, it would be on his terms. He was tired of being played. He cursed under his breath. First the government, then the army, and now this American . . . No. He'd risen from the bottom ranks as a child soldier to become a leader who could demand what he wanted when he wanted it. Power, women, drink, whatever he wanted was at his disposal. And no one would be allowed to take away what was rightfully his.

"What's your name?"

"Ashley . . . Ashley James."

"You fool." He spat on the ground beside her, then pointed to his wife, Eshe. "She could have died because of your foolishness."

Eshe lay on a mat beneath the shade of a mango tree with their newborn child nestled at her breast. He knew the complications childbirth brought with it and he had heard her screams in the night as she struggled to free the child from her womb. Ashley James was lucky the ancestors had granted the child safe entrance into the world, or she wouldn't be standing in front of him right now.

Ashley's chest heaved. "The other women, they knew what to do. So when you assumed I was a doctor, I didn't want you to kill me . . . like my father."

Jonas slid the barrel of his gun down her jawline, feeling no pity for her loss. Death had become a frequent visitor, starting with his own parents when he was eight. He'd watched the soldiers hack them to death before they'd given him the ax and forced him to butcher his three sisters. Twenty years later, the scenario had replayed over and over again in his head when government soldiers turned on him and murdered his first wife and four children in front of him . . .

He pushed away the haunting memories. He was done working for anyone other than himself. Instead, he let the feeling of power work its way through him like a drug and smiled, knowing that if he wanted to, he could snuff out her life with one slight pull of the trigger.

Yara grabbed onto his leg and held on.

"Eshe, come get the child." He looked down at Yara, momentarily distracted. Big, brown eyes, a reflection of his own, stared back at him. He ordered her to return to her mother, but instead her chubby fists tightened around his leg.

Ngozi walked up from behind him, grabbed the child, and handed Jonas another beer. "Let the American be for now. Even if she's not a doctor, she's more useful to us alive than dead. And besides, we have planning to do."

Jonas popped off the metal cap with his back teeth. "She lied to me about who she is."

"It doesn't matter. You have a bigger bargaining chip now. You heard the radio broadcast. Her family has money. They'll do anything to keep her alive."

"He's right." Ashley's eyes pleaded with him. "My family will pay anything for my safety out of here. Please."

Jonas pulled back his hand to slap her again for interrupting then stopped, instead letting the idea of a ransom play around in his head. Perhaps his original intention of using her as a pawn in this game was too shortsighted. "I suppose the daughter of an oil executive and a well-known celebrity could be worth something. We take the money and once the others are released, we disappear into the DRC or maybe down into South Africa."

"Do you have a satellite phone?" Ashley asked.

He nodded.

"You can call my family and have them transfer what you want into an off-shore account."

Jonas smiled. Things were working out better than he'd hoped. The ransom money would guarantee them the resources they needed to win this war. He glanced at the other American and the nurses who'd been kidnapped from the camp. He'd keep them alive as continued leverage with the UN. For now.

"Get the satellite phone." He nodded at Ngozi before turning back to the American. "I have a friend who will be pleased to make the arrangements with your family. It's time to see just how much your life is worth, Miss James."

THIRTY-EIGHT

Wednesday, February 23, 11:27 a.m.
Near The Village Of Dzandoni, Kingani Region
Sunlight streamed through the edges of the tree line as the forest opened up into a thick savannah. Beyond the tall grasses waving in the morning breeze, fields of cassava spread out along the landscape, finally meeting a road that meant help.

Nick squinted as his eyes adjusted to the light. "How much farther?"

Samson pointed toward the dirt road. "The nearest village shouldn't be far. Three, four kilometers at the most."

Nick pulled off his baseball cap and wiped the sweat from his brow with the back of his hand, thankful to be out of the seclusion of the forest. They might still be in the middle of nowhere due to the lack of modern conveniences, but he still felt as if he'd reached civilization. He glanced at his arms, eaten alive by the mosquitoes. "After the past few hours of hiking through the jungle, a dirt road sounds like a walk in the park, if you ask me."

"No kidding." Brandon glanced at Nigel, who stood half a dozen paces ahead of them, then turned back to Nick. "If you ask me, we're lucky we made it through there alive."

Nick caught his meaning, but was still not convinced that Nigel was a mole. If he was working with the rebels, chances were they'd all be dead by now. That fact made him want to give Nigel the benefit of the doubt.

"How's your hand?" Nick called out to Nigel, who held up the wounded limb. "The bleeding seems to have stopped, though it still hurts like hell."

Samson quickened his steps. "There's a small clinic in this town where they should be able to bandage you up properly."

Nick held up his cell phone and searched for a signal.

Nothing.

So much for modern conveniences. He turned to Samson. "You're sure there's a cell tower in this town?"

"I can't guarantee what the soldiers have done to it, but yes. There is one."

"Let's hope so, because I'm not feeling

too keen on extending today's trek to the next village."

And as far as he was concerned, the quicker he could get back to the camp the better. Leaving Paige and the others at the mercy of the rebels had soured his stomach, because he'd gone that route before. If anything happened to her — to any of them — he'd never forgive himself.

Thirty-five minutes later, they stood at the edge of the village of Dzandoni. Wooden stalls lining the main road were bursting with activity as dozens of sellers competed for customers. If the rebels had been through this village, there would be nothing left to sell. Perhaps it was simply a matter of time.

Nigel undid the top button of his shirt, an action that no doubt did little to alleviate the sweltering heat. "I need to get something to eat."

Nick swallowed any remaining suspicions and nodded. "What about you, Samson? Do you need something?"

"I'm fine for now." Samson leaned up against a tree in front of a brightly painted shop, advertising Coke and selling everything from liquor to car parts to fabric. "I'll just wait here for you."

Nick nodded. "Then let's all meet back

here in fifteen minutes."

He watched Nigel walk toward the market. If the man was one of the rebels, there was nothing he could do at this point. He held up his phone and prayed for a signal.

Two bars.

"Anything?" Brandon asked.

"There's a signal, but it's not great."

Nick headed toward the edge of town where the cell tower loomed, then stopped and turned to Brandon. "I think we should follow Nigel."

"So my suspicions are rubbing off?"

Nick tugged on the bill of his baseball cap, unable to ignore his unease. If Nigel was with the rebels, he probably had a way to communicate with them. And having their position compromised wasn't a chance he was willing to take. "Yeah, along with a bit of my own gut instinct."

"I saw him turn into the market."

"Then let's go."

They rushed back down the dirt road and entered the market from the west. Women sat behind colorful piles of fruit — mangos, bananas, and papaya — and vegetables — onions, tomatoes, and cucumbers. Nick searched the crowded venue for Nigel's red shirt.

Brandon spotted him first. "There he is!"

"He's got a radio!" Nick started running, barely avoiding a collision with a woman carrying a large bowl of pineapples on her head. "Nigel?"

Nigel hesitated for a moment, then turned to run farther into the market. Nick quickened his pace, dodging customers along the narrow aisle as he ran past a row of bicycle parts, but Nigel was too far ahead.

Samson appeared on the other side of Nigel, running toward them and forcing Nigel to search for another escape, which gave Nick and Brandon time to catch up. Nigel spun around, clipping the corner of a wooden table full of dried fish as he turned. The table tipped, spilling piles of the fly-covered fish across the narrow pathway.

Nigel dropped the radio as Samson grabbed his arm and pinned him against the ground. "I had a feeling this man was dirty. Philip's death . . . it was too easy."

"We thought the same thing." Nick kicked aside one of the fish, ignoring the barrage of onlookers gathering and the shopkeeper's protests. "You've been in radio contact with the rebel base camp the whole time, haven't you? Then Philip found out that you were the mole and you killed him."

Nigel spat at the ground, barely missing Nick's shoe. "Do what you want, because it doesn't matter. In the end we will win."

Nigel reached for the radio, but Samson's grip held him tight.

Nick picked up the radio. "Don't even try it. What did you tell them?"

Nigel didn't respond.

Brandon stood beside Nick. "Why not just kill us all when you had the chance?"

"I was told to bring in the Americans alive."

Samson tightened his grip. "So I would have been next?"

"If you'd started asking questions."

Samson looked at Nick. "What do we do with him?"

"Good question." Nick folded his arms across his chest. "I say we hand him over to the crowd. I don't think they will take too kindly to having one of the Ghost Soldiers back in town."

Nigel jerked his head back. "They will kill me."

"Probably." Nick folded his arms. "Which means we now hold the advantage. Tell me what the plan is and what you told your boss when you checked in just now, and we might make sure they don't feed your dead body to the vultures."

"I . . ."

"You can start with the plan."

"Fine. I was just supposed to watch you and check in every twelve hours. If there was a plan to bring in the army, I was supposed to tell them where and how many."

"What did you tell them just now?"

"Nothing, I —"

"The deal was that you tell us everything so we don't feed you to the lions."

"They know that there were five of us who left to get help, but I couldn't pick up radio signal in the forest, so they don't know where we are. I didn't have a chance."

Brandon folded his arms across his chest. "Do you believe him?"

"No." Nick shook his head. "But whether we like it or not, this is a situation for the authorities to handle. Not us. Keep your eyes on him, Samson. I've got a call to make."

"Trust me. He will not be going anywhere."

Nick walked out of the noisy market until his phone registered four bars. Five minutes later he was finally connected with Paul Hayes at the embassy.

"Paul, this is Nick Gilbert."

"Nick, it's been a long time. I thought I heard you'd left the country after last November's fiasco in the capital, but then your name showed up across my desk a couple hours ago as one of the aid workers still up in the Kingani region. Where exactly are you? Our offices have been trying to reach the camp the past forty-eight hours, with no luck."

"That would be because rebels shot down my plane and have cut off all access points and communication. Several of us managed to slip past them and hike through the forest so we could get cell-phone coverage, but these guys mean business. Besides a recent attack on the camp, they're holding six people as hostages, including two Americans and four of the local medical staff."

"What do you know about the group climbing Mt. Maja?"

Nick stared at the ground, hating being the deliverer of all the bad news. "Robert James is dead. He was killed up on the mountain Monday night during a raid."

"And his daughter?"

"She was in the group taken hostage. The two other hikers, Brandon and Jodi Collins, are alive. There were also four Canadians scheduled to come down the mountain the next day, but so far we haven't heard from them." Nick scuffed his foot against the ground. It was time he got some answers as well. "I need to know what can be done about the situation in the camp. We figured someone would have figured out something was wrong by now and sent in the army."

"The local military is stretched to the limit, and until Washington decides to intervene, my hands are tied."

"That's not good enough."

"I haven't given up yet, but I'm going to need some time."

"Time is one thing we don't have."

"What do you mean?"

Nick shifted his weight to his other foot. When he'd flown Black Hawks for the air force, they were always ready. Choppers fueled up. But limited resources here changed the picture completely. Which put lives on the line.

"There's another issue that we need to deal with. On top of the cholera, there's an outbreak of measles about to erupt in the refugee camp. With enough vaccinations, we might be able to curb the spread. Dr. Ryan said if you contact Volunteers of Hope, they were already in the process of putting together a large-scale vaccine campaign and should have the vaccines available. The biggest issue, then, will be the logistics of getting them past the rebels and into the camp."

"Sounds simple enough." Paul groaned. "I might not have access to a U.S. warship or their marines, but I could work on getting a couple helicopters and a few marines and local soldiers together until I can get the ground forces up there."

"How long to pull something like that together?"

"I don't know. I'm not exactly prepared to launch a large-scale mission, but I'll do what I can."

"According to Dr. Ryan, we've got a window of about forty-three more hours to put a curb on this disease before it starts spreading like wildfire."

"I'll have to come up with some sort of leverage with the government to get them moving."

Nick sighed, irritated at the amount of red tape when lives were at stake. Unless . . . "What if I told you I had something to get them moving?"

"Like?"

"Knowledge of where the rebel base camp is."

"You know where it is?"

"We've got it narrowed down. And I'm pretty sure I've got a guy who could lead you there." Nick passed on the location he'd circled earlier on the map.

"Paired with satellite photos, this might give us enough for our intelligence people to work with. The government needs the rebels out of the picture as much as you do, which also means I should be able to get what I ask for, including military backup."

"How long?"

"Let me make a few phone calls and see what I can do."

"What about us?"

"Can you get to Kingani?"

"Theoretically we should be able to take public transport, but why Kingani?"

"I want you to work with Digane and the officials there to see if you can coordinate another ground shipment of supplies to the camp, this time under heavy guard. I'll call you as soon as I have a timetable for the vaccines and military support."

A minute later, Nick flipped his phone shut, then turned to Brandon and Samson. "Looks like it's time to hitch a ride."

THIRTY-NINE

Paul dropped his cell phone onto his desk, hoping he hadn't just made a promise he couldn't keep. Putting together a rescue operation wasn't the biggest problem he faced. The greater obstacle was going to be actually getting the vaccine into the camp, and all foreigners out, before things escalated even further.

Nick's report wasn't all that had his head pounding like a jackhammer. He dug through his top drawer for another round of cold medicine and a couple of pain relievers before buzzing for Mercy. He'd finally talked with Maggie on the phone early this morning. She'd listened to his apologies and excuses, then told him her ultimatum still stood. He'd used every tactic in the book to try and get her to see things his way, but she was as stubborn as they came. Funny how her tenacity had been one of the things that had attracted him to her in the beginning.

But that had nothing to do with his current dilemma. Like it or not, he couldn't just walk away from this job. Or could he? The decision burned in his gut. Walking away meant putting the lives of dozens of American citizens in further danger. And staying meant losing his kids and the one woman he'd ever loved.

"Mitch Peterson, Ashley James' fiancé, is on the phone again."

He glanced up at Mercy, who stood in the doorway, and groaned. Mitch Peterson was the last person he wanted to talk to right now. Ashley's fiancé might have his sympathy because of the situation, but that was it. He had no patience for the man's presumptuous attitude or his belief that he wasn't doing his job. Drag him away from his plush life and plop him in the middle of nowhere, with no telephone lines, cell-phone service, or other means of communication, and see how long he survived. Maybe then he'd understand what they were up against.

Paul downed the cold medicine with a swig of lukewarm water. "Tell him I'll call him back. Right now, I want the deputy of foreign affairs on the phone."

"I'll . . ." Mercy hesitated. "I'll do my best, sir."

"Wait." Paul waved her back. He was going to play this game differently. "Forget the phone. Tell the deputy I want him here in my office."

Mercy's forehead wrinkled. "I don't see how —"

"Simply tell him I have information that we believe will lead to the whereabouts of the rebel base camp. That might get him moving."

Mercy's frown faded. "I'm on it, sir."

James Ngani took the bait. Forty-five minutes later he arrived at the embassy and was immediately ushered into Paul's office.

Paul stood by the window, arms crossed, drinking some nasty herbal tea Mercy had convinced him would relieve his cold symptoms. It might, if the taste didn't kill him first.

Paul nodded to one of the open chairs on the other side of his desk. "Thanks for coming. Have a seat."

While waiting for the deputy's arrival, he'd had time to put in a dozen calls to organize the delivery of the vaccines. He'd done his part. Now he just had to convince Ngani that his government needed to do theirs.

Ngani remained in the doorway, suspicion clear in his expression. "The only reason I'm here is because I was told you have information about the location of the rebel base camp. If this is another attempt on your part to accuse my government of not doing their job . . ."

"I know why you're here. Have a seat."

Ngani hesitated. "Where's the camp?"

Paul motioned again to the open chair, then sat down behind his desk. "Here's the deal. I've got a situation that has just come up, and we're going to play this my way. We all know that despite the gallant efforts of your government to make it look as if you're in control, that's far from the reality of the situation."

"You don't understand."

"I don't understand what? The fact that your government is hiding behind a bunch of lies and people are dying because of it?"

He knew all too well the complications of the situation and the probable consequences of his lack of diplomacy, but he was done playing games. The situation in the refugee camp was nothing more than a ticking time bomb. As food became scarcer and nerves began to fray, violence would grow. It had to be stopped now.

"I just received a phone call from an

American humanitarian worker still in the Kingani region," he continued. "Apparently, despite your government's reassurances, the refugee camp is now in control of the rebels, and has been for the last forty-eight hours or so. We already know that the convoy full of supplies was hijacked by the rebels, which means that food and medicine will be running out soon. I need to organize an air transport of supplies, including a measles vaccine, to the camp."

"Measles?"

Paul clinched, then released his fists. He wasn't going to listen to a bunch of excuses. "On top of the cholera crisis, there's been an outbreak of measles in the camp that will become an epidemic if we don't do something about it."

Ngani's tone changed. "What else do you need from me?"

"I've already contacted Volunteers for Hope International here in the capital and they are working on getting the vaccine ready for transport, but it has to arrive at the camp quickly in order for it to be effective."

"I'll work on the transport."

"And I'll send four of my marines with your pilots and crew. I want two helicopters and your best men." Paul folded his hands in front of him. "And I want them in the air, along with sufficient ground cover, in the next twenty-four hours."

"That's not possible —"

"Why? Because sending in the army would be admitting that the government isn't in control? I want you to make this possible. While your government is worried about the UN discovering the situation has soured, your people are dying. In exchange, I'll provide you with our intel on the rebel base location."

"Do you even have the exact location of the camp?"

"I'll have the exact location by the time those helos are ready to take off."

Ngami stood, looking as if he was still debating on his answer. Finally he tugged on the bottom of his suit coat and nodded. "I'll call you as soon as I can arrange something."

As soon as Ngani had left, Paul closed his eyes, grateful the conversation was over. Somehow, he was going to find a way to save these people — and his marriage — at the same time.

FORTY

Wednesday, February 23, 4:12 p.m.
Somewhere Between Dzandoni And Kingani

Nick's head smacked against the back of the seat, jarring him from a restless sleep. He fought to remember where he was. The smell of perspiration and diesel filled the humid air. A chicken squawked, a baby cried . . . His eyes focused on the battered leather suitcase halfway across his lap and the plump woman beside him as his memory began to clear.

Samson leading them through the forest, Philip lying in the ravine, Nigel's confession, talking to Paul at the embassy . . .

It had taken forty-five minutes to fill the derelict taxi that ran from Dzandoni to Kingani, and according to the heap-of-junk's driver, it would take another hour-plus to reach their destination. If they managed to make it there without breaking down.

The taxi hit a pothole, smacking his knees

against a metal bar in the seat in front of him. He glanced around the crowded van. Seventeen people were crammed into the twelve-passenger vehicle and with the way his luck was running, they'd stop and pick up more in the next town.

Brandon sat next to him, looking far more alert than Nick felt. "You've been sleeping."

Nick glanced at his watch. "How long?"

"Not long, but I don't know how you can sleep at all. When you mentioned hitching a ride, I wasn't counting on putting my life into the hands of some maniac driver."

Nick slowly rolled his neck and shoulders to work out the kinks, then jumped to his feet while the van rumbled beneath him. "You should have waked me up."

"Why? There's nothing you need to do — Samson's got it under control."

"I suppose you're right. Nigel's not going anywhere."

Nigel sat against the window next to Samson in the seat in front of them. Bringing him with them had seemed like the safest thing to do at the moment.

Nick took off his cap and wiped the sweat off his forehead as they passed a scattering of compounds with mud-brick dwellings and thatched roofs. Little changed in the scenery beyond trees, compounds, and the occasional town.

"What's wrong?"

"I don't know." Nick glanced at his phone before shoving it back into his pocket. Three bars meant they were near a town, but there were no missed calls, no messages. Which hopefully meant that the plan was still on track. But that didn't take away the gnawing feeling in his gut. "I just can't shake this bad feeling."

"What are you worried about?"

"Nigel might not have been able to let the rebel leaders in on the plan, but that doesn't mean they don't know exactly where we are."

Brandon unzipped his backpack and started digging for something. "Stop being paranoid. You've been watching too many movies."

Nick laughed. "I wish. The last time I saw a decent movie was . . . I don't even remember."

"It's just as well." Brandon pulled out a couple of power bars and tossed one to Nick. "Hungry?"

"Yeah."

"Just remember that this is the RD." Brandon handed another one of the bars to Samson, who nodded his thanks. "And from what I've gathered in my short time here, no one has the resources of a specialized ops team, including the rebels."

"Maybe, but the rebels are not only organized and well armed, but they've got a collection of satellite and VHF radio equipment they've managed to get a hold of."

Which meant they were probably at least as well equipped or better equipped than the army. And Nick had left the camp, and everyone in it, as vulnerable as a battalion in the middle of a war zone with no means for cover. Things never should have gotten this far out of hand.

Nick's phone rang. He grabbed it from his pocket and took the call. It was Paul. "I'm hoping this means you have some good news?"

"It's progress. I spoke with one of the administrators with Volunteers for Hope, and not only do they have the vaccine, they are able to help."

Nick pressed his fingers against his other ear so he could hear better. Procuring Volunteers for Hope's help was the easy part. "And the help we'll need from the local army?"

"I also had a conversation with the deputy of foreign affairs. I think we'll get what we want."

Nick breathed out a sigh of relief and gave

Brandon a thumbs-up. "So I guess we got our miracle."

"Your info on the camp ended up being the trump card, but while we might have narrowed it down, we're going to need an exact location in the next few hours."

"What kind of time frame are we looking at?"

"Another twenty-four hours."

Nick weighed the situation. At least with the vaccine and other needed supplies on their way, they'd have a chance to get the situation at the camp under control. Now they'd just have to hold off the rebels as well.

The line crackled. They were almost out of the cell tower's range.

"Listen, the line's breaking up. I'll call you as soon as we get to Kingani."

"I'll wait for your call, and Nick —"

The phone went dead, cutting off Paul's response. Nick flipped his phone shut and shoved it back in his pocket. At least they were making some progress.

The van hit another pothole, then started slowing down.

"Flat tire?"

"I don't think so." Nick strained his neck and looked out the window. The van was pulling off to the side of the road. "Police stop. It shouldn't take long."

Nick's attention shifted to the four armed policemen approaching the van. Their driver rolled down his window and started speaking rapidly in Dha. A twinge of concern twisted in his gut. This wasn't a typical license check. Something was wrong.

One of the policemen pulled open the side door of the van and cocked his weapon. "Everyone out of the van now."

Nick filed out behind the others, climbing over empty bottles of beer and luggage in the process. "And you thought I'd been watching too many movies."

"Rebels?"

"That's my guess. The police don't typically force passengers to unload."

"Unless they're looking for rebels."

One of the men cocked his gun and pointed it at Nick's face. "Or unless they're looking for us."

"On your knees."

Nick dropped to his knees beside Brandon.

"How'd they know we were here?"

"I don't know."

Nick searched for a way out, but a half dozen machine guns pointed in his direction didn't leave him with many options.

One of the rebels stopped in front of him.

"Nick Gilbert?"

Now how in the world did he know that?
"Yeah."

He shoved the nozzle of the gun beneath Nick's chin. "You and your buddies here are coming with me. But please don't try anything heroic. Or you will not wake up to see another day."

FORTY-ONE

Paige stared at the file in the dim glow of the light bulb above her and reread the nurse's scribbled notes. They'd diagnosed three more severe cases of cholera and seven cases of measles in the past twelve hours, which meant that they needed those vaccines soon or there was going to be no way to stop a second epidemic from sweeping through the camp.

Dropping the file onto the desk, she dug through her medical bag, pulled out a couple of Tylenol, and swallowed them with what was left of the warm water from her plastic bottle. What she wouldn't do for an ice-cold Coke and a deep-dish pan pizza. Except such cravings seemed frivolous. Because the state of the camp wasn't the only thing that had multiplied her prayers.

Over twenty-four hours had passed and

354

Nick and the others hadn't returned. Which left her with the dozens of scenarios that had flooded her mind all night. They'd been attacked in the forest, stumbled into the rebel base camp by mistake, and were taken hostage . . . She let out a low groan. There was no way for her to know, but that didn't stop the questions from coming.

I need them here, God. Things are only going to keep getting worse.

"Dr. Ryan?" One of the nurses set a plate of rice and beans on her desk. "You've barely eaten or slept for days."

She nodded her appreciation, but the smell of food turned her stomach. "Thank you. Have the security details checked in yet?"

They'd set up extra security details throughout the camp before Nick and Samson's departure. They might not have weapons to fight the rebels off if they attacked again, but at least they'd have some warning.

"About twenty minutes ago. There has been no reported sign of the rebels near the camp."

"Good." Paige rubbed the muscles at the base of her neck with her fingertips. As long as they didn't have to handle another attack by the rebels, they'd be able to deal with

355

the medical situation. "Anything else?"

"Jodi's awake and says she's hungry, and Raina's been calling for her mother."

Paige pushed back the stack of paperwork and stood. "I'll check on them both now."

"And your breakfast?"

"I'll eat it when I'm done checking on them." Paige caught the nurse's disapproving look. "I promise."

Inside the isolation tent, Jodi lay on her side, her cheeks a soft tint of pink instead of the pale they'd been all week. When she saw Paige, she tried to push herself up with her elbows before falling back against the bed.

"Slow down. You might be feeling better, but you're still very weak." Paige felt her forehead. "Your fever's broken."

"A good sign?"

"A very good sign. I think you're going to make it."

Jodi's left eyebrow shot up. "Was there ever a time when you thought I wouldn't?"

"To be honest, I was worried. The gunshot wound lowered your resistance and added to the chances of infection." Paige checked the bandage on Jodi's shoulder. "Thankfully, it's healing nicely."

"Can I ask you a question?"

"Of course."

"Brandon's told me what's going on in

the camp, but to be honest, I'm not sure what's real and what I've dreamed up. I feel as if I've been living in a fog the past couple days."

"Three days, to be exact."

"And the rebels? They're here at the camp?"

"They've stayed outside the camp for the most part, but they've got us cut off from the outside. Several of the men left yesterday to get help."

"Including Brandon."

Paige sat down on the edge of the bed. "Yeah. He went because he knew you needed medical help I can't provide here. The last forty-eight hours have been touch and go."

"He said something about having the measles."

"Believe it or not, you do."

"But I was vaccinated as a child."

"Unfortunately that vaccine isn't always effective. The nurse told me you were hungry?"

"Starved, actually. I don't suppose you've got a T-bone steak and a side of mashed potatoes lying around somewhere."

Paige laughed. "You'll have to settle for hot porridge at first. I don't want you to overdo it."

"I guess I can handle that for starters." Jodi rolled over onto her back and managed a small smile. "When did you last hear from Brandon and the others?"

"It's been about twenty-four hours, but I'm sure they're fine."

"That's not what your eyes tell me."

Paige dropped her gaze, hating that she was so easy to read. "I knew it would take them awhile to get back. They've got to get hold of enough vaccines, arrange transport, coordinate with the army . . . I'd just hoped they'd be back by now. And since we can't phone them or radio them, we have to pray and wait."

"But do you think something went wrong?"

Paige shook her head. The last thing she wanted was to add to the woman's worries. "There is simply no way to know what's happening out there."

"This whole thing is crazy." Jodi fiddled with the frayed hem of the sheet that covered her. "This isn't exactly the way I planned to spend my honeymoon. When we signed up, climbing Mt. Maja seemed like a big adventure. Even when they told us about the potential problems with the rebels in the north, I guess I thought I was immune to them. You never think something like this could happen, do you?"

"No. Until this week, I thought that being a humanitarian worker would keep me safe." Paige noted the tension in Jodi's face and changed the subject. "The RD is probably the most unique setting I've heard of for a honeymoon. How did the two of you meet?"

"Brandon and I?" Jodi's smile widened. "I was in a car wreck about eighteen months ago — thus the hardware in my ankle. A drunk driver slammed into me from the side. At first, the doctors didn't think I'd make it, but I pulled through. Brandon was my physical therapist."

"Really? How romantic."

"It was. We connected right away, but I was focused on getting back on my feet — literally — and not falling in love, so it took awhile before we actually got together."

"Your first date?"

"I would have preferred hiking, but I wasn't exactly up for anything strenuous at that point. So instead he took me to a jazz concert in the park. It was perfect. He was perfect. Turned out we'd both been climbing for years and wanted to travel more, so for our honeymoon we wanted something different and a bit exotic. Trekking across Africa seemed like the perfect combination.

This was to be the last part of our trip. Not too strenuous, which was something Brandon insisted on, and add to that the view from the summit of Mt. Maja is incredible. What I didn't expect was a bunch of rebels to ruin the climb."

"None of us did."

Jodi propped herself up with her elbow. "What about you? Did you leave someone behind in the States?"

"Me? No." Paige felt her cheeks flush. "I guess I've always had a hard time balancing the hectic schedule of my profession and a relationship. Romance never seems to work out for me. Most guys want a wife who's home to cook them dinner every night and wash their socks. I don't think I could live up to that standard. I'm a horrible cook and I hate to do laundry."

Jodi laughed. "Maybe you just intimidate them."

"Well, I'm not sure about that. I always planned to have the whole package — husband, kids, and a white picket fence — but now I'm looking at my biological clock starting to wind down."

"You're hardly old."

"Once you hit your, uh, early-thirties, you start wondering if love hasn't passed you by for good."

"That's nonsense. My mom was happily single until she was thirty-eight. She had me a year later." Jodi's eyes brightened. "What about that good-looking pilot I've seen you talking to as I drifted in and out of reality? Or was he another one of my dreams as well?"

"Nick? He's no dream . . . well . . . I'll admit he is dreamy." Paige felt her heart flutter. "But he just happens to be stuck here with the rest of us."

"And . . ."

Paige shook her head. "And?"

"Anything else?"

Paige felt another blush. "He kissed me before he left."

"And what did you think about that?"

"That I wished we had time to get to know each other under normal circumstances."

Jodi laughed. "Somehow, I don't think either of you is destined to have a normal life."

"Funny. I'm not even sure what normal is anymore."

Paige glanced across the room at Raina. "I need to check on Raina, then I'll have one of the nurses bring you a big bowl of porridge."

Raina sat on the edge of her bed, her feet

dangling in front of her.

Paige crossed the room and shot her a smile. "You're sitting up this morning. I'd say that's tremendous progress. How are you feeling?"

Raina shrugged. Hollow eyes stared at the floor. What had this girl seen?

"How are you feeling?"

She looked up beneath long lashes. "Have you heard from my father?"

Paige touched one of the neat rows of tight braids on her head. Raina flinched and Paige pulled back her hand. "Not yet, but when he does return, he'll be returning as a hero."

"And my mother?"

Paige's gaze dropped. She wished she had answers for the girl. Some ray of hope she could give her, but as far as she knew, her mother had yet to arrive at the camp. Which meant there was a good chance she hadn't survived the raid.

"I don't know where your mother is, but we won't stop looking. I promise."

Raina stared straight ahead. "I woke up, and they were all gone."

Paige's jaw tensed. "Your family? Are you talking about the night your village was raided?"

"Everything was burning. Then there was

no one left. My mother, my father, my sisters . . . Asim."

"Did the men hurt you?"

Raina's chin quivered. "They smelled bad, but I could not run. They wouldn't let me. Then they hurt me."

Paige pulled out a square piece of blue-patterned paper and began folding it. "There's a lot of beauty in this world, but there is also a lot of evil."

"I couldn't stop them. Why doesn't someone stop them?"

Paige continued folding, then opened up the butterfly and handed it to Raina. "I want you to keep this, and when you feel afraid, it will help you remember that someone — that many people — are trying to stop them."

"Dr. Ryan." One of Paige's nurses stood in the entrance of the tent. "We need you at the clinic."

Paige gently clasped Raina's hand. "We'll talk some more later, but for now, I want you to rest. You need to build up your strength. And as soon as you're not contagious, I'll let you see your brother."

"They won't come back, will they?"

Paige pressed her lips together, fighting off tears. Sometimes life was so unfair. "I promise I'll do everything in my power to keep you safe, Raina."

Raina nodded, then lay down as Paige stood and walked quietly from the room. She glanced back before leaving the tent. The little girl's emotional scars would far outlast the physical scars, because sometimes all the wishes in the world couldn't magically make all the pain go away.

FORTY-TWO

Ashley stared at the runny sauce and mush on her plate and felt her stomach turn. She shoved aside the food and began picking at her chipped French nails instead, wondering what in the world had possessed her to have them done before trekking across Africa. Even Mitch, who hardly ever noticed things like manicured nails or highlighted hair, had rolled his eyes at her before kissing her good-bye. At the time it had seemed important. Today it seemed a useless extravagance.

The rebel compound was quieter than the refugee camp, but held the same woodsy scent of smoke in the air. Women cooked over smoldering fires and children played beneath the shade of a mango tree while the men lazed beneath a morning sun that was already over halfway to its zenith. She brushed a layer of dust from her khaki pants and let out a deep sigh, afraid that even her father's money couldn't get her out of this situation. Her mother had promised to send the ransom, but coming up with five million dollars in cash quickly, even for her family, wasn't going to be easy.

Taz plopped down beside her, his plate already empty. "How are you doing?"

She quirked her right brow. The guy was way too perky. "You really want to know?"

"I wouldn't ask if I didn't want to know."

"Well, let's see. I'm being held hostage by a group of rebels who are apparently intent on taking over the world. Or at least this small part of the world. Which makes this one of those terrible, horrible, no good, very bad days —"

Taz's nose wrinkled. "I used to love that book. My mom used to read it to me over and over and over. I'm sure I drove her crazy."

Ashley pulled her knees toward her chest and wrapped her arms around her legs. "She must be a great mom."

"She was your typical car-poolin' PTA chairman Sunday school teacher who never missed one of her only son's games." Taz stared off into the distance. "Yeah, she's a pretty great mom. Now she sends me care packages and calls me once or twice a month."

Her own memories of her mother were overshadowed with at least a dozen different nannies and full-time maids. "You're lucky. My mom was always busy with one charity or the other while I was shuffled from one activity to the next by nannies and chauffeurs."

"Sounds lonely."

"It was."

"My dad was the absent one. I guess my mom was always trying to make up for his not ever being around. They divorced when I was eight. I haven't seen him since."

"I do see both my parents frequently, though they separated years ago. I guess we both have our share of a few bad days."

"This one does rank up in the top ten, but I'm not sure it quite compares to my six months in North Africa." He looked up at her and caught her gaze. "You wouldn't believe the conditions there."

"Worse than being held hostage by a group of ruthless rebels?"

Taz chuckled. "I'll admit, it's a close running, but then I'm assuming you've never been to Chad."

Ashley shook her head. "This experience excluded, I'm typically not the thrill-seeker type who books a plane ticket just to say I've been there."

"I had a couple friends who told me that if you were willing to risk the dangerous militia and government forces, along with the horrid roads and highway bandits, the beauty of the country is worth every minute of the risk."

"Like I said, I think I'd pass on that one."

"Not me. I was posted along the northern border on the edge of the Sahara, which has got to be the most desolate place in the world. Fierce sandstorms rise up from the Sahara and last for days at a time. And as far as lawlessness, well, it's a bit like the Wild West, and water was their gold."

"Water?"

"Imagine the wind and sand drying you up like a shriveled prune while the winds and the sand storms suck out moisture from everything that breathes. And on top of that, there were constant raids by the rebels, despite the curfews that were put into place."

"Sounds wonderful." This guy really was crazy.

"I worked in this field office with no air conditioner and no heater, and believe me, you'd do anything for both there. In the day, it can easily get up to a hundred and twenty, then *bang* —" He snapped his fingers. "—drop to freezing at night. Every day brought with it a new set of problems."

Ashley studied his face, trying to figure out if he was pulling her leg, or if he really got his kicks from risking his life. "Is this how you make me feel better? By insinuating that things could get even worse?"

"Is it working?" He wiggled a nose that was red from the sun.

"No."

"You're smiling."

Boy, he was good at trying her patience. "No, I'm not. I'm thinking that you have to be completely insane to find anything to smile about in this situation."

"Oh, I definitely saw a smile there."

"Stop." Ashley's laugh came out as a snort through her nose. "I don't know how you do that."

"Make you smile?" Taz leaned back against his elbows and watched her. "Surely you've got someone in your life who does that on a regular basis."

Homesickness pinched her insides. "His name is Mitch. We're getting married in June."

"Congratulations."

"Thanks." Ashley squirmed, wondering how his probing questions made her feel as if he could see straight into her soul. Not that it mattered. He wasn't her type by any stretch of the imagination. Even if he could make her laugh.

"And he is a . . ."

"A Harvard grad lawyer."

"And do you love this . . . Harvard grad lawyer?"

"Of course I love him."

Ashley frowned at the question and tried not to wonder when the last time was that Mitch had made her laugh. Lately, he'd spent most of his time working on cases and racking up billable hours. And she'd been so busy, she hadn't really even noticed.

"Besides." She went back to picking at her fingernail. "Don't you think that's a rather personal question?"

"I don't know." Taz jutted his chin toward the cinder-block wall of the compound. "Last time I looked, there were four armed rebels guarding the perimeter of the compound. I think the typical social and etiquette rules can be dropped. And the last time I looked, there wasn't exactly a whole lot of things filling up your social calendar."

She cleared her throat. "You never told me where the name Taz came from."

"Trying to change the subject?"

"Definitely."

Taz laughed.

"So . . ."

"My real name is Timothy Gregory Michaels III."

"That's quite a mouthful."

"Taz is definitely easier to remember. It just happens to be one of those crazy nicknames that stuck. According to my mother, I was a child with boundless energy and an insatiable sense of curiosity. My uncle told her I reminded him of the Tasmanian Devil on Looney Tunes who never stopped running. Thus the name Taz. I guess I was destined for a career that keeps me running."

Ashley looked up at him. "Sometimes I wonder if I've found what I was destined for."

"What do you mean? You're Ashley James. Famous Emmy-nominated actress —"

"But that's not who I am."

"Whom do you want to be?"

"I don't know."

"Your life can't be all that bad."

"Trust me, it's not." She flashed him a smile. "Five-star hotels, manicures, parties . . . I'd do anything for a five-course meal at Le Fleur de Lile right about now."

"Then why all the reflecting?"

"I don't know." Ashley shrugged. "Coming here has made me see for the first time how much of the rest of the world really lives. And with it I have this odd sense of compassion toward them I hadn't expected. Paige tried once to talk to me about her faith and why she decided to come here, but I haven't exactly been the type to hang onto religion."

"Did you ever think that coming here can be motivated by something more than religion?"

"All I know is that it would take a lot more than religion to get me to stay."

"It's not religion that brought me here, but a person. Jesus Christ changed my life."

"From what? A suburban boy scout?"

Taz chuckled. "You'd be surprised how far astray a hyperactive kid from the suburbs can go."

"I still can't imagine living where I didn't have a party or a premiere to go to every night, or month-long vacations in the Caribbean."

Taz sighed. "A white, sandy beach sounds fantastic right about now."

"You'd love it there."

"Not sure I'd exactly fit in with your friends."

"Why?" She flicked an ant from her pants, then caught his gaze. "Because you're a fearless, risk-taking humanitarian worker who wears a floppy safari hat and a cheap tourist bracelet?"

Mitch would never be caught dead in Taz's hodgepodge wardrobe, but for some crazy reason it suited Taz.

He held up his arm and pointed to the bracelet. "I'll have you know that this bracelet is genuine giraffe hair and was a gift from a twelve-year-old boy I met in one of the refugee camps in Kenya. Not only do I never take it off; I'll take everything you just said as a compliment."

Ashley's gaze moved to one of the armed guards standing ten feet away at the edge of the compound. "I just wish I was half as fearless as you are."

"If they were going to hurt us they'd have done it by now. Besides, we're worth more to them alive at this point. You especially. Your mom won't give over the money without proof of life."

Proof of life.

She shivered. That phrase was supposed to be reserved for Hollywood movies and best-selling novels. Not her life in the middle of some African rebel base camp.

She nodded slowly and searched for a spark of courage inside her trembling body. "Let's just hope you're right."

FORTY-THREE

Jonas stood in the corner of the room and watched his daughter Yara sleeping on the thin mat. Smoke from the cooking fire filtered through the open door of the mud hut, filling the room with its haze and burning his eyes.

He folded his arms across his chest. He should be preparing for tomorrow, not worrying about domestic issues. But even he hadn't been able to ignore Eshe's request.

"What's wrong with the child?"

One of the nurses squatting beside Yara looked up at him. "Measles."

"Measles?"

Jonas bent down beside Yara and touched her forehead where dots of perspiration glistened beneath the yellow light of the lamp. When Eshe had asked him to have the nurses from the refugee camp check on

374

several of the children who had runny noses and coughs, he'd complied, but he hadn't expected this.

He recognized the telltale marks of the disease — tiny dots on the inside of Yara's mouth — because he'd seen it in one of his own children. First the spots, then the cough, then the struggling to breathe . . . Afterward, he'd watched his wife cry as he wrapped the child's lifeless body, then buried her in the field beyond the walls of their compound.

He backed away from Yara's small body. Why had the ancestors insisted on sending their curses upon him now?

Ngozi entered the hut and stood in the doorway behind him. "Yara is not the only one. It is spreading. Abah and Zaid are now sick as well."

Jonas stroked his stubble and stared at his friend. Ngozi might be one of his oldest friends, but the birth of his children had made him forget the injustices they faced together and why they fought against President Tau and his men. But this disease was not something he could control like the men who now followed him. He might as well attempt to control the winds blowing across the vast savannah.

He turned back to the nurse. "Where did

this illness come from?"

She stood and brushed her hands on her skirt, fear still lingering in her eyes. "There has been a measles outbreak in the refugee camp. It could have come from there or maybe from one of the surrounding villages, brought in by your men."

"So what do we do?"

She shook her head. "There is no cure for measles. As long as there are no complications, she should be fine in a few days. In the meantime, we isolate anyone who is sick, make sure they stay hydrated, and control the fever. Beyond that —"

Ngozi stepped forward. "What kind of complications?"

"They . . . they can be common, especially if malnutrition is involved. It becomes a secondary issue of the disease. If the child becomes dehydrated or gets pneumonia, then . . . then they can die."

Jonas stepped outside and drew in a deep breath.

Ngozi followed. "We need medical help."

"And tell me who is going to help us? The talks in the capital are going nowhere, which means despite everything we have done, nothing has changed for any of us."

"You told me you'd sacrifice your life for revenge, but look at your daughter. Is it really worth it? Our wives, our children, are without medical help, and we live on the run."

Jonas' stomach burned. "I'm starting to question your loyalties. Don't you remember what they did to us? Why we have to stand up?"

Ngozi dipped his head. "Of course I remember."

"Look at me."

Ngozi's mouth tightened, but he kept his gaze lowered.

"Look at me! They killed our fathers in front of us, raped our women, and yet now we are the ones the world sees as evil, all so they can rake in more foreign aid that will never leave their pockets. They made us who we are."

Ngozi pressed his shoulders back and looked Jonas in the eye. "And who are we? Soldiers who fight blindly, taking every order as we kill our own people? I am no longer convinced this is how it must be done. Nor do I want to sacrifice everything I have just to have my throat slit by the president's army."

"Once again, you have forgotten that my brother lies rotting in one of their prisons along with the rest of our leaders."

"I have not forgotten, but I do want to

know one thing: you have risen to be our leader, Jonas, but where do you lead us? I'm no longer convinced I want to go where you are taking us."

"Because you have forgotten the truth. We started this for the sake of freedom —"

"But you now seek revenge, not freedom."

Jonas felt a twinge in his shoulder and reached up and touched where the soldiers had shot him. "I will not go through life cowering at the government's whims, and then, when the noose begins to tighten, find out that it is my neck ensnarled in their rope."

"But for what? To what end?" Nzoni reached up and ripped the amulet from around his neck, throwing it on the ground. "This was to make me invisible to our enemies, yet they have found us. There is no longer anywhere to hide. They will find us, and when they do, there will be nothing left . . . not even a marker above our grave. And our children won't even remember to pray to us."

Jonas crushed the charm with the heel of his boot. "Then we die, but at least we die fighting for our freedom."

Ngozi spat onto the dusty ground in front of him. "I will stay and fight, but we need medical help here or this disease is going to wipe out everything worth fighting for."

"Then go back to the camp, and this time bring back the doctor."

FORTY-FOUR

Nick heard the roar of the vehicle before he saw the headlights through the cracks of the metal gate of the compound. Besides the constant chatter of insects and the occasional wail of an infant, there had been little noise from inside the rebel base camp since their arrival just before midnight, making the middle-of-the-night entrance even more pronounced.

Rolling over onto his elbow, he tried to count the shadows of the guards who had jumped into action to unlock the gate, but above him clouds blocked out the stars, leaving the humid night shrouded in black and allowing him to see little of the surrounding compound.

He slapped at the annoying buzzing in his ear. Sleeping outside with no mosquito net meant a constant barrage of the offensive insects that had continuously feasted on him during the long night. Which was yet another reason he'd lain awake on the reed mat, trying to come up with a way past the armed guards. But so far, every idea he'd come up with seemed too risky a plan for civilian hostages.

The heavy metal gate creaked open and allowed the vehicle to enter. A moment later a 4×4 screeched to a halt inside the walls of the compound, stopping inches from the base of the knotted trunk of a shade tree.

Paige stumbled from the vehicle.

Nick felt a rush of adrenalin surge through him. "Paige?"

He jumped to his feet, stopping only at the sound of the cocking of an assault rifle behind him.

He held up his hands. "I just want to make sure she's okay."

Ngozi's familiar form exited the car behind her. "She's not here for you."

Paige moved in front of the car to where the vehicle's yellow beam of lights illuminated her profile. But even her steady stance couldn't hide the look of fear — and surprise — marking her expression.

She turned to Ngozi. "I'll need his help."

"We have nurses from the camp here —"

"You want me to treat your patients? I

need his help."

Ngozi hesitated, then nodded. "Fine. Take her to the isolation hut."

Paige walked toward Nick. For a moment, all he could see was the last time he'd told her good-bye, but for the moment he needed to forget the memory of their kiss. The only thing that mattered right now was their safety. And the anger simmering behind her expression told him she wasn't done fighting, which was good. It was going to take every ounce of courage they had to get them all out of here alive.

Paige jutted her chin toward Ngozi, who was momentarily distracted talking with one of the guards, then followed him to the hut. "Is he the leader here?"

"Second in command, from what I can figure out, and the father of one of the sick children."

"An advantage?"

Nick nodded. "He's genuinely worried about the child."

"What about Brandon, Samson, and the others?"

"Long story short, Brandon and Samson are fine, but Nigel was a mole and murdered Philip. He let them know where we were; then they brought us here."

She took a moment for the information to

sink in. "What are the chances of escape from here?"

"Extremely risky."

Clouds overhead opened up, allowing a sliver of moonlight to shine on the courtyard and letting him catch the intensity of her gaze along with the fatigue marking her expression. She'd probably fallen asleep in her scrubs in the clinic, then been jarred awake by the rebels. And now, her attempts to assess the situation were the only way to find a measure of control in the nightmarish situation.

Nick rubbed his stiff neck with his fingertips, longing for the same control she did. "The only problem in escaping is that even Samson, who knows this region better than any of us, isn't sure where we are. And we could tell from our arrival that the area surrounding the camp is heavily forested."

"And heavily guarded."

"Yeah." He stopped in front of the isolation hut. "You looked surprised to see me here."

"Shouldn't I be?" She glanced up at him, her eyes widened, her voice laced with resentment. "You were supposed to be out arranging our rescue. There are people dying in that camp."

"So you think this was my fault? I —"

"I'm sorry." She shook her head, reached out, and brushed her hand against his forearm, then dropped her arm to her side. "None of this is your fault. I'm exhausted, scared, and struggling with the daunting reality that I can't fix everything. And sometimes . . ." Her gaze dropped. "And sometimes it's hard to hold onto the fact that whatever happens around us, God is still in control of this mess."

He opened the solid wooden door to the isolation hut. She wasn't the only one struggling. "He is still in control."

"I know."

"I talked to Paul at the embassy, so he is aware of the situation at the camp." He kept his voice to a low whisper. "But our taxi was hijacked on the way to Kingani. Brandon and I believe that there's a mole somewhere in the embassy as well."

"So Paul doesn't know where you are now?"

"No." Nick hesitated at the doorway. "He's probably wondering why he can't get a hold of me."

"Nick, this has to end. The number of cholera cases has slowed some, but now measles is trickling through the population, and there's nothing I can do about it. I need to be at the camp, and I need those vaccines and supplies."

"I know." Nick glanced at Ngozi, who now walked toward them. "Let's deal with things here, then see what we can do about getting you back to the camp."

Nick ducked and entered the thatched-roof hut. The one window was shut, blocking out any chance for a breeze. He took in a stale breath of air. Sleeping outside on the hard ground hadn't been his first choice of accommodations, but it had obviously been better than the stifling heat inside one of the huts.

Inside the small room, six or seven mats covered the dirt floor where those diagnosed with measles slept. Along the edges of the room were bags of rice and corn and an assortment of pots and pans. Paige joined one of the nurses on the far side of the room where a little girl's forehead glistened in the light of a candle set on the table.

Paige opened up her medical bag and pulled out her stethoscope before addressing the nurse. "How many are sick?"

"Five children and one old woman."

Movement to the right caught Nick's attention. One of the children stiffened, then began to jerk. Nick shoved aside the pile of metal pots stacked beside the small girl's head. "Paige . . . she's having a seizure."

Ngozi pushed his way into the room. "What is happening?"

"I need you to move back now." Paige crossed the room. "Nick, hand me that blanket on the floor beside you, then time how long the seizure lasts."

Paige took the blanket from Nick, laid it beneath the young girl's head, then turned her onto her side. Nick pressed the light on his watch and started counting.

"I said, what is happening?" Ngozi's voice rose above the commotion in the hut. "That's my daughter."

"Please, sir. I need you to move back."

"You told me she had the measles."

Paige turned to the nurse, ignoring the man's interruptions. "Has she had a seizure before?"

"No."

In less than a minute, the jerking movements stopped. Paige leaned down and checked her breathing.

"Nick, hand me my medical bag."

Nick shut the door on the crowd gathering outside the hut, then stepped across the row of crying children to get the bag from the other side of the room.

Paige spoke to the nurse. "What are her other symptoms?"

"Fever, headache, rash . . . Just like the

386

other children. I thought it was the measles."

Paige glanced up at Ngozi, who hovered over his daughter. "What's her name?"

"Abah. Two days ago she was running and playing beneath the afternoon sun." Ngozi's expression darkened in the flickering candlelight. "Tell me what is wrong with her."

Paige wiped the back of her neck and shook her head. "It's impossible for me to be one hundred percent certain because I can't do any tests, but it looks as if she's contracted encephalitis. Typically, cases are mild and many even go unreported, but it can be life-threatening."

Ngozi took a step closer. "What is that?"

Abah lay still on the ground, her breathing regular again.

Paige set Abah's head against the mat, then rolled onto the balls of her feet. "Sometimes, when a child contracts a disease like the measles, they end up with secondary infections. More than likely, her immune system overreacted to the foreign substance in her, which in this case is the measles."

"What can you do?"

"I can try and treat her, but measles isn't the biggest problem here, and there are a number of risk factors working against her.

Her age, her weakened immune system . . . For now, we need to work to reduce both the fever and the brain swelling." Paige stood and faced Ngozi. "Your daughter is very sick, and while I'll do whatever I can to help her and the others who need medical help, I expect to be taken back to the camp once I'm done here."

"I don't believe you understand that you're not in a position to make demands—"

"I don't think you understand the severity of what is going on here, because what happens in the camp obviously affects what happens here. Some of your men have families in the camp, which is why the disease is here, isn't it? And that is why this disease will continue to spread and some of your wives and children will die if you don't let me do things my way."

"I had my orders to bring you here from the camp and to ensure no one leaves this compound."

"Do you have other children?"

Ngozi's gaze dropped. "My son's in here and I have another one due to come when the rains come again."

"Then you know how important it is to protect them. You've seen your daughter. I promise to do everything I can to help her, but there's an even bigger problem out there that I intend to deal with."

"I have my orders. The two of you are not going anywhere."

Paige stared at the door as Ngozi left the hut, slamming the door behind him. "What do you think?"

"He's scared he's going to lose her."

Paige knelt down beside her newest patient, who now lay sleeping again on the thin mat. "So am I."

FORTY-FIVE

Ashley squeezed her eyes shut to block out the morning sun. In a perfect world, she'd have pulled the shades before she went to bed, set the air conditioner to sixty-eight, then slipped under her down comforter and slept until eight or nine. She glanced at her watch. It wasn't even six o'clock. She never woke up before six. And the bubble surrounding her perfect world had long since burst.

Rolling onto her side, she groaned at the dull ache that spread throughout her legs and back. She'd pay a thousand bucks for a room with an air conditioner and a soft bed that didn't poke her arms and the back of her stiff neck with its scratchy reeds. She flinched, then itched beneath her elbow where a dozen mosquito bites added to her misery.

Several armed men sat on the other side of the compound eating and laughing and reminding her that her deplorable sleeping quarters were the least of her worries. She'd been right. If she somehow managed to avoid getting murdered in her sleep, she'd end up dying from some infectious disease.

Closing her eyes again, she drew in a smoky breath of air from the cooking fires and wondered how long it would take her mother to come up with the five million in cash. By now, she should have already contacted their lawyer and the bank and Mitch —

"Ashley?"

Ashley slit open one eye and let the blurry image of Taz register before she shut it again. "What do you want?"

"Good morning. Did you sleep okay?"

"There is nothing good about this morning, and once again, you sound far too perky. Do you know what time it is?"

"Time for breakfast. I just returned from talking to the cook, who told me that the menu for the day includes eggs Benedict, croissants, sausage, and fresh-squeezed orange juice."

She opened her eyes and shot him a dirty look. "Either I'm still dreaming or you've lost your mind, and for some reason I'm quite sure the first isn't true."

"Croissants and sausage is what I'm dreaming about at the moment."

Ashley studied the stubble on his face — reds and browns with a hint of gray. "It should be a federal offense to talk about buttery croissants when I'll be given some sort of . . . of mush for breakfast, if I get anything at all."

"Hmmm . . ." He brushed his thumb across her chin, then chuckled.

"What?"

"You smiled again."

"No, I didn't."

"Oh, you definitely did."

Ashley propped herself up on her elbows, annoyed with the way he could make her smile. And where their conversations always managed to take her train of thought. She should be thinking about Mitch. Not how much she enjoyed being with this geeky-lawyer-turned-humanitarian.

"Is having the ability to make you laugh such a bad thing?"

Ashley closed her eyes for a moment and pictured Mitch decked out in one of his expensive suits at one of their parties — rich foods, conversation, too much champagne . . . "It's not even six o'clock, so yes, that's a bad thing."

She pushed back a strand of her oily bangs, feeling self-conscious. No makeup, unkempt hair, and not even a chance to brush her teeth or take a decent shower for days. Mitch would be horrified at her unruly appearance. Taz didn't seem to notice.

Instead he sat down on the three-legged stool beside her, some of the worry he tried to hide seeping into his expression. "They brought Paige here last night after Nick and the others."

Ashley's eyes widened. "Is everyone okay?"

"Yeah. She and Nick are inside the isolation hut taking care of the sick children."

Ashley drew up her legs Indian style, then glanced around the compound, trying to convince herself there was nothing to worry about. Her mother would pay the ransom, they'd release her, and this whole nightmare would be forgotten, along with Taz and all the others.

Her breathing quickened. That was what she wanted. But experiences like this weren't things you brushed away like unimportant dates on one's social calendar.

The nurses from the camp sat talking in a small huddle. Brandon dozed on his mat, and Samson sat staring off into space. Scattered around them, the rebels guarded them, machine guns in hand, a reminder that they were still calling the shots.

She pulled out a long, dried piece of reed from her mat and twirled it between her fingers. "Do you ever think of dying?"

Taz flipped up the rim of his hat and peered at her. "Sometimes."

The dried reed crumbled between her fingers. "It scares me."

"My mother used to always tell me that death is a part of life. We just don't know when it's coming for us."

"And your faith?" She'd never looked for answers before. Never needed to. "What does it tell you about death?"

"That I can have confidence of where I'll spend eternity because of Christ's death on the cross and then his resurrection."

"He triumphed over death." She knew some of the lingo. What she didn't know was this man who claimed to be the Son of God. Didn't know why someone claiming to be the Son of God allowed things like this to happen in the world He supposedly created.

A car horn sounded from outside the compound, interrupting their conversation. Someone opened the gate, and two 4×4s entered the camp.

Ashley leaned forward. "What's going on?"

"I don't know. Jonas left late last night. Looks like he and some of his buddies are back."

Two more vehicles arrived and parked outside the compound. Car doors slammed shut and several more men, all wearing fatigues, entered through the metal gate.

Ashley reached up and touched the tender spot where Jonas had slapped her. "None of them look very happy."

Jonas stopped in the middle of the compound and fired a shot into the air. "I want you all lined up on that log. Now!"

Panic swept through her. "Taz . . ."

"Everything's going to be all right." Taz reached out and squeezed her hand. "They need your money, so they won't hurt you."

"You don't know that."

"Trust me." Taz kept hold of her hand and led her toward the fallen log, where they sat down on the end beside Samson, Brandon, and the four nurses.

Jonas paced in front of them, his fingers tight around the weapon. "Where is the doctor?"

A minute later, Paige and Nick emerged from the isolation hut in front of one of the guards.

Ashley dropped her gaze to the line of ants marching in front of the log. She closed her eyes and fought to breathe, trying to convince herself that Taz was right. Killing her would only guarantee they didn't get the ransom money. Something they wouldn't do. Her mother would never send money without proof of life. She just needed to take in a few deep breaths and remember that her mother would wire the money and all this would be over soon.

Jonas pulled a small digital camera from his pocket and tossed it to Ngozi, along with a wrapped-up newspaper. "I want individual photos of each of them holding up the front page."

Paige sat down on the other end of the log beside Nick. Apparently being a doctor didn't make her any more immune from the lineup than herself being worth a hefty ransom. Ngozi started at the far end and began snapping photos of each one of them.

Ashley's stomach burned.

Proof of life.

But Taz had been right. She was worth far more to them alive. They all were.

Jonas stood in front of them, his stance rigid, his expression cold. "Apparently, my government, along with the rest of the world, believes that our current demands are nothing more than a game, and if they simply ignore us, we will eventually disappear like a case of the measles."

Ngozi stopped in front of Ashley and handed her the newspaper before aiming the camera at her.

Oh God, if you are out there, please don't let this be the last photo my family sees of me.

"Until today," Jonas continued, "we've held negotiations in the capital, where we have sought a fair exchange for the release and amnesty of our leaders, but it is strange how quickly they have forgotten their own guilt. Seventeen years ago, my brother fought to help President Tau overthrow the old president to become our new president, but now? No one seems to remember."

Ashley squeezed Taz's hand. "Is he drunk?"

"I don't know."

Anger burned in Jonas' eyes. "We burn their villages, rape their women, and kill their men, but all they do is tell the world that everything is under control. That we are no more a threat than . . . than all of you are. But I'm through playing their diplomatic games. Tired of being the weak link they believe they can utilize as their scapegoat. So we've made a decision."

Jonas walked forward and stopped at the other end of the log. He lifted Paige's chin with the tip of his gun. "You think I am crazy?"

Paige's gaze dropped. "No."

"They made me what I am today and now they want to stop me."

"I think —"

Nick started to speak, but Paige tugged on his shirt and shook her head.

Jonas moved in front of Nick. "Let him say what he wants. I'm sure it is no different from what the rest of the world believes. They see us as savages who only want to butcher our people, but they do not know everything."

Nick cleared his throat. "Tell us what happened at the talks. Maybe one of us could go with you and help negotiate."

Jonas' laugh ran hollow. "You'd like that, wouldn't you? No, I have a much better idea. We've done everything to prove that we are serious and yet nothing has changed. Which means it is time for me to change things."

An ant crawled across Ashley's arm. She brushed it onto the ground and struggled to catch her breath. They were going to kill her. Kill all of them. Her life would end in the middle of some godforsaken country without a chance to say good-bye to Mitch.

Jonas continued down the row. One of the nurses sobbed silently. The wives and children of the rebels had vanished into the huts, but the men gathered around them, their attention on Jonas.

Jonas rested his hand against his hip. "There's only one thing that will make the rest of the world believe we're serious. Killing our own people has done nothing. Killing one of you . . . that will make them stop and listen."

"You're wrong."

Jonas spun around to face Nick, who was leaning forward. "Excuse me?"

"Violence hasn't changed the situation yet, and it's not going to now. If anything it will make them more determined to put a stop to what you are doing."

"Enough." Jonas swung the weapon toward Nick. "You have lost your privilege to talk. All of you have. All you suggest is more diplomacy, but I am finished walking down that path."

Ashley gasped for air. "Taz."

"Take a deep breath, Ashley."

"We've made a decision." Jonas continued his pacing in front of them. "As for now, the rules have changed. And you will pay the price."

Ashley felt her body go numb.

"Here's the new deal." All emotion had vanished from Jonas' face "One dead, every twelve hours, until they agree to our demands. Maybe then the world will finally decide to listen to what we have to say."

Paige gasped from the other side of the log. "You can't —"

Jonas pointed the gun in her direction. "Oh, but I can. I just haven't decided who will go first."

Jonas moved down the line slowly. He paused, aimed his weapon at Brandon's head, then kept moving.

Ashley's heart pounded in her throat. It was Russian roulette, and one of them was going to die.

Taz squeezed her hand. "Whatever happens, you're going to be okay."

Jonas hesitated in front of her. "Five million dollars will extend your life . . . for now."

He took another step to the left and stopped in front of Taz.

Ashley felt a scream swell in her throat, but she couldn't move, couldn't breathe. Taz's fingers slipped from hers. The sky above her began to spin. Her vision blurred.

Jonas pressed his gun against Taz's head and pulled the trigger.

FORTY-SIX

Friday, February 25, 7:01 a.m.
U.S. Embassy, RD

Paul turned up the radio and leaned back in his office chair to listen to the broadcast, nursing his sore throat with another steamy cup of hot tea. He didn't have to listen to the news to know that the situation was turning into the nightmare he'd hoped to avoid. All he had to do was look outside the embassy's front windows at the chaos brewing in the city streets.

. . . many believe that what started out as a plea for amnesty has now turned into an attempt to overthrow President Tau's government. Fear has forced hundreds to flee to the U.S. Embassy compound and other foreign agencies, many with everything they own, in an attempt to find refuge from the rebels and their newest rampage in the capital.

Organizations like the UN and Volunteers

for Hope International, a nonprofit organization that provides temporary medical staffing, have already lost hundreds of thousands of U.S. dollars worth of medical supplies, communications equipment, and food when the rebels hijacked a convoy and raided food warehouses earlier this week.

With the rebels now roaming the capital, the government has extended the state of emergency from the Mponi region to the entire country and has imposed a six o'clock curfew that is being enforced by checkpoints and truckloads of armed soldiers. But fears continue to escalate as to whether or not that is enough to contain the rebels, and if the government's slow response will end up costing more lives.

One of the biggest concerns at the moment remains with the humanitarian workers who were taken hostage in the northern section of the country. Rebels have publicly announced that they have threatened to execute a hostage every twelve hours until their long list of demands are met.

A State Department spokesman has verified that marine expeditionary units are on alert, and it is expected that they will head to the RD to aid in the evacuation of the roughly three hundred and fifty remaining Americans within the next twenty-four hours. Most of the

Americans currently in the country are religious and humanitarian aid workers, businessmen, and U.S. Embassy employees and their dependants . . .

Paul turned down the radio before grabbing the folder Mercy had brought him. He dumped its pile of black-and-white photos onto the desk in front of him. They confirmed his suspicions that his embassy held a mole. Until four months ago, he'd been lulled into thinking that the RD was different from places like Chad and Sudan, where threats of uprisings were often quickly squelched by a government whose aim was to paint a picture of democracy and peace to the rest of the world.

Nick failing to check in last night in Kingani had been the first clue that that wasn't true. The photos in front of him reconfirmed that fear. They showed proof of life for Paige Ryan, Nick Gilbert, Ashley James, Brandon Collins, and four national aid workers — and that Timothy Gregory Michaels III had been executed in cold blood. He glanced at the photo of Timothy's lifeless body in the middle of some godforsaken compound. Six years of humanitarian work in refugee camps from Kenya to Chad . . . The thirty-two-year-old former lawyer from Chicago didn't deserve this.

Man, he hated this place.

His cell phone rang, jarring him from his contemplations. He flipped it open and answered the call. "Paul Hayes speaking."

"This is James Ngani."

"I was getting ready to call you."

"I heard about the rebels taking the missing Americans as hostages."

Paul took another sip of his tea, thankful that any formalities and long-winded greetings had been saved for another day. His voice wasn't going to make it much longer, and neither was his patience. "They're not just empty threats. They killed the first hostage about an hour ago and are threatening to kill another one every twelve hours until all charges are dropped. Which means I can't wait another twelve hours."

He knew that Timothy's death, and that of the other foreigners, was merely a drop in the bucket compared to how many Dhambizans had lost their lives during the conflict, but if some fancy diplomatic footwork could put an end to the crisis, then it would end up stopping the loss of life on both sides.

"Ground forces are organizing now and should be heading out within the hour." Ngani paused on the other end. "What about the location of the camp?"

"Our military experts are working on it using satellites."

Paul ripped the wrapper off one of the cough drops in his pocket and popped the lozenge into his mouth, hoping it would ease his sore throat better than the hot tea. And hoping Ngani bought his exaggeration. If he had his way, American surveillance planes would already be in the air trying to pinpoint the rebels' location, but even in his position, he could only make things move so fast.

He cleared his throat, this time sprinkling a bit of truth into the mixture. "Congressional leaders were notified just after six-thirty this morning when we received these faxes. I haven't gotten the official go-ahead, but I am expecting the White House to agree to a rescue operation."

Paul thumbed the edge of one of the photos. Apparently it took a handful of dead citizens to get Washington to make a decision. Which might not be fair, but he was sick of red tape when people's lives were on the line.

"From the looks of the uproar in the capital, we're going to need all the help we can get." Paul crunched down on the cough drop. "So, like you, I need this to end.

Which means we need to locate not only the camp, but the location of every key rebel leader." Paul's mind flew through his limited options. "What about the arrested leaders? Can we dig information out of them?"

"We've tried, but our intelligence has confirmed that the rebels have moved camps since the arrests were made."

"Any communication between the two groups?"

"None. In fact, the rebels who were arrested are being transferred to a higher-security facility today to insure that doesn't change."

An idea took root in the back of Paul's mind. If they couldn't find a way to locate the camp, the next best thing was to defuse the rebels' fighting power by taking down more of their leaders. And in the process, they might just discover the location of the camp. "Who knows about the transfer?"

"Only a handful of people. Even I haven't been told where they're being taken."

Paul tapped his fingers against his desk. There were only three or four secure prisons in the country. Maybe it was time he used the mole to his advantage. "I've got an idea."

FORTY-SEVEN

Friday, February 25, 8:12 a.m.
Rebel Base Camp

Paige folded her hands together to stop them from trembling. The combination of lack of sleep and food had dropped her blood pressure and left her feeling light-headed. And the fact that in another ten hours one of them could be lying in a freshly dug plot beside Taz if something didn't change hadn't helped the rising panic pressing hard against her chest.

She drew in a labored breath. She'd been the one who'd frantically tried in vain to breathe life back into Taz's limp body, and now all she could see was the vivid image of Jonas' gun, Taz's body slipping from the log onto the hard ground, and Ashley scream-ing . . .

Her fingers clamped onto the fabric of her shirt as another wave of dizziness hit. She reached for one of the small, red bananas the women had brought with breakfast. As much as she didn't want to eat, not eating would only mess further with her blood sugar and make things worse. Not that the situation could get much worse. She hadn't believed Jonas would follow through with his threat. Hadn't truly believed he'd pulled the trigger. But he had. And now she couldn't help but wonder how many more were going to die before this nightmare was over.

"Paige."

She looked up at Nick, who sat beside her on the reed mat, and studied his day-old stubble and the creases along his forehead that seemed more pronounced today. They'd let him stay with her in the isolation hut, making him the one anchor in a world quickly drifting out of control, but even his presence couldn't erase the horror of the situation.

"I'm sorry." She shook her head. "I missed what you were saying."

"Don't be sorry. We're all distracted." Nick blew on the tin mug of coffee he held, then shot her a smile that managed to help calm the churning inside her. "How's Ashley?"

"I had to give her a sedative so she would sleep."

Nick scratched the back of his neck. "Unfortunately, things aren't going to get better unless we can find a way out of here."

Paige glanced at one of the rebels, who sat dozing under a shade tree. At the moment, no one seemed to notice their presence. Brandon and Samson had joined them a few moments ago without any comment from the guards, but she knew that the rules — whatever they were — could change in an instant and they could all be separated.

Brandon nodded at Nick's observation. "Especially now that it's clear the rebels have every intention of following through with their threats. We have to find a way to communicate with the outside world."

Nick took another sip of his drink, then cleared his throat. "We can be fairly certain that the embassy knows we're in the camp because of the photos they took, but as far as we know, no one knows the exact location of the camp."

"That is the problem." Samson spoke up for the first time. "We might have narrowed it down for them, but these forests are thick and dense and go on forever."

Paige's frown deepened. "It still could take days for them to locate where we are."

Nick tossed the rest of his coffee onto the ground behind them, leaving a dark line across the red dirt. "And time is not something we have in abundance."

"We could try to break into their supply hut." Samson nodded toward the far edge of the compound. "I am certain they have communication equipment stored in there."

Paige mulled over the idea. From what she'd gathered from talking with Nick, and from her own observations, this camp, while newly established, was the rebels' main base. Communication with the other rebel fronts scattered throughout the country was done by both radios and cell and satellite phones, which allowed them tactical coordination and the element of surprise. The fact that the RD didn't have the technology to trace those calls and locate their position gave them yet another advantage.

"All we need is access to a satellite phone." Brandon shoved his breakfast aside, clearly intrigued with the idea. "Most have advanced GPS signals, and if we called the embassy, there's a good chance the U.S. military could pick up our location."

Paige shook her head. In her mind, the risk was still far too great. "There are at least twenty-five to thirty guards surrounding this compound at all times. I don't see how breaking into their supply hut is even a possibility."

Nick picked up a stick and began doodling in the dirt. "She's right. They're everywhere. We'd never get past them."

Paige reached up and rubbed her temples, which wouldn't stop pounding. The pain didn't help when trying to come up with a foolproof escape plan. She looked toward the isolation hut where she'd spent the past few hours. She was only out here now because Ngozi had agreed she could take a short break to eat the breakfast the women had prepared for them. Her time could be up at any minute.

They needed that satellite equipment. And if they couldn't break in . . .

Paige's gaze snapped back to the hut. "What about Ngozi?"

"What about him?" Nick asked.

"I think I might be able to get him to help us."

Brandon shook his head. "Why would he ever agree to do that?"

"Because his daughter's situation is deteriorating." She pressed her hands against her thighs. "Serious cases of encephalitis are difficult to treat because too often the disease doesn't respond to medications. But there are some antiviral drugs that could help reduce the swelling and pressure in her skull. Without them, though, her chances to

411

survive are slim."

Nick's eyes brightened. "Which might just give us the leverage we need."

"Maybe." Brandon scratched the back of his neck. His motivation to leave came from more than just Jonas' threats. The fact that Jodi had been left at the camp with little if any medical help had them both worried. "But it still sounds like a pretty big risk to me. If he doesn't want to help us, then he'll tell Jonas, and we'll end up paying with our lives. Or what if he knows the call could be traced?"

Nick snapped his stick in half. "These guys were trained to be soldiers, and while their leaders might take precautions by switching phones and limiting their airtime, I doubt that most of them know much about this kind of technology."

"He's right." The guard stirred, so Paige lowered her voice as a precaution. "I'm not saying it's not a risk, but I don't think we have a choice. Ngozi is different from the others. He believes in the rebels' cause, but he also cares deeply for his daughter, and I don't think he's willing to let her die."

"You think you can convince him to let us use the phone?"

Paige nodded. "Just let me talk to him."

Nick glanced at his watch. "I think it's the

best option we've got so far. Whatever we do, it's going to take time to get someone here, and we're going to have to move quickly. I don't plan on burying another body tonight."

Brandon nodded toward the gate. "I haven't seen Jonas for the past couple hours, but Nzogi's here."

Nick grabbed Paige's hand, lacing their fingers together as she stood. "Be careful. Promise me."

Paige nodded at his tender expression, closed her eyes for a brief moment, then started across the dusty compound and started praying. She could do this.

"Ngozi."

He leaned against the cinder-block wall near the front gate, smoking a cigarette. "What?"

"I need to talk to you about your daughter." She studied his dark, leathery expression, praying for a way to invoke his help, not his anger. "She's not doing well."

"That is why I brought you here."

"That might not be enough. Your daughter is very sick, and if I don't get the proper medicines, she's going to die." Paige paused. "I need access to a satellite phone."

Ngozi flicked his cigarette butt onto the dirt, then turned back to face her. "You cannot be serious?"

Paige caught the irritation in his voice, but knew she couldn't back down now. "There are certain medicines that will lessen the swelling of the brain and stop the seizures."

Ngozi shook his head. "Even if I had access to one, do you actually think I would allow you to use it?"

"Your daughter's life is on the line."

"You are bluffing."

"No, I'm not. You've seen her. She'll die without the necessary treatment."

"Even if it is true, you know I cannot do what you are asking."

"Why not? I know you love your daughter. I've seen the way you treat her, and the way you ask about her. I want to help. We aren't near any hospitals, and even if we were, I would assume that as one of the rebel leaders your photo has been posted in every police station from here to the capital. This is the quickest way I know of to get her the help she needs."

Ngozi pulled out a matchbox from his pocket and lit another cigarette. "What exactly are you proposing?"

"Nick has a friend who could fly in on a helicopter with the medicine I need. All he would need to do is drop off the supplies, then leave."

"Jonas would kill me if he found out that I took a risk like this."

"Then we make sure Jonas doesn't find out."

Ngozi took in another long drag. "I don't know."

"We need that medicine, Ngozi. You can save your daughter. It's up to you."

"Jonas is gone and won't be back until late tonight." Ngozi glanced at his watch for a moment as if still debating his answer. "I could organize the drop site away from the compound, but only if Nick goes with me. And the only person I want on that aircraft is the pilot. No one else. He makes the drop and leaves while I hold a gun to Nick's head. If anything goes wrong, Nick dies."

Paige weighed her options. If they wanted to get out alive, this might be their only chance. And she knew Nick would agree. She drew in a deep breath, then nodded her head. "It's a deal. Now get me that phone."

FORTY-EIGHT

Friday, February 25, 4:04 p.m.
Fifty Kilometers From The Rebel Base Camp

The rugged 4×4 Land Cruiser rattled beneath Nick as Ngozi drove the vehicle down the narrow road edged by towering trees and thick, green undergrowth. Gripping the door handle to keep himself from whacking his head against the window, he glanced at the older man's weathered profile. Determination and concern marked his expression, but time would tell as to whether or not his concern for his daughter had truly triumphed over his rebel loyalties. Nick just had to make sure he didn't get caught in the middle of the man's conflicting ideals.

Ngozi hit another pothole, confirming Nick's belief that the truck's shocks and suspension were gone and making him wonder how much more abuse the vehicle — and his own body — could take. No air conditioner meant a constant barrage of

dust and thick, humid air that made breathing harder. A short stint on a paved road
and through a decent-sized town had been
sandwiched between long bouts of weaving
through the bush, past smaller compounds
with thatched huts and a mélange of animals, like chickens and goats, who ran loose
in the dirt yards.

But after more than an hour of rough
roads, he just wanted to put an end to this
mess. Which meant he had to rely on Paul
for more than just the medicine at the drop-
off site. The lives of Paige and Brandon —
all of them — hung in the balance.

Paige.

The thought of her sweet smile brought
with it a tinge of anticipation. He hadn't
expected his attraction to deepen into
something that made him long to be with
her, but over the past few days she'd become
the one light in the midst of a dark tunnel.
With the refugee camp as a backdrop, he'd
watched her skills as a doctor paired with
her strong sense of justice and a streak of
vulnerability.

Not that she'd ever admit she needed
rescuing.

He gazed out the window at the forest
with its layers of green bushes, ferns, plants,
and trees. The sun had already reached its

zenith, but his normal keen sense of direction had been thrown off by a road that had twisted and turned for the past fifty or sixty miles. Which meant all he could do now was trust Paul's ability to track the satellite phone Nick had used, so he could throw a rescue party together before Jonas made good on his threat.

Nick looked across the worn leather seats at Ngozi. After an hour in the car with no conversation, maybe it was time to break the silence. "I'm amazed at how you can find your way on this . . . well, technically, I'm not sure I'd call it a road."

Ngozi's frown deepened. Apparently, he didn't like Nick's attempt at humor. "I grew up in this region."

"And your family?"

"My parents and all my brothers and sisters are dead. All I have now is Jonas and the other men."

"And Abah, her mother, and brother."

Ngozi didn't respond. He simply stared out the cracked window shield.

"Dr. Ryan is an incredible doctor, and she'll do everything she can to save your daughter. You've got to trust her."

"Why?" Ngozi's fingers gripped the steering wheel. "I don't trust you any more than you trust me."

"Maybe not, but Dr. Ryan has a strong sense of duty, and she won't let any . . . any personal feelings get in the way of trying to save your daughter's life."

Thick brush opened into a small clearing, large enough for a helicopter to land, enclosed enough to provide covering. Ngozi brought the vehicle to a stop along the edge of a long patch of tall grasses blowing in the midday wind.

Ngozi turned to him and nodded. "This is the drop-off point. I hope for your sake your friend comes alone."

Fifteen minutes later, the helo touched down, bringing with it a swirling cloud of dirt and countless memories of landings in Tallil, where the surrounding terrain had been scarred by years of war. At the moment, things were no different here.

A twenty-something-year-old man stepped down from the chopper, shouting above the whirl of the blades. "It's good to see you, Nick. I've got the supplies you asked for."

Nick looked to Ngozi before sliding out of the vehicle. "All I'm going to do is pick up the medicine, and he can leave."

"Not without me."

Ngozi slid from the vehicle behind Nick, looking nervous. Fear from the possibility of Jonas finding out what he'd done? Or worse perhaps, that this was a setup. Nick sent up a short prayer, like he'd done a hundred times over the past week, because even he didn't know what the entire plan was. His conversation with Paul had been brief and to the point. All he could do right now was go with his gut and play this out.

Movement behind him shifted Nick's attention. Ngozi had drawn his pistol and was pointing it at the pilot.

"Ngozi! What are you —"

A shot rang out. The pilot slumped to the ground, landing face down.

Nick started for the man, then stopped at Ngozi's barking order and the telltale cock of the hammer.

"Do not move." Ngozi turned his weapon on Nick. "There has been a change of plans."

"He needs help."

"It is already too late for your friend."

Nick turned away. This wasn't supposed to have happened. The drop had been a way to get Paul the GPS coordinates and them the medicine they needed. Nothing else. And no one was supposed to die.

Just like in Iraq.

Nick turned back to Ngozi, the anger in his voice raw. "You didn't have to do that."

"You really think I am stupid enough to

trust you?" Ngozi aimed the weapon at Nick. "This was always about more than just picking up medicines, though I am grateful for your concern for my daughter."

Nick shook his head. "I still don't understand."

"I guess you wouldn't have heard about the state of emergency declared by our government, or the curfew they set in the capital in an attempt to squelch our movement. And apparently, with the recent attacks by some of our men in the capital, the government feared we might try and liberate our leaders ourselves and decided to move them to an *undisclosed* location. Fortunately for us, we know they are being transported today from the capital to a prison outside Kasili, making a rescue much easier than from a state prison cell."

"So that's where Jonas went this morning? To hijack a prison convoy?"

"It's a long drive across the north of the country, but he should have enough time to locate the transport vehicle before they reach the prison."

"How did he find out?"

"We have our own sources of intel inside your own embassy."

"And the plan now?"

"To kill you like your friend, of course."

"Except that would leave you with a problem, because you've just killed the pilot." Nick dug up his only trump card. "Fortunately for you, I can help. I flew Black Hawks in the Middle East for two years."

"Impressive, but your government isn't the only one capable of training their soldiers. I too am a pilot and perfectly capable of flying this helo without your help."

Any idea of escaping vanished into the humid, late-afternoon air.

"And since we promised to deliver another dead body —"

"It's not been twelve hours yet."

Ngozi glanced at his watch. "Close enough."

FORTY-NINE

Jonas pressed on the accelerator of his 4×4, ready to put an end to the almost twelve hours of driving. Killing the American might not have been his original plan, but neither had he anticipated the stubbornness of his government. He'd expected them to give in quickly to their demands in order to bury the problem. Instead, their unwillingness to compromise had become the motivating factor that had eventually driven him to make a stand they would not be able to fight against.

And this time he had no intention of losing.

He knew how these things worked. The death of one white man was enough to raise the sleeping giants from their slumber and for his government to finally see things his way.

A glance out the back window confirmed that the other two vehicles were right behind him. Warfare across the country had changed since his brother had first risen up as a leader. Satellite phones made it possible to communicate instantly with the next village or the other side of the country. Which meant all he needed to stay in business was a few Land Cruisers and a way to communicate that enabled him to run the battle they fought from anywhere. The phones also made assembling forces in the capital or coordinating raids in the Mponi region fairly quick and effortless.

Like today.

His mole in the American embassy had finally given him the break he'd been waiting for. And if everything went as planned, the attack would be over before anyone had time to even realize what had happened. Nor would it matter any longer what the ICC or the Dzambizan government said. In another few hours, five million American dollars would sit in his account, his brother would be free, and he wouldn't care where he was — as long as he was as far away as possible from here.

Jonas smiled as an unmarked vehicle came into view, matching the description he'd been given. He signaled the other drivers behind him, then sped to catch up. They'd prepared for weeks for a possible ground assault against the army, waiting only until an opportunity like today's to present itself. Within minutes, his brother would be free and the rest of the world would realize who now stood in control.

The rotating whirl of a helicopter caught Jonas off guard. A tire exploded beneath his Land Cruiser and the vehicle jerked to the right, spinning out of control. He fought against the wheel, his head smashing against the window. The sound of shattering glass and metal grinding pounded in his ears until, finally, the vehicle skidded to a stop.

Jonas fought to catch his bearing. Men, wearing fatigues and carrying assault weapons, exited the white van they'd been chasing and approached him. His men from the other vehicles stood nearby, their hands held high in defeat.

Jonas searched for an escape, but there was no way out. And no sign of his brother.

Blood dripped down the side of his face as Jonas stepped from the vehicle. He raised his hands and sank down against the African soil.

FIFTY

Nick caught a flash of movement out of the corner of his left eye. Something moved on the ground beside them.

The pilot?

Ngozi's gaze shifted momentarily. Nick's instinct to survive, paired with years of military training, took over. He stepped toward Ngozi, moving out of the line of fire, then struck hard above the man's wrists, knocking away his weapon before pinning the man to the ground.

The _dead_ pilot tossed him a pair of handcuffs. "Corporal Sam Mills, U.S. Marines, sir."

"Nick Gilbert, but I guess you already knew that." Nick shoved his knee into Ngozi's back and tightened his grip. "I thought you were dead."

Mills pulled up the bottom of his shirt.

"Thanks to a bulletproof vest and the fact that you've got lightning reflexes, I'm not."

Nick locked the cuffs, then jerked Ngozi to his feet, still dealing with the rush of adrenalin at almost getting shot. "And this was your plan?"

With a hand still gripping his chest, Mills nodded, then managed to stand. "Sort of."

"Sort of? He shot you point blank."

"I'd actually hoped I wouldn't need the vest." Mills pulled out the embedded bullet. The guy'd be sore for days. "And you're right: this was too close a call. But once I realized his intention was to kill us both, I decided playing dead might be our only way out."

"It was a very bad plan." Nick frowned. He was getting tired of close calls. "But at least you're alive."

"At least we're both alive."

"So what —"

Nick stopped midsentence. Two dozen uniformed soldiers emerged from the forest, guns cocked and looking ready for a fight.

You've got to be kidding.

"You're late, guys." Mills shouted at the men, then turned back to Nick. "Don't worry. These are the good guys. The ambush was supposed to be before I even got out of the helo, but I was worried that might alert your rebel friend that something was off."

"You did good, Corporal." Fatigue washed over Nick. "What are the rest of your orders?"

"We're to head for the rebel base camp to provide any necessary backup."

"Then let's get out of here."

Fifteen minutes later, the camp came into view. Mills landed the helo beside a second bird and a line of Humvees and army trucks. From the looks of things, the radio report they'd received en route was correct and the camp had already been secured by the RD army and a handful of U.S. Marines.

Nick exited the helo and entered the compound. Finding Paige was first on his priority list. Rebels lay facedown in the dirt, hands cuffed behind them, legs spread. Against the cinder-block wall lay a row of bodies covered with sheets.

Gunfire had been exchanged. Where was she?

He rushed past a group of women and children, looking for whoever was in charge. Someone had set up a communications center on a rickety wooden table, a contrast to the hi-tech satellite phone and other communication equipment sitting on top of it.

"Nick?"

Nick turned around. Brandon stood there, a heavy fatigue registering in his eyes. "You leaving?"

"Yeah. We just got word that the surprise attack on the refugee camp was successful. The military is going to airlift Jodi from the camp, and I'll meet her in the capital in a couple hours. I don't think I've ever been so relieved in my life."

"You should be. I know this trip has been a nightmare for you. Get back home, then take your wife down to some tropical locale in the Pacific for a couple weeks."

Brandon laughed. "Knowing Jodi and her stubbornness, she'll be begging to return so she can finally climb that mountain." His smile faded. "Something like this can only happen once in a lifetime, right?"

"Let's hope so." Nick's gaze scoured the compound beyond Brandon. "Have you seen Paige?"

"I think she was in the isolation hut when the rescue started."

"Thanks." Nick reached out and shook the man's hand before heading toward the familiar hut.

He found her on the far side of the compound, tending to the wounds of one of the rebel's wives. Relief flooded through him as he stopped to study Paige's profile. The strip of dirt smudged on her cheekbone, her dark hair pulled back in a ponytail, the mark of determination in her expression.

He stopped about ten feet from where she worked. "Paige?"

She looked up, the smile on her face all for him. She pressed her hands against her thighs, stood, and walked toward him. "Thank God you're alive. I was so worried something happened to you."

"Actually, I was worried about you."

"This whole experience has been terrifying, but I'm okay."

She wrapped her arms around his neck and nestled her chin into his shoulder. She smelled like campfire, smoke, and disinfectant, and he was sure all she wanted was a hot shower and a safe place to sleep for the next week, but all he could think about was how her nearness teased his senses.

Boy, he could get used to this.

"Trust me, I'm very much alive." He caught her gaze and grinned. The scene around him faded as he reached down and kissed her. He felt her respond, cautiously at first, then more intensely as the kiss deepened.

She took a step back after a moment, breathless, but still smiling. "My emotions are already so spun out of control, I'm not sure my heart can handle falling for such a handsome hero."

He entwined her fingers with his, realizing that for his own heart, there was going to be no turning back. "We can take things slow."

"I'd like that." Her cheeks turned a rosy shade of pink as she looked up at him beneath her long lashes. "I just talked with someone from the RD military. The refugee camp has been secured along with this camp, plus Jonas and most of the key rebel leaders have been taken into custody."

Maybe this nightmare really was over.

He cleared his throat and studied her expression, unsure of what her response was going to be. "I've been asked to return to Bogama for the next couple days. For security reasons, the embassy wants all foreigners evacuated until they are certain the situation is under control. I can get you to the capital in time for your flight out in the morning."

"I . . . I've decided to stay."

He wasn't sure he'd heard her correctly. "You're staying?"

"The thought of leaving has been on the forefront of my mind ever since I arrived at the camp, but now that it's time for me to go I realize that this is where I need to be right now."

"You're sure?"

"You sound as if you're trying to talk me out of extending my stay —"

"No." He brushed his fingers across her hair. "There's nothing I want more than for you to stay. I just . . . I just thought that you accomplished what you came for and were ready to leave. The cholera treatment center is up and running, the mortality rate has dropped almost to normal, you have the vaccines for the camp . . ."

"But there's still so much left I can do. It's taken me a long time to realize that while I might not be able to save them all, it's worth the risk for the ones I can save." He caught a new sense of peace in her expression. "The women and children in this camp have nothing now. We're going to transport them to the refugee camp temporarily until something permanent can be arranged. Samson will be coming back to the camp with me in hopes he can find his family."

He cupped her face with his hands and kissed her again, savoring the moment. "Then promise me you'll be careful, because as soon as I'm finished, I'll come find you."

She smiled up at him and nodded. "I'll be waiting."

FIFTY-ONE

Paul folded the letter-sized paper into thirds, slid it into the envelope, then dropped it onto his desk. The cold medicine he'd taken this morning had left him groggy without alleviating his symptoms, and over the past few days, his cough had turned into a nasty rattle deep in his chest. He eyed the bottle of Tylenol perched on the edge of his desk. He'd take one if he wasn't already overdosed on a half dozen other over-the-counter meds. At this point, he had a better chance of surviving a firing squad than getting rid of this cold.

"I understand congratulations are in order."

Paul glanced up at the open doorway. The ambassador stood leaning against the door frame, dressed in a blue button-down shirt and tie, with his arms folded across

434

his chest.

Paul cleared his throat. "Welcome back. I thought you weren't going to be able to get a flight in until tomorrow."

"I was able to catch a private plane from Kinshasa. And I apologize for missing all the action. Though I understand you did fine without me."

"It's good to have you back, sir." Paul took a step back and reached for a tissue to blow his nose. "But I wouldn't get too close if I were you. A week without sleep hasn't helped me shake this blasted cold."

"Then why aren't you at home?"

Paul tossed the tissue into the already full trash can beside his desk. "I had some paperwork to finish up, but I'm heading there now."

"Good, because you look awful."

Paul ignored the ambassador's grin. "Thanks."

"On the up side, helping to save an entire refugee camp and splintering what was left of the rebel group isn't bad for a week's work."

Paul dismissed the praise. While finding a way to divide the rebel forces between the refugee camp, the rebel base camp, and a bogus prison convoy had worked, he hadn't been one of the forces on the ground. "We got lucky, but we also had a lot of good men out there risking their lives."

"I understand your assistant wasn't quite so lucky."

Paul reached up and scratched his day-old beard. His attempts to trap the mole relaying information to the rebel base camp had worked better than he'd expected, but he'd never wanted to believe Mercy was behind the intel leaks.

"They arrested Mercy outside the embassy Friday afternoon after it was confirmed she was the one who had passed on the false information I gave her about the prison convoy. Turns out that one of the leaders of the Ghost Soldiers rotting in prison right now is her fiancé."

The subsequent arrests over the weekend of key rebel leaders and dozens of their soldiers had turned out to be a fatal blow to the rebel faction. And for Paul, it helped to alleviate the sting of Mercy's betrayal. It had also managed to scatter any remaining rebels, essentially guaranteeing that the bloody conflict was finally over.

The ambassador shook his head. "None of my ex-wives would have risked prison for me."

"And your current wife?"

Paul felt the automatic twinge of regret

over his too personal comment, but the ambassador only laughed. "One day when we've got a free afternoon and a full bottle of Jack Daniels, we'll discuss the vices of our wives."

"That day might have to wait, sir." Paul hesitated a moment, then picked up the envelope from the desk. "There is something else I need to mention."

"What's that?"

"I was going to give this to you tomorrow, but since you're here now . . ." Paul handed the envelope to his boss.

The ambassador ripped it open and started reading the letter. "You're resigning?"

"Yeah."

"I don't understand."

"My wife needs me, and it's time I was there for her."

"Wait a minute. You haven't slept for days, you need to see a doctor . . ." The ambassador leaned forward. "Listen. I'll grant you a leave of absence. As much time as you want."

Paul shook his head. "It's the end of the line for me. If I don't walk away now, my marriage will be over, and I don't want that to happen."

The ambassador tapped his fingers against

his chest. "Look at me. Vices aside, I'm juggling a marriage and a career. It can be done."

"Now that says a lot coming from a man who's now on his — what is it, third wife?"

"Fourth." The ambassador dropped the letter back onto the desk in defeat. "So don't use me as an example."

"I've taken my family for granted for too long. I've decided that it's time I started being a husband to my wife."

He already had it planned out. He'd find some quiet, nine-to-five job where no one was trying to blow him up or where he had to save the world. Come summer vacation, he'd take the kids to Disney World and Maggie away for their next anniversary. He was going to spend Christmas with his family, celebrate the twins' birthday with his parents, start going to church again, and maybe — if he found the time — write that book he'd always wanted to write.

"You're too good to walk away from this, Paul, and I'll make sure all my acquaintances in Washington know that. Besides, you'd hate working behind a desk all day."

Paul couldn't help but laugh. "So now that I'm quitting you're going to broadcast my worth to all of DC?"

"Just promise me you'll think about it."

The ambassador leaned against the desk. "I can get you a raise, a new post in Europe . . ."

None of that even mattered anymore.

"Twenty years ago I'd have jumped at the offer. But if I leave now . . ." He glanced at the photo of his twins. "I might just be able to save my marriage."

The ambassador moved toward the door, a sliver of approval registering in the older man's eyes. "If you ever change your mind, let me know."

FIFTY-TWO

Ashley stepped from the private jet and drew in a deep breath of LA smog. It seemed like a million years ago since she and her father had left for their trip to the RD. Even the hot shower she'd taken at the embassy had done little to wash away the grime of the past week. Or the raw reality that she'd returned without her father.

Her mom stood at the bottom of the mobile staircase, dressed as if she were going to one of her charity fund-raisers. Hair coiffured by Bobby, perfect French nails. Ashley felt her heart pound. This was her world. Had been her world. But as much as she wanted to simply erase the past week of her life she knew she never would be able to forget. And that because of it she'd never be the same.

Ashley slid on her sunglasses, hoping the

440

dark lenses would cover her red, swollen eyes. "Mom. Thanks for picking me up."

Her mom greeted her on the runway and kissed her on the cheek.

Grief engulfed her until she could hardly breathe. "Daddy's gone. I'm so sorry . . ."

"I know." Her mom pressed her lips together. Her tears would come later and only in private.

Hanging on to the last bit of composure she could muster, Ashley scanned the quiet airfield as they walked toward the private terminal. "Where's Mitch?"

"Mitch couldn't come." Her mom looped her arm through Ashley's. "He had something come up he had to take care of, but he promised to come over later tonight. We'll have a family dinner. Your brother and sister-in-law are flying in later today. We have funeral arrangements to discuss." Her mother's voice choked up. "I know your father and I didn't always agree on things, but I never stopped loving him."

"I know."

Her mom stopped just inside the entrance and handed Ashley a small, zippered bag. "You'll need to redo your makeup in the car. There is a press conference scheduled in less than an hour at your father's house. I told reporters you were flying into another airfield, or they'd be here right now."

Ashley shook her head. "A press conference?"

"When you and your father leave on some crazy mountain climbing adventure halfway around the world and one of you returns in a coffin it makes international news."

"I'm not doing a press conference."

"You have an obligation to your fans, and besides, it's good publicity."

"I'm not obligated to tell the press anything. My father died along with a good friend of mine. I'm not looking for publicity out of this."

Her mother's heels clicked against the tiled floor. "Don't be a fool, Ashley. Despite the horrors of the situation, this could help skyrocket your career."

Disgust washed through her, but before she could respond, an older woman stepped forward. Her clothes were plain, black slacks and a white-flowered blouse. Hair neatly combed, not styled like her mother's.

"I'm sorry." Ashley's mom stopped in front of the woman. "This is Mrs. Michaels. The mother of that boy who died over there in the camp. She called and asked if she could see you —"

"Taz?" Ashley's breath caught in her throat.

"I'm sorry to bother you. I just needed . . . wanted to meet you, and your mother graciously agreed. I understand that you were with him the past few days."

Ashley nodded, then stepped forward to give the woman a hug. "I'm so sorry for your loss. I didn't know Taz for long, but he went out of his way to help me in a very difficult situation. He was a good friend."

"Taz was always like that. He could never pass up helping anyone in need."

Ashley glanced down at her wrist, then tugged off the giraffe bracelet. "This was Taz's. I think he'd want you to have it. He loved you, and while I'm not sure I'll ever completely understand why he did what he did living over there, he died doing what he believed in."

Mrs. Michaels slid the bracelet back onto Ashley's wrist. "Somehow, I think he'd want you to have it."

Ashley felt the unexpected connection with the older woman. "We could go get some breakfast and talk."

Relief showed in the woman's eyes. "I'd like that."

"So would I."

Ashley's mom was shouting instructions to their chauffeur when they caught up. "Hurry up, Ashley. We're going to be late."

Ashley took Mrs. Michael's arm and felt the first sense of peace she'd experienced in days. "Coming, Mother."

FIFTY-THREE

Tuesday, March 1, 4:59 p.m.
Kingani Refugee Camp

Paige slipped off her rubber gloves and popped them into the trash before sliding into the chair at her desk. She drew in a deep breath, then exhaled slowly. For the past three days, they'd handed out vaccination cards and administrated the vaccine to the majority of the camp.

Every minute a child died from measles somewhere in the world. Maybe after their work the past three days, they'd been a part of slowing down that statistic. She rolled her shoulders to work out some of the knots in her neck and back muscles. Tomorrow they'd finish dealing with the mountains of used syringes and needles, but for now, with the clinic finally closed for the day, she was looking forward to a few moments of quiet.

Three of her national nurses worked quietly, checking on patients, administering medicine, and giving her the short reprieve she needed. She flipped on the radio, hoping to catch the hourly news brief — and hoping even more that Nick managed to make it back to the camp before dark.

. . . On Saturday, about fifty U.S. soldiers, primarily special ops, in conjunction with the Dzambizan military, carried out a daring surprise attack that included helicopter-borne paratroopers who landed both at a refugee camp in the north being held by hostile rebels and the rebel base camp itself, where ten hostages had been held since the previous Tuesday. It ended with the arrest of dozens of rebel leaders.

The decision by the U.S. to send in military reinforcement came after the execution-style murder of an American aid worker, with threats to continue executing hostages if rebel demands were not met. Including the three Americans who lost their lives during the conflict, it is estimated that over one thousand people were slaughtered during the rebels' month-long rampage in an attempt to gain amnesty for their leaders arrested earlier this year.

American actress Ashley James, who was in the country to climb Mt. Maja with her father and was taken hostage by the rebels, arrived back in LA early Sunday morning. She immediately cancelled a scheduled press conference, much to the surprise of the media, who are still waiting for the details of her ordeal and the tragic death of her father. It is also rumored that she has called off her engagement to Mitch Peterson.

Brandon and Jodi Collins, the American couple also taken hostage, have now been reunited with friends and family in the small town of Cherry, Illinois, where townspeople held a welcome-home parade in the city center over the weekend . . .

"Paige?"

She flipped off the radio and turned to see Nick standing in the doorway. "You're back."

"I brought you a surprise."

She crossed the room and offered him a wide smile. "I thought you agreed that there would be no more catered meals —"

He held out the box he was carrying and popped open the lid. Meat, cheese, olives, onions . . .

Her eyes widened. "Where did you get this?"

"I had to make a run to the capital before coming here, and I know this little restaurant in the hotel district that makes a decent pizza." He cleared his throat. "It's not deep-dish and it's cold —"

"I love cold pizza." And she was starving. She reached for a piece, then stopped.

Nick laughed. "It's all yours, Paige. After what you did this weekend, I'd say you deserve it."

She dropped the box onto her desk and took a piece. "Wow, this is good, but you're spoiling me again."

"That was part of my plan."

Nick's smile reached his eyes and brought a warm blush to Paige's cheeks. Maybe she had found her Mr. Right.

"Tell me about what's happened since I saw you Saturday."

She swallowed the first bite and reached for her water bottle. "With the rebels gone, we've been able to send out an exploratory team into the surrounding villages to assess how far the cholera had spread. While they've diagnosed a number of cases, the crisis seems to be over."

"That's wonderful news."

"We finished vaccinating the camp this afternoon, and while we're still handling a number of measles cases, it does seem to be slowing the spread of the disease."

"What else?"

"Last night, Samson's wife and daughters

showed up at the registration tent in the camp. They'd been hiding in the forest, foraging for food, unable to enter the camp because of the rebels."

"Are they okay?"

Paige took another bite, then sat down on the edge of the desk. "The emotional scars of the situation will carry on for a long time, but after Asim is released in the next few days, they're going to go back to their village and try and rebuild their new life. Not a fairy-tale ending, but seeing some closure helps. For all of us."

"I've got another surprise to add to your good news."

"Dessert?"

Nick tapped on his pockets. "Only if you want a handful of Tic Tacs."

Paige laughed. "Okay. Then what's the good news?"

Nick grabbed her hand. "Get the pizza and come with me."

"Nick?"

Two of the nurses giggled in the background as he hurried her out the clinic doors.

"I promise you'll like this."

He led her toward the airstrip that was adjacent to the camp. Instead of rebels, all she could see now were the wisps of white clouds lining the horizon beneath a pale-blue sky. And in the middle of the airstrip sat a bright-yellow plane.

Paige stopped. "What is that?"

"What is it? It's my brand-new Kodiak 100. Seats ten, including the pilot, doors open wide to allow stretchers to be boarded easily — you'll like that feature — the landing gear can be removed —"

"I mean where did it come from?"

"A rather generous donation from our favorite actress, Ashley James."

Paige stopped at the edge of the runway and let the wind tug at her hair. "You're kidding."

"Not at all. Apparently the woman has a lot of pull. She made some phone calls on the long trip home, and, well, there it is."

"I don't know." Paige wrinkled her brow. "I'm surprised they're actually letting you fly it considering your history of crashing —"

"Rebels don't count, and the other times —"

Paige laughed and nudged him with her elbow. "I'm kidding. It's wonderful. Really."

"I know. Ashley set up a memorial fund in honor of Taz so the legacy of what he did here will continue. And she's planning to return next year on a goodwill tour to promote the needs here."

"Wow." She followed Nick to the plane, then stopped to rub her hand across its sleek belly. "God really does work in mysterious ways."

"And that's not all."

"What do you mean?"

"There's a surprise inside for you as well." Nick flipped open the side door of the plane. "It was loaded with over a thousand pounds of supplies for the hospital in Bensi, including a generator, an infant incubator, anesthesia machines, OR lights, a portable X-ray unit —"

"Nick!" Paige handed Nick the pizza before stepping into the pea-green cargo hold of the plane and pulling open one of the boxes like a kid at Christmas. Scalpels, scissors, needle holders . . . "All this was Ashley as well?"

"Like I said. The woman has connections."

And apparently a heart.

She set the box of supplies down and grinned. "When can we go?"

"First thing in the morning, if you're up for it."

"Oh, I'm up for it."

"In the meantime, I have a question for you." Nick grabbed a piece of pizza, then handed her the box before sitting down in the wide doorway of the plane. "Are you still planning to stay?"

"I don't know how I could leave. There are too many Taylas and Samsons and Rainas for me to run." She took another piece of pizza and sat down beside him, letting her legs dangle over the edge of the cargo hold while the fading sunlight glistened against the side of Mt. Maja.

"I agree." He wiped off a dab of tomato sauce from the side of her mouth. "I'm finally ready to stop running, Paige."

"I like hearing that." She looked up at him and smiled. "Because I know this incredibly handsome pilot who once told me that all I had to worry about was one person at a time."

"He must have been a smart guy."

"Maybe a bit cocky at times." Paige laughed and leaned into his shoulder. "I think I'll always struggle over the suffering I see here, but I've decided the bottom line is that my circumstances, and the circumstances of those around me, don't dictate God's goodness. Nothing I do can ever change who He is. And He'll always give me the strength I need to make it through each day."

The ball of sunlight sank beneath the

mountain, spilling its golden rays across the white tents that dotted the vast savanna in front of them and promising hope for another day.

And for this moment, that was enough.

Dear Reader,

Thank you so much for taking this journey with me. As I started doing the research for this book, I found myself afraid that you, as a reader, would find the plot unbelievable. Surely the story of a humanitarian crisis dealing with so many issues — from cholera to measles to rebels — could only be fabricated and would never happen in today's world. Yet as I read story after story of individual refugees I found myself weeping with them over what they experienced. And I realized that, if anything, I had sanitized my story to make it more believable, because the facts tell another story.

According to the international aid organization Doctors Without Borders, there are forty-two million people in the world who have been displaced by war and violence. Read that again: forty-two million. So while the story behind *Blood Covenant,* including the setting, is fictional, the issue of those being forced to leave their homes with nothing more than the clothes on their back, often after witnessing murder, rape, violence, and kidnappings, is very real. But in spite of this horror, I didn't want to stop the story there. Drawing from my own experiences across Africa over the past twenty years I wanted to tell a story that went beyond the adversities and gave a message of hope.

The truth is we don't have to travel around the world to see people hurting and exploited and needing that message of hope. They're real people we pass every day, living in our neighborhoods and attending our churches and schools. They're empty and broken, searching for freedom and hope in an often hopeless world.

But maybe, like Paige — and myself — you often feel too small and inadequate to do what God is calling you to do. Paul says that it is through our weaknesses that we are made strong because of Christ's power. At the greatest moment of weakness from the world's point of view, Christ's death on the cross brought victory and allowed God to enter into a relationship with us through that sacrifice.

Interestingly enough, God has been doing the same thing in my own life as He stretches me with new opportunities. Lynne Gentry, a close friend and fellow author, and I have recently started The ECHO Project, a nonprofit organization where ordinary people like you and me can make a difference in changing the world one individual at a time through assistance with education, compassion, health, and opportunities.

It's tempting to believe one person cannot make a difference. But when we dare to become involved, the ECHO can be heard around the world. Find out how you can invest in an individual today in order to reap a changed world tomorrow by visiting our website at *www.theECHOproject.org.* For more information about the refugee situation around the world, visit my website at *www.lisaharriswrites.com.*

It all starts with each one of us, wherever we are, letting God take us on that amazing journey He's prepared for us.

Be blessed today,
Lisa Harris

DISCUSSION QUESTIONS

1. What character did you relate to most in this story and why?

2. Paige had to finally come to the point where she admitted her weaknesses and fears and continue on in God's strength, not her own. Has there ever been a specific time in your own life when you realized you needed His strength in order to continue?

3. Have you ever been challenged to ask yourself if you are living out God's purpose for your life? What was your response?

4. Have you noticed that the Bible is filled with inadequate, ordinary people? What was Gideon's response when God called him in Judges 6:15?

5. What was Esther's reaction in Esther 4:11 to her uncle Mordecai's request that she must go before the king and beg for mercy for him and her people? What was Esther's uncle's response to her hesitation in verse 14?

6. God led Gideon to victory with only three hundred men, some trumpets, jars, and torches. Esther was able to save her people in the face of possible death. Neither of them triumphed through their own strength, but through God's strength. The Bible is full of these kinds of stories. David was a shepherd who became the king of a nation. Rahab was a prostitute, yet because she feared God, she not only saved Israel's spies, but she became a part of the lineage of Jesus. Think of someone you know today whom God has used to do extraordinary things with His power and share their story.

7. What does Paul say God determined from the very beginning of time in Acts 17:26? Why did Paul say that God did this in verse 27?

8. Did you realize that He is talking about you in these verses? In the middle of your

ordinary, run-of-the-mill, take-out-the-trash-and-drive-the-kids-to-school routine, you've been called by God for this time. For this moment. To make a difference in the world around you. How do you see God calling you to make a difference in your world?

9. Ashley helps to represent the extreme dichotomy between the haves and the have-nots in this world. Her eyes were opened and she was changed through the difficult experiences she lived through. After reading this story, do you see your own life any differently? Do you see the world differently?